STUFFED
INTO
DARKNESS

STUFFED
INTO
DARKNESS

LIZ BRASWELL

Disney • HYPERION
Los Angeles   New York

First Edition, May 2021
1 3 5 7 9 10 8 6 4 2
FAC-020093-21078
Printed in the United States of America

This book is set in Jenson Recut/Fontspring; Cooper, Scratch, Neutraface Txt,
Helvetica LT Pro/Monotype; Bullet, Flyerfonts Distortion/House Industries
Designed by Tyler Nevins and David Hastings
How-to illustrations by Luke Newell

Library of Congress Cataloging-in-Publication Data
Names: Braswell, Liz, author.
Title: Into darkness / by Liz Braswell.
Description: First edition. • Los Angeles : Disney Hyperion, 2021. • Series: Stuffed ; book 2 •
Audience: Ages 8–12. • Audience: Grades 7–9. • Summary: "Foon's boy, Clark, is kidnapped
by an evil monster bent on revenge and Foon must enter the Darkness in order to save him"—
Provided by publisher. Includes instructions for making a stuffed mouse. Identifiers: LCCN
2020041715 • ISBN 9781368039185 (hardcover) • ISBN 9781368044431 (ebook)
Subjects: CYAC: Toys—Fiction. • Monsters—Fiction. • Camps—
Fiction. • Magic—Fiction. • Friendship—Fiction.
Classification: LCC PZ7.B73767 Int 2021 • DDC [Fic]—dc23
LC record available at https://lccn.loc.gov/2020041715

Reinforced binding

Visit www.DisneyBooks.com

SUSTAINABLE Certified Sourcing
FORESTRY
INITIATIVE www.sfiprogram.org
SFI-00993
Logo Applies to Text Stock Only

A quick refresher on determining your Stuffy's MPF (Monster Protection Factor):

For all normal-size or "medium" Stuffies, start with a base of 3.

Give them:

- +1 if they're bigger, –1 if smaller (for instance, beanbag Stuffies would be a 2, but for charm or zipper dangle–size Stuffies, start with a base of ¼)
- +1 for each additional offensive feature (fangs, horns, claws, weapons, etc.)
- +2 for handmade
- +2 for deeply loved
- + ½ for *sustainably imagined* features. Magic powers, hidden weapons, etc. that you can't see but have always imagined the Stuffy has. CANNOT be something you make up on the spot.

So, adding up all the stats for our hero, Foon:

$$
\begin{aligned}
&3 \text{ (base)} \\
+\ &1 \text{ (tusks)} \\
+\ &1 \text{ (horns)} \\
+\ &1 \text{ (claws)} \\
+\ &1 \text{ (weapon)} \\
+\ &2 \text{ (handmade)} \\
\underline{+\ &2 \text{ (love)}} \\
=\ &11
\end{aligned}
$$

Now might be a good time to determine the MPFs of *your* Stuffy army....

For Cleopatra Josephine Miccolis

Grow up—but not too much.
Be brave against all monsters, real and imagined.
Remember: Not all heroes carry weapons. Some wield words.

From the very first day the sun rose over the world there have been shadows;

For where there is Light, there is always Dark.

Ever since life emerged from the waters and walked on dry land, creatures have run from those shadows.

When early hominids left their safe nursery in the trees, the shadows trailed their footsteps.

Even as humans prospered and spread across the world, the Dark followed and waged its terrible, silent war for dominion.

Yet there is hope.

Humans are not alone in this fight.

They have golems and friends, powerful beings who are sworn to keep the enemy at bay.

This is but one tale of many in the fight against the Darkness, in the Saga of Foon the Hero.

So, by the Grace of the Velveteen, our story begins. . . .

PROLOGUE

Something that wasn't the sun shone sharp and black in a perpetually twilit sky.

Things gathered—the things that could move, anyway—in a dead and dusty square under the pale un-light.

"He mussst be punished!"

"He *must* be stopped!"

"kill hurt bloody kick stab"

"Curse the Emissary of the Light! Make him pay! Kill him and pull out all his Stuffing and put his head on a spike as a warning for all who would oppose the Dark!"

Everything yelled and shook its tail, claw, club, or tendril in fierce agreement and frothy anger. The Dark City rumbled from all the pounding, jumping, and stomping of bodies in shades of blood and grey. Horn butted horn; claws snapped and clicked.

"*Beings, Monsters.*" A voice slow as honey dripped and oozed over the crowd, quieting them.

The Great Pleticon loomed above the crowd. It had a surprisingly small head at the end of its very long neck and spoke with utter authority.

"Certainly we could simply *kill* Foon. Maybe even torture him a bit first. But is this easy ending really the revenge that we seek? Will merely getting rid of the Stuffy who took out my poor King Derker truly fulfill us—and punish him?

"*NO!*" it suddenly hissed, whipping its long neck out over the crowd. Its tiny black eyes blazed in fury. "We must draw out his agony. We must make him rue the day he ever took one of ours. We will force him to shed a tear for every precious black drop of ichor our King Derker spilled before it died."

"And the Lomer!" a Gorbel called out. "Don't forget the Lomer he killed!"

"Of course," the Pleticon said generously—though a flicker of annoyance shot through its eyes. "My darling King Derker, *and* the Lomer..."

"And the Silverfish!" a scaly Fuulary added. "He got, like, a bunch of them. Them's cousins to us Fuulary!"

"*And* the Silverfish, *and* the Lomer," the Pleticon said through gritted teeth (and fangs). "*For all of these reasons,* a simple execution will not be enough. We must *hurt* him—and send a message to *all* Stuffies who would dare attack us. So let us proceed in an organized fashion for once. Ever is our way to rush ahead with death and poison, unprepared for the reality of what we might actually face. We bring chaos and disorder—not results."

The crowd hissed and applauded (perhaps incorrectly).

"Chaos!"

"Disorder!"

"Entropy, Darkness, and Death!"

"Yes, yes, yes," the tall being said, moving its cumbrous body slowly among the littler ones. "All of that has its place. But sometimes, dear Monstren, a little forethought can go a long way. Sometimes what is *not* needed is—this." The creature gestured around it at the disorganized rabble with a claw that ended in feathers and tentacles.

"Sometimes what is needed is a *plan.* . . ."

BOOK I:

A CAMP IN DANGER

ONE

Here

"I don't think this is a good idea," Clark whispered.

"You *always* don't think *anything* is a good idea," D. A. said. But his voice may have cracked a little. "It's just dark. That doesn't *mean* there's anything down there to get us. Besides, we've got our weapons."

"D. A.'s right," Catherine-Lucille said grimly. "And anyway there's no other choice. Let's just go down the stairs and face whatever's there. Together."

"If we have to," Clark said with a sigh of resignation.

"The stairs are moist with the slimy blood and entrails of whatever came before," Anna told them. The candle flickered, casting ugly shadows around her face. "A cold breeze brings mist and the stench of something long dead—no, worse than that; something still half-alive.

"Or . . . *undead!*"

"ANNA!"

The bright overhead light snapped on, its chilly modern bulb illuminating every corner of the bedroom. The three kids—and one kid on a video screen—looked up guiltily as Mrs. Smith stood in the doorway, glowering at them.

"How many times have I told you? *No real candles in your room!*"

"We need it for the mood," Anna protested.

"Aw, Mom, we were just about to kick some zombie butt!" Clark grumbled, throwing down his pencil.

"Oh yeah, you sounded *so* thrilled about it." On the video call, Catherine-Lucille rolled her eyes.

"I'm a halfling thief," he pointed out. "We're not known for our bravery. I was playing true to character."

"Sorry, Mrs. Smith," D. A. said, pulling his cap down over his eyebrows. While the gesture was supposed to show that he really *was* sorry, Clark was pretty sure his friend knew its precise effect on adults, especially moms. They found it adorable and immediately forgave him everything. Clark wished he had a superpower like that.

"Guess we'll save the zombies for another time," Anna said—with a side-wink at Clark. This meant: *when Mom and Dad are out.*

"We have perfectly realistic battery-operated tea lights you can use," Mrs. Smith said, not quite catching the byplay, but obviously aware that some kind of silent communication was going on. She narrowed her eyes and blew a puff of hair out of her face. It was a new style, longer and more fluffy than the bangs-and-tight-ponytail she used to sport. Her job was changing in some way Clark didn't fully understand and now required face-to-face meetings, not just phone calls (she wanted to look *hip* but *trustworthy*, she said).

"I should probably go, anyway," D. A. said with a yawn. "B-ball practice tomorrow morning."

Clark wilted, disappointed that the game was ending so early. Even after they figured out how to bring Catherine-Lucille in, it had been hard to schedule everyone—and then to wheedle Anna into DMing. He picked up the green-and-gold dice that were D. A.'s birthday present to him and shoved them into their matching green velvet bag a little harder than necessary.

"Aw, buck up, Private," Catherine-Lucille's pixelated face said. "We'll see each other for real in a few days!"

"That's true," Clark said, brightening. It was more like ten days, but then the three of them would be heading to Camp I Can together for *two whole weeks.* Which meant they would be there for the special intersession camping trip! On the weekend between the two one-week sessions a small number of campers got to hike Mount Wantastiquet and spend the night at the peak, in tents.

(Clark kept the now-worn brochure in his pocket at all times.)

He was not unaware of the complete one-eighty of his feelings on the matter. Last summer he had fought tooth and nail against being forced to go to the camp known for *developing self-esteem* and *fostering independence.* It was the second-worst clash between him and his mom ever.

The reasons he didn't want to go were many and complicated. It wasn't just because he had never spent a night away from home before. It wasn't because Stuffies weren't allowed at camp and he had to sneak in the one his grandma had made (Foon, of course). It wasn't even that Probably the Best Grandma in the Universe had started chemo for her cancer that same week.

Mostly it was because his dad was slowly being drained by the King Derker who had haunted their house. Clark didn't want to leave his dad alone without constant Stuffy protection.

(But also his mom had used Clark's absence as a chance to try to get rid of his Stuffies.)

(That was the cause of their *first*-worst clash of all time.)

Eventually everything turned out all right, of course. Clark's new friend Catherine-Lucille helped him find an illegal phone that the counselors kept hidden in the woods. He used it to call Anna and make sure she was maintaining a Stuffy army around the house every night (she wasn't—but only because his Stuffies had been bagged up and put in the basement). When he finally got home, Foon made short work of the Monster.

(At least it seemed that way: Clark found Foon the next morning all torn up from what looked like a pretty fierce battle. And his dad suddenly began acting normal again. Coincidence? Unlikely. Plus, there were all those weird Stuffy eyes scattered across the basement floor. . . .)

Grandma Machen had taught Clark how to fix Foon, stitch by stitch, while he kept her company at the hospital during her chemo. Both patients recovered completely and were soon back in action. Clark's dad, free from the terrible King Derker, also regained his health, and even took the family to a monster-truck rally—without, ironically, understanding that it was a Monster that had been making him sick.

Anyway, this summer was different. Clark was no longer terrified of being alone, far from home. His parents were now completely safe. He and D. A. might even be in the same cabin, Catherine-Lucille would be a short walk away. It would be like one never-ending playdate!

During the school year the three friends had texted, called, video-chatted, Discorded, *every*thinged, but it wasn't the same. Even when they managed to meet up a couple times in real life it was always awkward, at least at the beginning. Besides the usual not-seeing-a-friend-for-a-while uncomfortableness, there was also the added bonus of parents being there. They made everything weirder.

Now the three friends would have two weeks together! Without parents. *And* a camping trip!

Clark had always been intrigued by the Boy Scouts—from a distance. He loved the idea of earning badges (real ones that you sewed on, not in-game ones), and bonfires and marshmallows and stargazing. It was the "lots of other boys he didn't know or who might not like him" part that wasn't thrilling. Here he would get a bonfire, a tent, and stars—but with his best friends.

No badge, though.

That was kind of a shame.

Clark helped Anna and D. A. pick up all the bits and pieces

of a really good D&D campaign: dice, pencils, character sheets, candy wrappers, popcorn and chip bags, miniature pewter figurines, empty Japanese soda bottles.

"Hey, you guys see that video that's been going around?" Catherine-Lucille asked from her screen the moment Anna left the room. "The one of the kid taken over by the Shawgrath?"

"No! Put it on!" D. A. said eagerly.

Clark was…less eager. He knew it was important to stay up-to-date on the world of Monsters and keep himself educated about them. But it was still scary. His dad had almost been devoured by a Monster. Sometimes he wished he could go back to wondering if they were real—wondering, instead of *knowing*.

"Here." Catherine-Lucille's fingers moved below the screen and a link popped up beside her face. D. A. clicked it and turned up the volume.

At first it was hard to see anything, like all of the videos of this type. A dark room with strange things gleaming or glowing in the infrared of the night camera. Squinting, Clark could just make out the outlines of a bed and someone sleeping in it.

Suddenly the kid sat up.

Her eyes shone white in the black-and-white world—and she didn't blink.

She just sat up and stared, like a confused zombie.

"Aw, that's nothing," D. A. said disappointedly. "Just some little kid who had a nightmare or has to pee or something."

"Shh. Watch!" Catherine-Lucille ordered.

After a few moments of stillness the girl in the video got out of bed—jerkily, like a puppet. She stood in the middle of the room and again froze, doing nothing. Then she whirled suddenly, lurched over to the corner of her room, looked up—and *began talking.*

There was no sound, of course. Her lips moved and her eyes shone like she was having a serious conversation with the cobwebs—or Cowbers—on the ceiling.

Then, as she spoke, something—her breath, a shadow, a thin stream of vapor—began to seep out of her mouth.

"Pause it," Clark ordered. D. A. did so without hesitation. "Go back, like, a half second and enlarge the screen."

There was no doubt about it.

The stuff coming out of her mouth wasn't like the fog on a cold day. It was stringy and sticky-looking, long threads like a parachute spider might spin before floating away on a morning breeze. If that web was a foot long and inside a girl's head.

"Oh man," D. A. said in wonder. "That's so weird! And... disgusting."

"*Definitely* a Shawgrath. Or maybe an Ergootz," Catherine-Lucille said thoughtfully. "Like, a tiny one."

"Why weren't there videos like this before?" Clark demanded. "I mean, you're finding them all the time now, and before I met you I'd never seen a single one."

"That's because you didn't even know to look for them. Or

what to look for," D. A. said with a laugh. "Plus, this is C. L. here. She's the Monster Expert."

"No, that's actually a good point," the Monster Expert said unexpectedly. "There *do* seem to be more and more sightings and posts."

"Yeah, by accounts like..." D. A. leaned in to read the name of the video's creator. "'Akidsbedtimestory.' That could totally be a fake."

"Who would make a little kid act out something so scary?" Clark wondered. Not a good parent. Not even a halfway decent big sister. Anna had done a lot of questionable things, but nothing that put Clark into a potentially nightmare-inducing situation.

"A jerk who wants to make a lot of money off the internet," D. A. suggested. "Okay, guys. I gotta jet. We can totally discuss all this at camp, though."

"Gonna be hard," Catherine-Lucille said, tapping her tooth in thought. "Since we can't show videos. We can only trade notes. The club should come up with a system for ranking videos by how believable they are, and how trustworthy the sources."

"Hey, uh..." Clark cleared his throat. He didn't want to sound like a baby, or desperate. "So...uh...about the club..."

"Oh, Clark, relax," Catherine-Lucille said with one of her rare smiles. "You're in. We'll properly induct you the first night we formally meet. Okay? Stop worrying so much. You're with me. You're in. *HEY*, idiot, that's *my* cupcake!"

It took both boys a moment to realize she wasn't yelling at them, but at someone at her house, offscreen.

Anna popped her head back into the room. "Clark? Mom says you gotta wipe the table and sweep and then go take a shower."

"Sigh. Okay. See you later, C. L."

Clark closed the "Catherine-Lucille" computer; she was already gone and yelling at one of her cousins.

D. A. grabbed his bike helmet. "I'll see you online when I get home."

"Yeah, at least until nine," Clark said, walking him downstairs. They bumped knuckles at the front door, drawing their hands out afterward and wiggling their fingers like tentacles.

The sun was just setting. An orange spill of syrupy light spread out behind the houses across the street. Bright pink clouds couldn't hide behind the trees, whose topmost branches were as dark as the darkest, most starless night.

Clark felt a strange mixture of things. Wonder at the beauty of the sunset. Relief he no longer feared the night quite as much as he had.

(Why would he, now that he knew for certain that his Stuffies protected him?)

He watched D. A. pedal down the dim street, the only noise the *swischt* of his rubber tires against the sidewalk. His headlight bobbed up and down in the dusk like a will-o'-the-wisp going out, getting smaller and smaller until it disappeared.

Clark was torn between envy that the other boy was allowed the privilege of biking at night and a strange wistfulness he couldn't name. Something about lights dimming into the distance. Something about summer ending, even though it was only the beginning of August.

He stood for a moment, puzzling over it, then finally turned and went back inside.

TWO

Here, Night

If an adult staying up for the late-late show had not been lulled to sleep by the magic of the Moon—and had looked out the window—she would have seen a strange sight.

There were two groups of small, lumpy objects outside, under the streetlights, that moved a little when they probably shouldn't have.

They seemed to be interacting.

It would be hard to tell from far away what the things were made of: There were no sharp angles, no smooth sides, no shiny facets of plastic or metal or rock.

Foon, Hero of the Basement, Emissary of the Light, Ground Commander of House Clark, was shaking the hand—wing—of Dredful Duck of House Maya. Over the property line that divided their two realms, as was customary. Accompanying the duck was her cohort: Macow, Aramdillo, Dog, and Frank. With Foon were Winkum, Draco, Fang, Bo Bear, Dark Horse, and Kevin.

"We thank you for all your help," Dredful said, bowing deeply. Her bill almost touched the grass. It was worn through right to the Stuffing. She was loved, very much indeed, and therefore worthy of the greatest respect. She easily had an MPF of Ten—which was pretty amazing for a duck. "It was a terrible infestation; I don't know how long it would have taken us to clear out that nest of Sorvors."

"I'm sure you could have accomplished the task yourself in time," Foon said generously. "But we were honored to be asked to help."

He too bowed, saluting her with the tip of his trident, Focus, as his soft sock-body bent in half. It was a graceful, elegant gesture and all of House Maya were suitably impressed by it and his words.

"I am concerned, however…" the duck added thoughtfully. "We do a routine House check and perimeter search every night—I don't know how that nest even got built there without our noticing. And it was a corner of the attic closest to *your* house. The vent practically overlooks your second floor."

"Is it not usual for Sorvors to nest in dark and lonely attics?" Foon asked.

"Yes, but…news of your renown has spread far and wide,

friend," the duck said with a twinkle in her eye. "If I were a Sorvor, I would want to nest as far away from *your* House as possible. You are death to Monsters. Unless there was some other reason for it."

Foon bowed his head humbly. "You do me great honor, Dredful Duck. But Monsters have no thought or plan or reason. I am just glad I was able to rid you of their foul presence."

"Oh, absolutely, Foon. That is what's truly important here. Henceforth let there be an alliance between our Houses. *For where there is Light…*"

"There is always Dark," Foon finished.

They gravely saluted and parted, each group of Stuffies returning to their own Houses.

Those of House Clark hopped one on top of another and made a tall, swaying tower that reached the doorknob of the Front Door. After a little wrangling they finally managed to open it, tumbling inside in a happy pile of softness. Not Foon: He did a flip on the way down and landed on his paws, ready to spring back into action if anything threatened.

Nothing did, of course. His House was a sanctuary, a beacon of the Light.

His friends were in high spirits.

"Let us cut through the kitchen and say hello to the Ap-Lionses!" Kevin cried. The small beanbag polar bear was always a little more outgoing than the rest, perhaps because Clark carried him around the Outside so much.

The Stuffies marched in line, chanting:

> *Yarn and thread and fur and string*
> *We will fight most anything*
> *Moon and stars and needle and pin*
> *We will fight and we will win!*

"What ho, little Stuffies!" the Espresso Maker called genially from above. "Victory, was it?"

"An entire clutch of Sorvors!" Bo Bear called back in his surprisingly deep voice. He was small and very light green.

"We freed House Maya of their Monsters; it is now a complete sanctuary of the Light," Foon explained.

"Well done, all, well done!" the Blender cried, whirring his blades.

All the Ap-Lionses made noises of congratulations: clicking, clinking, beeping, and grinding. The Stuffies waved and laughed and marched through while blue and white and green lights flashed on and off like a fireworks display.

Foon smiled, watching his friends enjoy their moment of triumph. But his smile faded when they passed the basement door. He shivered, remembering the Lomer, and the eyes, and the well-spoken but evil King Derker who almost killed him.

Even after they won, it was months before Foon could speak or think properly again. His injuries were extreme.

The Stuffies reached the living room and turned to go upstairs. A few Dust Pugs, delighted by the show, joined in the parade, bouncing and rolling along behind. They all marched down the hall and into the Boy's Room.

Snowy had been left in charge; the owl clapped her giant wings twice in greeting.

"Well met, Foon! I assume from all the noise you have had a great success!"

"Well met, Snow Killer! We have indeed! With any luck, we shall soon have this entire neighborhood free of the Dark, creating a safe haven for all who stay in the Light!"

"That would be a great and mighty thing," Winkum, the oldest, most loved horse, said with a kind smile. "But let us celebrate our current victories now and think of the future later."

"Of course," Foon said quickly, ashamed of his boastful words. *Of course* they should honor the bravery and accomplishments of his comrades tonight and not belittle them by focusing on the greater war and the future instead.

Winkum was so very, very wise. Foon wondered if there would ever come a day when *he* would have as much wisdom to bestow on younger Stuffies.

It didn't seem possible.

THREE

Camp, Ho!

Clark hoped he had packed everything on the list.

He still had some camp stuff from last time—the duffel, the backpack, the hat, the towel. . . . But his parents needed to order him all new shorts and T-shirts because he was two sizes bigger now. He packed a new journal, pencils and pens, and a couple of books.

(Still no modern series or licensed properties allowed. He chose *The Fellowship of the Ring*, *The Once and Future King*, and *Half Magic*.)

Clark *also* packed his D&D books, a small game called Fezziwig, and a pencil case that Anna had given him for Christmas. She had made it herself; it was black leather with a black embroidered dragon whose eyes were red jewels. The dragon was hard to see unless you looked carefully, but Clark loved it; he decided that it was a Night Dragon with Invisibility or Camouflage.

The D&D stuff was a little bit of a risk; technically it was "licensed." And there were so many other things to do at camp that he probably wouldn't have time for a real campaign. But maybe he could get people to make characters and then talk them through an introductory scene at a tavern or two, get them kitted up.

He carefully wrapped in socks the compass his parents had given him for his birthday.

(His mom had attached a note that said *So glad you're heading in the right "direction," Champ!*)

He thought about throwing in the old-fashioned fire-starting kit that they had also given him (it had real flint) but decided he might get in trouble for it.

He *snick*ed back and forth across the house, up and down the stairs, a smug sort of energy tickling his feet. He felt like a grown-up preparing for something important. A business trip, maybe.

Well…he *was* going to officially join the secret club Catherine-Lucille ran. No longer would he be a timid little petitioner, an outsider. He would proudly sit next to Saneema and Scooter as *one of them.* Having Catherine-Lucille as a close friend was great; having a whole secret cadre of friends who knew about Monsters and Stuffies—and often shared their illicit candy—was off-the-charts awesome.

(Plus, Scooter seemed like the type who would definitely maybe play D&D. Clark was dying to ask.)

James, on the other hand, was a little bit of a worry. He had been at the very edge of being too old to be a camper *last* year. What if he wasn't there this year?

There was also Jaylynn, who was *not* in the secret club, but whom Clark was very much looking forward to seeing again. She had been his canoeing partner; they had bonded over Star Wars and soaking other paddlers in splash fights. They had a *lot* to catch up on.

So many things to look forward to!

But first: packing.

Mr. Smith was in the living room working on getting a boring-looking electronic device and the house's internet to talk to each other. A light or the heater or something. Mrs. Smith was in the kitchen putting together a spaceship-in-a-bottle. She had read somewhere that hobbies like that keep your brain young and improve fine motor skills.

"Won't this look great on your shelf?" she asked, beaming at him over the top of her weird double-magnifying-glass binocular things. They made her look like a cheap Star Wars extra.

No doubt she had chosen the spaceship to match the space mural she had installed in Clark's room (appreciated, but without his permission).

"Sure, but a dragon might be nice," Clark said carefully.

"A dragon-in-a-bottle? Who's ever heard of *that*?" his mom asked, laughing.

The same people who have heard of a spaceship-in-a-bottle, Clark decided not to say aloud.

He poked his head into Anna's room. She had been awfully silent that day, occupied with her own things.

She was going to college that fall—Miskatonic University, all the way in Rhode Island. Clark kept pretending that it wasn't happening, but it was hard with the brightly colored course catalogs all over the living room and the boxes and bins on her bed. Her walls still had black-and-white posters of old bands and just-the-limit-of-Smith-household-acceptable gory art (a tiny copper skeleton from Mexico, the skull of a rodent that she had told her parents was resin—it wasn't really), but the shelves and closet were looking a little barer than they should have been.

"Whatcha doing?" Clark asked.

"I'm packing, too, squirt. Want to make sure my dorm room is properly dark and moody. I got a text from my roommate." She made a face and held up her phone to show him.

Her roommate-to-be was ridiculously pretty, like someone from TV: all perfect brown skin and white teeth and smiles. Her name was Zarah.

Her words were all smiles, too, and exclamation points.

Clark was both smitten and worried for the girl's future.

Anna could be a little . . . temperamental.

Then he saw the box Anna had on her lap. It was lined with a purple satin blanket, like a cuddly nest for a just-hatched vampire kitten. In it, lying with their arms crossed over their chests, were her three fang dolls. Fat Bob, her pillow rock star, and Siouxsie, her toothy white rabbit, rested on either side of them.

"What are you doing?" Clark demanded.

Anna made a funny little face.

"Putting them away, Clarky-boy. Mom made some noises about using my room as a craft den, or she-shed, or something weird like that. Better I pack up my own stuff than let her get her cold, itchy little fingers on them. And then bag my dolls up like garbage. Remember last summer?"

"Of course I remember last summer! But—you don't have to put them *away* away," Clark protested. It looked like she was going to close the box and bury them in the backyard, like they did their goldfish. Permanently. He grabbed Siouxsie and shoved the Stuffy at her. "You'll need them more than ever when you're—you know, away from home."

She gave him a look, but he couldn't put it any other way. He couldn't say the words aloud. He knew that people went off to college and then to jobs or more school and then the rest of their lives. He really did know that. He just didn't want to think about it. It was better to imagine that college was just like summer camp, but in reverse. She would be back for the holidays and summer.

Anna reached out and ruffled his hair, the same way their mom did. He was better about keeping it brushed these days—a little better, anyway—but her fingers still found some thick brown locks to get tangled in.

He shook Siouxsie at her.

She sighed and took the rabbit, putting it in the "to take" pile along with her underwear, laptop, and makeup.

Clark sighed in relief. She would be safe.

Anything more than that—any feelings of *good-bye* or little lights fading into the distance—were less important. The main thing was that now Monsters like the Shawgrath in the video couldn't get her.

Even all the way in Rhode Island.

☆　☆　☆

The entire family drove Clark to Camp I Can, including Grandma Machen, who was offered the front seat but took the middle backseat, saying that she preferred to be squished between her grandkids than to survive an accident. For the occasion she wore an ONLY YOU CAN PREVENT FOREST FIRES Smokey Bear trucker's hat. Also purple leggings, in deference to the camp's ridiculous color scheme.

"You're bringing Foon again, I see," she said, her quick bird-black eyes noticing the little Stuffy's head peeping out of Clark's backpack.

"Also DangerMaus," Clark said proudly.

He had just finished the Stuffy that morning. The mouse was tiny, but had a mouth full of sharp metal teeth and *sustainably imagined* poison sacs just like a shrew's. These gave him an MPF of Three rather than the One his size normally would have allowed. Clark had designed and sewn the Stuffy mostly by himself, with Grandma Machen and his mom figuring out how to permanently attach the safety-pin teeth.

The day passing outside the car windows was half beautiful and half glare-y. Bright white sunlight shone between roiling grey clouds like an old religious painting. They took the slower, scenic route, so whether they were in shadow or brightness the entire landscape looked constantly dramatic. On a whim they stopped to pick their own blueberries.

(Blueberries were, of course, thrown. And not just between Clark and his sister, either. Mrs. Smith got Mr. Smith pretty good above his left eye, so Mr. Smith took one and smooshed it into her hair. Grandma Machen flicked a berry at each of her grandkids before returning to stuffing her own face with them. They paid for an extra pint at the tent with the cash register, having eaten at least that much.)

So Clark was already in high spirits—and sporting slightly purple lips—when Camp I Can appeared on the crest of the far hill.

For a moment he was confused: It was as if this scene were overlaid with a different one that was almost exactly the same—but that other scene was a memory, and felt very different.

The last time he had seen this view he was being forced to spend a week away from home when he didn't want to. A clammy, grasping fist of fear had squeezed his heart then.

This time he felt a thrill: Here was where he had met Catherine-Lucille, and braved the woods by himself, and made

Hedwig the Hippokoukou to protect his dad, and learned to canoe.

"You okay there, squirt?" Anna asked over their grandma's head. He must have looked a little strange as these two emotions battled it out in his brain.

Anna was trying to dress more college-y. To see him off at camp she wore black velvet pants—wayyy too hot for the weather—and a white collared shirt under a dark purple sweater—wayyy, wayyy too hot for the weather. On the left side of the sweater was a patch that *sort* of looked like something fancy, like a lion or a crocodile or a shield—but when you got up close it turned out to be an angry tentacled thing with too many teeth.

"Yeah, it's just...I dunno," Clark said, searching for the right words. "It's strange coming back here a year later. I'm happy now, but I was so scared before, but I want to go back now, and isn't that weird?"

"They put something in your Kool-Aid to addict you to the place," Anna said solemnly.

"It's growth, kiddo," Grandma Machen said (just as Mrs. Smith opened her mouth to reprimand her daughter). "Oh geez, speaking of growth—like cancer—I forgot to take my poison pill today."

"Mom!" Mrs. Smith cried.

But her mother just kept rummaging in her bag, looking for her pill case. "What? That's what it is. A poison pill to keep the cancer away. It tastes yucky and makes me tired all the time. Poison."

"But it keeps the cancer away," Mrs. Smith said through gritted teeth.

Grandma nudged Clark and rolled her eyes. Exactly the same way Anna did when their parents said something obvious and ridiculous. Clark wondered if things like that—gestures, reactions—skipped generations. His mom certainly never rolled her eyes.

Would his grandkids be able to pop their knuckles louder than anyone else in class?

Mr. Smith pulled onto the long gravel driveway and kept to the right, out of the way of the vans and tarps laid out on the ground. When a woman in a bright yellow shirt with the purple Camp I Can logo came over, clutching a clipboard, he gave her a warm smile.

"Camper Clark A. Smith reporting in. Bags on the tarps over there?" he guessed before she could open her mouth.

The woman blinked in surprise. Clark gave her credit for only taking a moment to process this before smiling back.

"An old pro, huh? We love returning campers!" She peered into the backseat and waved at Clark. "Unless it's Grandma here who's coming?"

"Do you have blackjack and waterslides? Because if so, I'm in," Grandma Machen said with great dignity.

"Waterslides, no." The woman laughed. "Blackjack—well, we do have game night. We might could fit you in there with something. Something a lot more like Crazy Eights, though. Gambling is not a Path to Success!"

At this *everyone* in the backseat rolled their eyes.

The woman didn't notice.

"Okay, Clark! This year it's…*Fishercat* Cabin for you! Mustelids all the way!" The woman slapped the car lightly like it was the flank of a horse and moved on to the next, her face resetting itself as she got ready to give her spiel again.

"She seemed to have independent thought," Anna said contemplatively. "Not like the robots you said the counselors were."

"There's a theory among campers that there's a robot hierarchy," Clark said, pleased to share this insider info. "The regular counselors are the lowest level, while the administrators and cafeteria workers have basic reasoning skills and emotions."

"Clark," Mr. Smith said in a warning tone, "that's not a nice way to talk about people."

"Wait, but what about the ones who live in the cabins with you?" Anna asked curiously, ignoring her father. "Like, senior counselors or whatever?"

"Cyborgs. Given human brains so they can act normally sometimes. But only sometimes.…So maybe they're just teenagers."

"Nice. *Jerk.*"

DangerMaus!

As you'll find out in about eleven chapters, DangerMaus, despite his tiny size, becomes extremely important in the quest to save Camp I Can...well, sort of. But no spoilers. So it is of utmost importance that *you, too,* learn how to make a DangerMaus! *Lots* of DangerMauses.

(DangerMoose.)

Because of his tiny size, DangerMaus can be deployed in any situation where you don't want Grownedups—um, adults—to know you're keeping an eye on the situation. And because he's so easy to make, you can build up an army of DangerMaus extremely quickly. Like action figures, Stuffies grow strong in high numbers.

Gonna assume you read *Stuffed* and know the basics of how to sew a Stuffy, so we won't repeat them all here. If you have questions, go back and reread the *Stuffed* chapter called "D. A.'s Amazing Zipper Dangle How-To!" That will refresh you on how to thread a needle, tie a knot, etc.

What you need:

STUFFY SKIN (cloth)
Felt or another stiff cloth is best and easiest, but whatever you have to work with.

NEEDLE

THREAD
Whatever you got. In a pinch, dental floss works.

SCISSORS

STUFFY STUFFING
Fiber fill *or* cotton balls (pulled apart and made fluffy) *or* crumpled-up other cloth.

TAIL MATERIAL
Thick yarn, thin rope, braided string, etc.

Optional but helpful:

TAPE
For holding the cloth together, or your pattern to the cloth.

GLUE
Fabric glue is best, superglue second-best, but almost anything will work except for glue sticks.

EYES
Googly eyes, buttons, beads, pieces of cloth cut into tiny circles.

HEART
Something small that you feel will make the Stuffy real.

OTHER COLORED THREAD and/or CLOTH, PENS, FABRIC, or ACRYLIC PAINT
For details.

READ THROUGH ALL THE INSTRUCTIONS FIRST!

Step 1
Drawing and cutting the Stuffy's shape out of cloth

- You need to cut out three pieces of cloth in the shape of the template seen here. IMPORTANT: The pieces do not have to be all the same cloth or color!

- If you're working with a thin cloth, you can trace the template directly from the book using a pen or pencil.

- If you're working with felt or another thick cloth, trace the shape onto a piece of paper, cut it out of the paper, and then trace around the paper shape onto the cloth.

*See full-size template on page 392

Step 2
Sewing your Stuffy, or: Welcome to the blanket stitch!

- Thread your needle and tie a knot in one end.

- At the pointy tip of one of the three oval pieces, push the needle through and pull the thread until the knot rests up against the cloth.

- Take a second piece of oval cloth and hold it up against the first one with the knot sandwiched in between them (this is so the knot remains on the inside of the mouse, unseen).

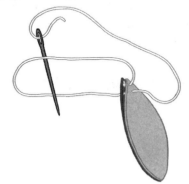

- Now take the thread up and over the top of the two pieces of cloth. Push the needle through the back of the back piece and all the way through to the front of the front piece. Make sure it comes out next to where the needle first came through, when you were anchoring the knot. BUT DO NOT PULL TIGHT YET. (If you did, the universe wouldn't explode or anything; you'd have a perfectly good whipstitch. But you've graduated, Corporal—that's why we're moving on to the blanket stitch!).

- Take the needle and put it through the loop of thread you have just made, from the back.
- *NOW* pull tight!
- What you should get is a neat little stitch that sort of rides on top of the two edges of cloth, *and* a stitch that goes across, from front to back of the cloth.

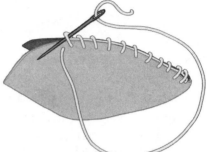

- Keep doing that: Always push the needle from the back of the back piece of cloth, through and out the front of the front piece of cloth half a centimeter or so away from your previous stitch, and then through the loop of thread you made, before pulling the thread tight.
- Continue this until you reach the point at the other end of the oval of cloth.

Step 3
Sewing the other pieces

- Now put the third piece of cloth in between the other two, so there are two sets of *two unsewn edges* along each other. (Don't worry if they don't fit exactly! Once you finish sewing and stuffing, the curves will all work out.) Now, without tying a knot or cutting the thread, blanket

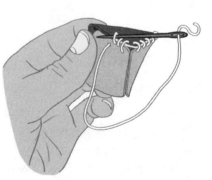

  stitch *up* the next two pieces of cloth. And when you get to that end . . .
- Yup, you guessed it! Sew the final seam. BUT NOT ALL THE WAY TO THE END! Leave about an inch unsewn. Because you have to . . .

Step 4
Stuff your Stuffy!

- You know how by now!

Step 5
Make a tail and sew 'em closed!

- Tie a big, thick knot at the very end of the tail material. Tie a knot several times if you have to, making it a sizable ball. Put the knot on the *inside* of the mouse, at the tip you haven't finished sewing yet, and let the long tail hang *out.*

- Finish sewing the Stuffy closed (trapping the tail knot inside, just like you did at the beginning with the thread knot). Tie a knot close to the cloth and clip the thread.

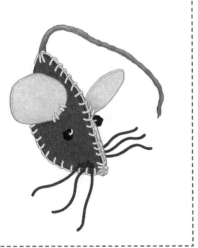

Step 6
Detail time!

- This is where you can really get creative. You can make ears by tracing quarters onto cloth, cutting them out, and sewing them on. Sew or glue beads for eyes! Or googly eyes! Or you can draw them in—along with a nose and mouth, too. Or embroider a nose (sew over the tip again and again). You can pin a whole bunch of tiny safety-pin teeth along his snout just like the original DangerMaus. Embroider on whiskers or paws, using the backstitch from the "Pro Skills" epilogue in *Stuffed*! Go crazy, or crazy cute!

Bonus Points

- For level-two whiskers: Thread a needle but *do not tie a knot in the end*. Sew once through the snout, in one side and out the other. Leave about a two-inch tail on either side, and snip the rest of the thread off. Then *tie a knot* in the thread as close to the snout on either side as possible. See? A knot on both sides keeps the thread from pulling out and looks adorable. Make as many whiskers this way as you like!

Pro Skills

- To keep your stiches super even and exactly the same distance apart, use a pen to make two marks on the tip of the thumbnail of your left hand (right, if you're a lefty), about half a centimeter between them. Then, when you're gripping the fabric, you can line your thumbnail up with the seam and put your needle through the cloth exactly above the mark.

FOUR

Camp I Can

Mr. Smith carefully pulled the car into an empty space in the merry, chaotic lot. Clark practically leaped out before the car had come to a full stop. He slung his pack over his back, put his camp hat on, and looked around eagerly to see if any of his friends were arriving. He didn't recognize anyone yet—but maybe they would be at the gathering place in the pine grove, waiting for him.

"C'mon, Clark, your luggage isn't going to carry itself," Mrs. Smith said, popping open the back of the car.

He grabbed his duffel bag. Anna helped Grandma Machen get out. Mr. Smith stretched and put his arm around his wife.

"I'd like to go to camp," he decided.

"Really?" Mrs. Smith blinked and looked around: at the trees, the sunshine, the kids with backpacks. "We could do a family camp. I think this place does that in the off-season. We could all sleep in a tent and do yoga on the beach and cook hot dogs over a fire! That might be fun!"

She immediately pulled out her phone and started tapping on it, searching.

Clark carried his bag over to the tarps and dropped it on the one labeled *Fishercat*. He had looked up all the cabin animals for eleven-year-olds before coming (he sort of hoped he would get *Catamount*). Fishercats were weird but pretty fierce, like weasels the size of dogs. He wondered why no one made Stuffies of them.

A man (also with a clipboard) came over and started to talk. Clark was feeling generous and let him.

"Okay, young man, it looks like you know what you're doing! You're prepared! You read all the literature! You're an A-plus student! No, wait, we're not supposed to say that. No talk about grades. You're trying super hard and *succeeding!*"

"Thank you. Can I ask who else is in my cabin?"

"Of course you can ask!"

The man smiled at him nicely but vacantly. Waiting.

It took Clark a moment to realize why.

"Um, so who—else—is—in—my—cabin?" he asked, slowly.

"Glad you asked!" the man responded immediately with a flashy smile. "Well, we're really not supposed to reveal it ahead of time, but if there's a buddy you particularly want to know about, I might be able to let a secret or two slip."

"D. A. Lee," Clark said, trying not to stand on his toes and peek.

"D. A.... You mean Derleth August? You're in luck! He is absolutely in your cabin! Tell you what, we'll see if we can get you guys in the same bunk. What d'ya like, top or bottom?"

"Either. I don't care." This wasn't entirely true. He kind of wanted the top—it was cool having a bird's-eye view of the rest of the cabin. He had the bottom last year and it was snug and safe-feeling, but he was ready to move on.

"Okay, little guy! I'll put you down for that! Great initiative for asking, by the way! High five!"

Clark grinned and slapped his hand.

The rest of the Smith family had witnessed the end of the conversation and looked at each other, baffled.

"Huh," Mr. Smith said, trying to sound neutral.

"See? *Robots*," Clark said triumphantly. "But nice ones."

He didn't want to be rude. But as they walked down the path through the main drag of the camp, his legs kept speeding up of their own free will. His eagerness to see his friends was literally pulling him ahead. He noticed that the canteen and the mess hall had fresh paint and new signs; the stuffed purple platypus was already hidden somewhere in the camp (if you found it you got a free bag of candy from the canteen). Clark wondered how the platypus felt about that, and if it was lonely wherever it was hidden.

The lake was as cold and black and foreboding-looking as ever despite the bright blue sky and green of the trees around it. Monsters could have been lurking just under its surface.

(Epic fantasy monsters, like Nessie. Not *Monsters* that could really hurt you.)

This somehow comforted Clark. Like: Check! All was the same as before, including the creepy lake.

Also the same was the sense of peace he immediately felt upon entering the pine grove. Silence and sweet smells draped over his shoulders like a hug, like nothing bad could ever happen there. As if it had been a place of serenity and safety since the beginning of time.

He spotted a very welcome, very familiar face.

"Catherine-Lucille!" he cried.

She had grown some over the past year, but since he had seen her a few times it wasn't immediately noticeable. Instead of having her hair in two long ponytails on the sides of her head, she now kept it in a single long braid down her back. Her ears were pierced—had they been before? He couldn't remember. She wore two little sparkly stones in them now. Her skin was darker than usual, much darker than Clark's. She had gone to visit relatives that summer and sent pictures of the amazing beaches she spent all day on, the same way Clark's family did at the lake.

She smiled at Clark and waved.

He was so overjoyed at seeing her in person he wanted to run over and hug her—and must have somehow betrayed that urge.

Her smile immediately disappeared.

She looked very, very alarmed.

Catherine-Lucille was not a hugger. She wasn't a cheek-kisser, shoulder-tapper, high-fiver, or fist-bumper, either. She just wasn't.

Clark managed to rein himself in. But she didn't relax until his hands were in his pockets and he *way more casually* strolled up to her.

"Private," she said, acknowledging him with a nod.

"Catherine-Lucille," Clark's mother said formally.

"Mrs. Smith. Mr. Smith. Anna. Um, Grandma."

Catherine-Lucille had never actually met Grandma Machen.

Grandma's eyebrows rose a little at this greeting, and then her black eyes twinkled merrily. Clark felt sure he was going to hear more about "his little friend" later. Hopefully his grandmother wouldn't be *too* hard on him.

"Where are your parents?" he asked.

"Are you kidding me? They dumped me and ran. My little sister has this extreme soccer camp she got accepted into and my cousin is going to some sort of chess nerd camp near there."

"Aw! Well, come sit with us!" Mrs. Smith threw her arm around Catherine-Lucille's shoulders and led her toward the benches. Clark's friend shot him a very unhappy look. He cracked up. There was nothing he could do. There wasn't a power in the universe that could counter his mom's hugs. Not even Catherine-Lucille.

They found an empty bench halfway up the gentle, shaded hill and settled in. Clark wished he could take Foon out and sit him on his lap to watch—it was such a beautiful place, he wanted to share it. But this was the *last* camp on the planet where that would be acceptable. Stuffies—and action figures, and dolls—were forbidden here. So Foon and DangerMaus stayed in the bag.

"Hey, Clark!"

Over the growing sea of heads Clark saw that D. A. was waving frantically and leaping up and down, pushing his way through the crowd toward them.

"And where are *your* parents?" Mrs. Smith asked when he got there.

"Oh, we're *mammals* now," D. A. said with a shrug.

Mr. and Mrs. Smith and Anna all looked at him blankly.

"I should hope you are," Grandma Machen said.

"Not Sunfish or Axolotls now, I mean," he said—as if that explained everything. "*Fishercats.* All the way!"

"*Fishercats!*" Clark cried, and the two boys bumped knuckles and did the tentacle thing with their fingers.

"*And* Golden Moles," Catherine-Lucille added. "We rule!"

"Those are our cabin units. Our age groups," Clark explained to the adults.

"Yeah, we're eleven and don't even need to do this whole drop-off thing," D. A. said. "The songs and the good-byes and stuff. We can just go straight to our cabins. So my parents left after dropping me and my stuff off. But I wanted to wait here for you guys."

Clark pondered this information. Why *wouldn't* D. A. want his family to come into camp and then say a proper good-bye? It was part of the tradition.

Then he wondered about Catherine-Lucille's answer when asked where *her* parents were. He was sure it was mostly true—she never lied, not even to avoid embarrassment or hurting someone else's feelings. But it might not have been the whole truth. Maybe there were other kids in the family to drop off at other camps...but maybe she also wanted them all to leave quickly.

"Do you want us to go now, too?" Clark's mom asked.

The cool thing would have been to say *Sure* or *Whatever* or *Yeah, I'm totally fine*. And then he could start chattering and gossiping with his friends immediately.

Clark wasn't a cool kid. He knew it, and (most of the time) he was just fine with it.

"No, it's okay, you're all already here, and besides, um, so is Grandma this time. It was a lot for her to come."

He wondered if that last bit sounded as false as he thought it did.

"Oh, *thank* you," Grandma Machen said archly. "It *was* so much for me to come here! I made a *special point* of tearing myself away from that *afghan* I was *crocheting* and the *old ladies' flower club* and my *stoh-ries* on the afternoon *TV*."

Clark blushed.

Catherine-Lucille broke into a wide grin at this obvious falsehood—and gentle put-down of her friend.

"HELLO, CAMP I CANNERS AND FAMILIES! WELCOME TO CAMP I CAN AND LAKE WANTASTIQUET!"

The man who shouted this wore a yellow polo shirt with

CAMP I CAN written across it in big purple letters. But he was not the camp director from last year.

"Hey, where's Park?" Catherine-Lucille demanded in a whisper. "He's been camp director since *forever!*"

"I dunno—it's weird," D. A. whispered back, frowning. When Clark looked at him questioningly, he explained. "Maxwell Park is a Camp I Can lifer. His parents sent him to Camp I Can when they first came to America. Then he started working here during the summers, and then sent his own kids. He's been camp director for, like, twenty years and does fundraising for it during the rest of the year. That's how my mom first heard of this place."

Around them, all the returning campers were similarly whispering to each other about similar things.

"I CAN SEE THAT SOME OF YOU ARE PROBABLY WONDERING ABOUT MR. PARK," Camp Director Not-Park said. "HE WAS CALLED AWAY ON URGENT AND SADLY UNAVOIDABLE FAMILY BUSINESS. BELIEVE YOU ME, HE IS *EXTREMELY* DISAPPOINTED THAT HE'S NOT HERE TO GREET YOU.

"AND YES, THERE HAVE BEEN A FEW OTHER LAST-MINUTE STAFF CHANGES.... BUT REST ASSURED, EVERYONE WHO WORKS AT CAMP I CAN IS AN EXPERIENCED CAREGIVER WITH EMERGENCY TRAINING AND BACKGROUND CHECKS. EXCEPT FOR THE COUNSELORS-IN-TRAINING, OF COURSE. THEY'RE LAKEBAIT."

The three friends cracked up at this.

"It's an inside joke," Clark whispered to his family. "The real counselors always make them test out the temperature of the water first. Sometimes in their normal clothes."

"Ah. *Shenanigans*," Mr. Smith said, nodding wisely.

"SO LET'S SKIP THE SONGS THIS YEAR...."

"Skip the *good-bye songs*?" Catherine-Lucille asked in horror. "Disgraceful!"

"AND LET'S KEEP THE PARTING SHORT AND SWEET. OUR CAMPERS CAN GET STRAIGHT TO HAVING FUN AND BECOMING THE MOST!"

There was some awkward but mostly cheerful clapping at this abrupt ending.

"The most what?" Anna asked.

"It's a new thing this year," Mrs. Smith said, pulling out the brochure and reading. "'Here at Camp I Can we help your children become the *Most*. The Most em-powered, en-abled, en-ergized, en—'"

"En-chilada?" Grandma Machen suggested.

"En-cephalitic?" Anna asked.

"En-gulfing the en-tire planet in a vengeful fire of doom?" Catherine-Lucille proposed.

"Whoa," D. A. said, impressed and horrified.

Mrs. Smith gave them all a withering look.

Then she sighed.

"Well, at least I know that you're in, if not *good* company, then at least *friendly* company here. Good-bye, Clark." She hugged him and kissed him on the top of his head, and he didn't care.

"Bye, squirt," Anna said, giving him a noogie—lightly—and then hugging him. *"Check your sheets."*

Clark had no idea what she meant. Bedsheets? Paper sheets? Whatever it was, it would probably be weird, possibly creepy, but definitely interesting.

"Bye, Clark," Mr. Smith said, squeezing him around the shoulders. Not jokingly; it was a real hug and he didn't fake-hit him on the back the way a lot of dads did.

"See you in two weeks, kiddo." Grandma Machen kissed him on the cheek and ruffled his hair. Her own hair had finally started to grow back in now that her chemo and radiation treatments were over, but it was still terribly short. She kept threatening to dye it blue—like, really blue, electric blue—with Anna's wholehearted encouragement, but never seemed to get around to doing it.

It was strange watching the four walk off, a family without him.

"Your folks are weird," Catherine-Lucille said. "Like, good weird. But weird."

"Mom's totally normal," Clark protested.

Both of his friends gave him the side-eye.

"She's got a job and she makes dinner and she reads books," Clark pointed out.

"And she writes weird little notes on Post-its addressed to

herself stuck to the mirror. That actually say 'Dear Self,'" D. A. pointed out. "And she makes you weird food with faces and stuff. And remember that time she took us to the kiddie mini golf—which was weird—and then had to ask the guy how to keep score? In *golf*? Kiddie golf? And then kept yelling 'Take that!' to the little kids behind us whenever we beat them?"

"And that time when I came over and she walked around the house with, like, all kinds of weird makeup on her face," Catherine-Lucille put in. "Cheek stuff and two different eye shadows and her lips were all striped with five separate shades of lipstick? *All day.* Even outside. Even when you guys dropped me off at the mall."

"She wanted to see how it looked in different light. Which colors were the best..." Clark said, and it made sense, but sort of totally didn't at the same time, so he trailed off at the end.

"Wonder what's really up with Camp Director Park and all that staffing stuff," Catherine-Lucille said thoughtfully, ignoring him like the matter was already settled. "I'm gonna have to look into that. Catch up with you later? Saneema and the others are going to be looking everywhere for me."

"Later—at the secret meeting place?" Clark asked, trying to contain his excitement.

"Nope, never on a Sunday night," D. A. said, laughing good-naturedly at his friend's impatience. "Too many new campers wandering around all over poking their noses into stuff. Let's meet in Fishercat Cabin. After dinner."

"Copy that." Catherine-Lucille nodded curtly and stalked

off, an intense look in her eyes Clark was *pretty* sure was a kind of happiness.

Clark and D. A. fell into an easy stroll, watching all the other campers and families interact. The dramatic clouds from earlier in the day had won, and the sky was now entirely blanketed with them. This new darkness lent a fecund quality to the trees, bushes, and grass. Everything smelled moist and twilighty, but not in a bad way.

It felt like the quiet before the storm. All sounds, including the happy shouts of campers, were strangely muffled. Even D. A. seemed predisposed to contemplation and quiet.

Clark was just thinking about how the scents outside at camp were different from the scents outside at home—when they came upon a heart-wrenching scene. A tiny kid, a cartoon of a boy, all large eyes and wet lashes, was silently weeping under his sideways Camp I Can hat. His parents looked on, upset and perplexed, unsure what to do. They were clearly trying to leave.

"Hey, it's okay," Clark said, patting the kid on the shoulder. "I was sad the first time I came here, too."

D. A. nodded and looked like he was agreeing, but it was probably just to show sympathy—he wasn't the type of kid who was ever sad about anything except for the proper things: pets dying, getting grounded, breaking an arm.

The crying boy blinked at them slowly, like a goldfish (if a goldfish could blink).

The parents' faces grew cautious, hopeful smiles.

"You'll love it here, I *promise*," Clark said.

"Yeah, it's dope," D. A. added. "You can stay up after dark and play cards without the counselors knowing, and the canoe splash fights are the best thing ever on a hot day."

"And the color wars are super fun! My name's Clark, by the way. Fishercat Cabin. You can come see me if you still feel sad later, okay?"

"Okay," the boy finally whispered, drawing a finger across the bottom of his drippy nose.

He didn't look *happy*. But maybe, just maybe, he was a tiny bit intrigued.

(His parents looked ecstatic.)

D. A. and Clark walked on; their work there was done.

"You just did what my uncle would call a mitzvah," D. A. said appreciatively.

Clark shrugged. He didn't want to talk about it. It was sort of embarrassing. But hearing D. A. say that—without knowing exactly what a mitzvah was—made him feel all warm inside.

And then the moment was ruined when something ice-cold and hard fell from the sky onto the back of his neck.

Several ice-cold things.

"What the...hail?" Clark yelped. He reached under his shirt and picked them out. Hoping desperately it was indeed hail and not a bunch of ticks or something gross like that.

It wasn't hail.

But it wasn't ticks, either.

Three different-sized googly eyes sat in the palm of his hand.

"'What the *hail.*' Priceless!" D. A. was still laughing at Clark's unintentional joke when he suddenly realized what his friend was holding. His jaw dropped and his eyes went wide. "Whoa."

Clark looked up into the tree but could see nothing except for the thick wall of leaves, dark green impenetrability.

"Must be from some dumb art project? From the craft cabin?" D. A. said, also looking up. "Like someone made a face up there or something?"

Sure, that was possible.

But Clark had found other random googly eyes the morning he also found Foon all torn up in the basement. And plastic and glass Stuffy eyes.

This was just a coincidence, right?

He shivered and threw the eyes away from him, feeling sick.

FIVE

You're a Good Man, Clark A. Smith

Then Clark felt bad about littering and picked up the eyes—despite his revulsion—and threw them into the nearest garbage can.

SIX

THE GREAT PLETICON SPEAKS

Ah yes, the Lomer... Well, what can I say? You go to war with the army you have. They are some of the smarter Higher Monsters, believe it or not. I needed someone I could trust to run ground operations in the World of Light.

I know there are those of you who have had doubts about the Great Plan. Especially after deploying the Sorvors close to the House of Foon for spying did not work out as I... er, *we*, had planned.

There were too few of them. They were dumb. They were easily discovered and destroyed.

A mistake I shall not make again.

This time I have sent out *many* Monsters of all different sorts into the World of Light to scout out the disgusting, tasty children, and figure out which one is our prey.

First were the Shawgrath. They did the job of removing any

pesky adults who would protect the boys and girls at camp, and were put into place *weeks* ago. They set the scene and made it safe for the rest to invade and tackle the next task: to identify *which* of the children is Foon's.

This should be relatively easy; it is whichever child keeps Foon close by.

For that, the Chowgun have been sent in. They are fast and can quickly search the tiny houses and belongings of the children with their graspy and prehensile claws. And if they find any Stuffies who *aren't* Foon, well, we can take care of them as well.

Crellans will take to the liquids: lake, toilets, swamps, and sinks. They will slither and slide into their hosts and drain information from the children's skin and blood. If the Chowgun fail, they are our next-best bet to find Foon's child.

The foul-smelling Vormonths are weak, true, but also invisible and can be anywhere, everywhere, even in the daylight. The ultimate spies. Even if they are discovered, no human will ever suspect them because in the humans' belief system only the one who smelt it, dealt it.

(I've also sent in a few Glimers to haunt their machines and devices. Just to, you know, spread chaos. Why not? Chaos is tasty!)

And since my own Monster self is too, ahem, *large* and *mighty* to cross over into the World of Light, the Lomer acts in my place. I trust it can get over its addiction to eyes and its childish sense of humor and get to work.

Finally, once all is in place and we have the child singled

out, held captive away from all help...well, the Grindel is ready for him.

And hungry.

We have five days, my Monstren. I know we can do this.

SEVEN

Sunday Night

It was mac 'n' cheese night. *The first night of camp.*

Obviously the "staff changes" were affecting every aspect of life at Camp I Can.

Bright yellow rubbery squares were piled high on trays like children's blocks. Their sides revealed cross sections of elbow macaroni held in a benthic suspension of cheese. Bets were taken as to how long a cube of the stuff would continue to wiggle after someone gave her plate a shake.

Still, if you ignored the texture and concentrated on the taste, it wasn't *too* bad. You had to chew a lot, of course. Some kids puckered their cheeks and squeezed the yellow pulp out between their teeth like zombie puke.

Mac-a-cheese

Don't you sneeze

Yer snot will hang down to your knees!

"Someday, *I'm* going to come up with a camp song," the girl next to Clark vowed.

"I don't think anyone's done anything with shepherd's pie yet," he pointed out helpfully.

"THERE IS NOTHING TO BE DONE WITH SHEPHERD'S PIE," the boy on the other side of him said, eyes haunted.

Thinking about it, Clark didn't disagree.

There was a flag-lowering ceremony in the playing field after dinner, and a big girl played "Taps" on a trumpet—not too badly, either.

When it was over Clark practically ran back to his cabin. He hadn't even bothered to make his bed yet, so he did that now while waiting for his friends. Carefully unfolding each sheet and blanket and pillowcase and looking closely at each piece of cloth (as per Anna's warning).

Yep.

There it was.

Anna had very meticulously dyed—and then embroidered a nice chain stitch around—a giant fake yellow puddle of pee in the middle of his bottom sheet.

"Not funny, Anna," he muttered.

But he was impressed with the amount of time and effort she had put into the prank. It was incredibly realistic. The fake pee even looked a little orange in places.

He quickly made up the rest of his bed, including the big down comforter, which was an upgrade from last year and absolutely not necessary considering how hot the nights were.

(He put it on just to bury the prank as deeply as possible.) There was a note tucked into his pillowcase.

Sorry—but it's pretty hilarious, right? You have to admit.
  Love, Anna
  PS: There is a bag of Starburst in your undies. According to the interwebs, they are fun to roast on a stick over a campfire.

Clark grinned. Anna was like... chaotic neutral. *And* even-handed. For every evil action there was an equal and opposite good action.

D. A.'s bed was somehow already done, albeit sloppily. He had thrown on a bottom sheet without actually pulling the fitted elastic corners down around the mattress. Then he just tossed his sleeping bag on top of it all. Clark shook his head and fixed the sheet. Maybe they could turn the whole bunk into their own private hideout, hang a blanket or something from the top to make curtains....

D. A. came in a few minutes later, throwing the cabin door open dramatically. "Wow, that was sick—I mean, literally sick. I'm going to be sick for days from that mac 'n' *skeeze.*"

"You didn't have to eat three servings of it," Clark pointed out as D. A. launched himself onto the lower (neatly made) bunk and belched.

"Hey—find any more weird eyes?"

"Um, no. Thank goodness."

"NO GIRLS ALLOWED!" another boy in the cabin suddenly shouted.

(Clark thought his name was Amir or Amos or something.)

Catherine-Lucille stood in the doorway with her arms crossed, her giant hiking boots planted like they were never going to move. Without breaking eye contact with Amos or Amir, she tossed her head, flipping the long braid from her shoulder to her back. Clark thought of nature shows when a bull paws the ground and lowers its head threateningly, or a tiger chuffs.

"No girls in a boys' cabin *after nine o'clock,*" she said loudly and clearly.

"That's the *camp's* rules." The boy stepped forward into her space—he had a good four inches on her. "There's also *cabin* rules. No one wants you in here."

"*I* want her in here," D. A. said. "Hey, C. L. Come on in."

She neatly stepped around the other boy and headed over to her friends—all without breaking eye contact with her adversary.

"*I'll see* you *later,*" she mouthed at him, pointing with two fingers from her eyes to his.

Amir or Amos finally had the sense to look worried.

Catherine-Lucille sat down on Clark's bed and looked around, nodding approvingly as if it were a new apartment. "Nice—you guys got a double together. I got a new girl below me. She's all right, I guess, but she laughs realllly loud at dumb things, and she says she snores. I think it's the braces."

"Did you find out anything about Camp Director Park? Or any of that other staff stuff?" D. A. asked.

"Yeah, it's real weird." Her eyes narrowed. "So, the counselors—including the 'nutritionist' and health aide—all came down with the same thing. Something gross like mono or hepatitis or something. Miz Shirley got it, too, I guess? But she got better. She's back. But all the stories about *Park* are different. Some say it was a family crisis, some say he got a better summer job, some say he just didn't show up on the first day. All really, really suspicious."

"Is a crazy craft lady one of the ones who got sick?" D. A. asked. "'Cause a bunch of googly eyes fell on Clark today and it was super weird. Maybe she got delirious and climbed a tree. Hoarding supplies in the trunk like a squirrel."

"Crafts falls under Occupational Therapy and Mindful Living. It doesn't have its own senior counselor—it's just handed off from one dumb teen CIT to another. That's why it always falls to me. There *is* no crazy craft lady."

D. A. and Clark exchanged significant looks. Fortunately for their health Catherine-Lucille didn't notice.

"But what kind of eyes were they?" she asked curiously. "Show 'em."

"They were just regular plastic googly eyes, not like Monster or human eyes or anything. They were cold and gross and it was weird that they fell on me out of nowhere. I threw them away," Clark admitted, now feeling stupid about it. But the horror he had felt when holding them had been very real. He just *couldn't* have kept them. "Actually, they were a lot like the ones from the morning I found Foon all torn up."

"Hmm." Catherine-Lucille looked thoughtful. "Mysteries. Something for the club to work on...*after* we induct you, of course."

Clark tried not to grin uncontrollably.

She got all comfy, drawing her legs up crisscross-applesauce, and began to go through her backpack. "So, who did you guys bring? I got Freya—" She didn't bother taking this Stuffy out of her bag, although the nose and antlers of the large creature peeped out the top. Freya the Reindeer was well known to D. A. and Clark; no introductions necessary. "And this little monster guy I was telling you about—not Monster," she added quickly. She pulled out a little green furry Stuffy with slit eyes and fangs and adorable twisted horns. "My aunt got him at the Renaissance Faire. I'd say he's an got an MPF Three. Maybe Three and a Half. He's small, so that's minus one from a base of three, which gives him a two. But he *does* have fangs and horns, each of which *should* be a plus-one, but...I dunno. His horns don't seem like they'd be too useful. So I'm just giving him plus one for both."

D. A. and Clark nodded. It all made sense.

"And *this* is Doris, whom I made myself," she said proudly. Doris was a bit of a shock.

She was a doll—a *doll* doll. Oh, she had dog ears and a mouth full of sharp teeth and paws for feet and very unlikely-looking stubs of jet-black wings coming out of her back. But her arms were slender and delicate, her hair a carefully sewn-down bun of very thin yarn, and her brown eyes had white highlights that were a little off-center but mostly professional.

"Wow, you made this?" Clark asked, marveling at the tiny pair of jean shorts she wore.

"Yeah. With help. From my cousin."

"What's her, um, backstory?" D. A. asked. There were just too many details for her not to have one.

"I think she works at a technology place or credit-card company all day and no one notices her at her cubicle. She goes through all these numbers, accounting or something, and she likes it, but she's a little lonely 'cause no one can see her, you know? And then at night she goes out and kills bad guys."

"What's her MPF?" Clark asked.

"Well, she's tall, but skinny, not like a meaty stuffed animal, so I think again I'm going to take away one from the base of three," Catherine-Lucille said thoughtfully. "But she *does* have a mouth full of sharp teeth, that's plus one, and her little knife there, which is also plus one. Also, she is very, very smart. So for *sustainably imagined* brains and tactics I'm giving her half a point. And half a point for *sustainably imagined* speed—she is very fast, and dexterous. So I think she's an MPF Five altogether."

"Wow, she's amazing," D. A. said. "Deadly. And like a Barbie but soft. Ha—C. L., this is so not like you! She's so girly."

"Shut *up*," Catherine-Lucille snapped. But she didn't deny it.

"Why a cubicle?" Clark asked curiously. "Why a technology place?"

"I don't know." She looked at the doll for a moment, seriously considering the question before stuffing Doris back into her bag. "She just…she sort of really belongs to the forests, but there aren't big ones left anymore? Or she didn't fit in there anymore? I dunno."

Clark decided his friend was done and probably wanted the attention taken off her.

"I have Foon, of course, and DangerMaus." He pulled out both, not caring if anyone else in the cabin saw. DangerMaus was small and blue and made from three pieces of eye-shaped cloth sewn together to make an oblong shape. A piece of leather cording served as the tail. The pointy teeth were too small to easily see from a distance; he could have been a cat toy.

"Classic," D. A. said, giving a thumbs-up. "Nice teeth."

"What about you?" Catherine-Lucille asked. "Where's your Pinky? Or Jaguar?"

"Oh, I just brought some Star Wars action figures this time, and a couple Avengers," he answered carelessly, stretching so that his hands touched the back wall.

"*WHAT?*" Catherine-Lucille demanded in outrage.

"Yeah, I dunno, there just wasn't room. I didn't feel like it. Couldn't choose."

That was too many very different answers for one unasked question: *Why?*

"But," Clark said.

"But," he said again.

"Why?" he wanted to say, but that question had already been answered. Three times.

"This summer," he said instead, which didn't mean anything at all. But also everything at once. D. A. had come over dozens of times; he said the Smiths' yard was better for playing. They hung out all day in the bushes and on the big flat rock and in Clark's bedroom playing with their Stuffies and action figures, tallying up armies, and of course playing lots of video games, too.

"What's wrong with you?" Catherine-Lucille demanded.

"I'm fine. It's safe here," D. A. said, again shrugging.

"But we *always* bring them. You never know," she persisted.

"Well, maybe I don't bring them. Now."

He said it lightly, with yet another shrug.

But the weight of his words fell heavily on the lower bunk. Clark didn't know where to look: at D. A., to see if his face changed under intense scrutiny, or at Catherine-Lucille, to try and guess what she was going to do or say next (or for warning signs to get out of her way, quickly).

"I bring action figures," D. A. added as if it was part of what he had said before. As if there hadn't been a very long pause. As if it wasn't long enough to almost mean that it was the start of an entirely new conversation, not a continuation of the old one. "That's what I do."

"D. A.," Catherine-Lucille finally said. She spoke evenly, without begging. If it were Clark he would have begged. "We even talked about this—like, a week ago. We all know you 'do' action figures. But—what, like, suddenly you 'don't do' Stuffies anymore? Today?"

"Whatever—what are you getting on my case for? I have action figures. Let's set 'em up. I have an Ultron with two fire-able missiles I haven't lost yet. Check it out."

He swung himself out of Clark's bed and up onto his own.

Clark watched Catherine-Lucille, afraid she would just stand up and go. He tried to get her attention, hoping for a patented Catherine-Lucille double eye roll and look of disgust. But all she did was frown a little, staring into space. Thinking her own thoughts.

D. A.'s legs dangled over the edge of the bed, like Monster appendages hoping for a victim.

They were swinging, in danger of—but never *quite*—whacking Clark and C.L., in the head.

EIGHT

Monday:
Four Days until the
Cabin on the Mountain

The next morning Clark stared into his bowl of Soggy-Os cereal, brooding.

Catherine-Lucille had *not* stomped off the night before. She had reluctantly stayed and the three had gone through D. A.'s—pitifully small—group of action figures. There were a couple cool new ones that were from the Avengers comic books and not the movies (D. A. and Catherine-Lucille both read them avidly; Clark didn't. He loved hearing about all the story lines that were different, though). Also, D. A. had a very cool limited-edition Ahsoka. By the time they had to get ready for bed and Catherine-Lucille had to leave they were all in pretty good spirits again.

But now that Clark thought it over, it did seem kind of strange.

D. A. was the one who had introduced Clark to the world of Stuffies and Monsters, and MPFs. And *he* was the one not bringing any? He hadn't mentioned anything about it the last time they hung out.

Also, the weather at camp that morning was weird and uncomfortable and made Clark even more irritable. It was hot and still—no wind at all. Sleeping had been hard until early in the morning. The sky was an ugly, alien grey.

Clark refocused on his breakfast. Floating in the middle of his bowl was a cluster of four and a half Soggy-Os, melded together. They looked like evil eyes that might fall out of the sky on you.

"GROSS," Backward-Baseball-Cap Boy (Shawn) declared, looking at them over his shoulder. "Whyncha grab some of those French toast sticks instead?"

"They were all gone by the time I got here," Clark admitted.

He picked up his tray and grudgingly threw out the murky milk and its questionable contents. He felt bad about wasting food, but he was pretty sure his mom wouldn't have objected if she had seen it herself.

Anna, on the other hand, would want to take a photo.

"Gotcha covered," BBCB said, tossing him one of the five sticks he had crammed into his jacket pocket. Clark caught it with only a little fumbling. "Hey—didja hear about the thing they found in Praying Mantis Cabin?"

Obviously it was *new* news; the other boy continued gleefully without waiting for an answer.

"No one knows what it is. Grey slime all over this poor kid's stuff... Everyone says it's like rotting salad, but *I* think it looks like cat puke. Not like *puke* puke, but when they cough up a furball, you know? Dark and grey."

"Um, yuck."

A cold drop of fear began to crystallize in Clark's stomach.

"Totally ruined the kid's backpack. *Plus* when they were going through it, the counselor found a stuffed animal. Clearly contraband—so they seized it. Too bad. It was really cute, actually," BBCB said, thinking about it. "A little harp seal pup, all mottled and totally realistic-looking. And they *took* it. Can you believe it? Some animal or something yarfed up all over his stuff *and* they took his seal away. What a bad deal."

"That's terrible," Clark said, feeling for the kid. He sorely hoped it wasn't the crying boy he had comforted the day before. "And super weird. Um, thanks for the French toast, though."

"No worries. But remember, you owe me!"

Clark gave him a thumbs-up and bit into the fairly yummy, crunchy stick. He wondered what form the future favor would take.

After Morning Assembly was Canoeing. At the dock he looked around for Jaylynn but didn't see her anywhere. She wasn't at the swim test, either. He made Leopard Frog this year, which was better than Eft but worse than Axolotl, and was partnered up with a younger camper named Shannon. Shannon was tiny and energetic and fairly coordinated. He picked up on the basics very quickly but only wanted to talk about Korean pop bands, about which Clark knew very little.

(He knew a lot more by the end of the session.)

After this, but before lunch, was Quiet Time—free time. Clark went to the Crafts Cabin to see what was going on.

Catherine-Lucille was hunched over a table, brow scrunched in concentration, fixing a much older camper's ragged-looking Encouragement Banner. At least that's what Clark assumed the long piece of cloth was, since a giant neon schedule poster on the wall said SESSION THREE: ENCOURAGEMENT BANNERS! YAY ON YOUR TRUE SELF WITH A BRIGHT-COLORED REMINDER HANDMADE BY YOU!

(Or handmade by Catherine-Lucille, as seemed to be the case.)

"Hey," she said, not looking up from where she was pulling stitches out.

The much older camper suddenly yelped in pain.

"Lo siento," Catherine-Lucille said through gritted teeth. "But you got a bit of *your own skin* stuck in there, too."

Clark suddenly realized that the older camper was looming far too closely to his friend because she had sewn her own shirt into the hem of the banner.

"The idiots in charge got rid of all the seam rippers and 'potentially deadly' tools—you have to sign out for a pair of *pinking shears* now," Catherine-Lucille grumbled. "How does that encourage self-esteem and empowerment?"

The older camper nodded desperately, apparently agreeing with anything her potential savior—the one wielding a giant pair of scissors close to her navel—said.

"Then again, maybe with noobs like *this one here* it's not a bad idea," Catherine-Lucille muttered.

"But it wasn't my fault!" the other girl cried. "The sewing machine just...It was like it *leaped* at me. Like it was possessed. Maybe it was a power surge or something."

Catherine-Lucille rolled her eyes.

"I'm gonna be busy with this for a while," she told Clark. "I'll see you at the—you know, the meeting place, later. We got a *lot* to discuss. Besides your induction. There's something strange afoot at the Circle K."

"What does that mean? Is that code? Should I know it for tonight?" Clark asked anxiously.

"Nah, it's just something my cousin says. It means weird things are going on."

"Oh yeah. Did you hear about the slime?"

Clark hoped he didn't sound too eager. He *never* got to be the one to deliver cool news.

"Which Cabin? Praying Mantis or Banana Slug?"

He was torn between disappointment that she already knew—and excitement at the *new* new news. "I only heard about Praying Mantis. Was the slime in Banana Slug also on someone's stuff? Like duffel bag or backpack or whatever?"

"Boy, was it. Yech."

"And was there a Stuffy there, too?"

Catherine-Lucille looked surprised, and then thoughtful— *and then impressed.*

"Yes, in fact...there was. Very interesting. Nice work, Private. I didn't make the connection before. We definitely have a lot to talk about."

"Copy that!" Clark said, trying to sound professional. Or army-like. Or something. It was hard to concentrate while overwhelmed by the glow of her praise.

"Great— Stay *still* or I'm gonna accidentally cut your butt off!" Catherine-Lucille swore at the other camper, who was trying very hard not to whimper.

Clark smiled and went back outside. While he felt rosy from the compliment, he still wondered: Would he ever have *that* kind of respect? Where people came to *him* with problems that he had the skills to fix—like sewing—or looked to him for decisions and leadership, like in a secret club?

"Hey, Clark?"

A girl tapped him on the shoulder, surprising him out of his thoughts.

It was Jaylynn!

She had grown ... a *lot* in the last year, and now towered over him by several inches. Her hair was longer, too, in lots of little braids (sadly, with no Star Wars–themed beads on them).

(She *did* have on what looked like a really fancy expensive necklace whose delicate gold pendant was the starbird, the symbol of the Rebel Alliance.)

"Hey! You're not in Canoeing anymore!" Clark said accusingly.

It wasn't what he meant to say when he first saw her.

But she laughed.

"You know, I don't really think rivers and lakes are my thing. I think trails and hiking are my thing."

There *was* something sort of especially hike-y/outdoorsy about her. Her sneakers looked almost like hiking boots, her belt was woven and had a very technical-looking pouch and water bottle attached. Besides her fancy Star Wars necklace she wore a kind of thick lanyard with pretty enamel pins of mountains and outdoor things on it.

"What's all that?" Clark asked.

"My grandparents took me to the Great Smoky Mountains National Park at the end of last summer, and we all went to the Grand Canyon for Thanksgiving. It was *amazing*. I hiked so much! Someday I want to hike the whole Appalachian Trail. And I'm trying to get my school to include trail running as a sport."

"Wow, that's cool."

There was an awkward moment of silence.

"You see that new Star Wars show? The animated one?" she eventually asked.

"HAVE I SEEN IT?" Clark exploded.

Jaylynn grinned. "I gotta get to Archery, but you want to meet after dinner tonight? I have some real issues with the weapons the bad guys use in it...."

"*WHO USES BLASTERS ANYMORE, RIGHT?* But I'm hanging out with some other friends tonight. Tomorrow night? *Please?* I have been *dying* to talk to someone who gets it! My sister just doesn't."

"You already have plans this evening? It's the first real day of camp!" she said, laughing. "Wow. Popular kid. Okay, tomorrow.

Hey, I heard you're the man when it comes to orienteering. You're in Advanced Orienteering—Geocaching?"

"Yeah! It's supposed to be like a video game, but in the real world."

"Okay, I absolutely want to know more. See you tomorrow night."

Clark was so full of goodwill and joy he almost started skipping (he stopped himself in time). Everything was awesome, slime or no slime, googly eyes, weird D. A., whatever. Camp was going to be great this year. Even better than last year.

He wandered around the main campus happily, waving to people he knew. Eventually he found D. A., hitting the tetherball ball back and forth with a new camper: a tall, lanky boy with a head that sort of hung off the end of his neck like it was stuck on as an afterthought. He had big square glasses and short dark curly hair and a smile Clark didn't like.

"Hey, Clark, this is Kris," D. A. said, catching the ball and holding it for a moment. "We met in Swimming. Kris, this is my old buddy Clark."

Clark found himself immediately warming. *Old buddy.* They had only known each other for a year, but D. A. was already referring to him as his *old buddy.* How ridiculous he had been last night, and this morning! D. A. was the same *old,* same as ever.

"Hey," Clark said. "Nice to meet you."

"'Nice to meet you.' *Classic,*" Kris said, cracking up, but he didn't say anything else.

Clark narrowed his eyes. Not a good beginning.

"So, what's your 'exciting challenge to overcome'?" he asked politely.

Everyone went to Camp I Can because of one of those...at least at the beginning. Last year, Clark's "challenge" had been to overcome his love for—and collecting of—Stuffies (he didn't).

"Well, here's the thing," Kris said with a sigh, looking piteously down at the ground. "I'm...just...too cool."

D. A. laughed and hit the ball at him.

Kris caught and held it for a moment before hitting it back—back to D. A., not on to Clark. "It's been a real hurdle in my development as a person. For real. Too cool for school."

"Must be hard," Clark said, rolling his eyes.

D. A. nodded at Clark and aimed the ball at him: *You ready for this?* Clark nodded back and prepared to spring.

"PHOTO BOMB!" Kris screamed, throwing himself in between the two, smashing the ball wildly out of the way.

The ball sailed high and hard as if hoping that it would finally escape its tether—only to be yanked back at the last moment with an unpleasant *twang* and then *thump* against the pole. For some reason this sound drove nails straight through Clark's ears and down his spine.

D. A. laughed. "You're such a freak, Kris."

"It's not even a photo," Clark muttered, walking away.

And even though he wasn't *quite* the same bullied little kid he was the year before, he was still unsurprised when the ball then hit him in the back of the head. Not hard enough to get D. A. upset; just hard enough to make a point. Clark made a note of that. Despite their brief interaction, it was already pretty obvious that Kris was the sort of kid who stayed *just within* the boundaries of nonpunishable behavior. He was sneaky. Clever.

Formidable.

Unlike the Ben Eldritches of fifth grade, who were simple in their attacks. Strong but not clever. Surrounded by loyal henchmen, true—but most of them could be avoided with just a little bit of forethought and skill. And that kind of nemesis lived for no higher purpose than immediate gratification, be it (literally) lunch money, a snack, or a momentary feeling of superiority.

What did Kris want?

Clark ran a hand down the back of his neck, subconsciously feeling for eyes but finding only beads of perspiration. Sweat didn't go anywhere in this strange weather and stagnant air. When there was any breeze, all it did was raise ugly prickles on his skin, moving the droplets along but not taking them anywhere.

He looked suspiciously at the huge old maple in the center of camp as he walked by, watching for more falling eyes. There weren't any—but he noticed something else strange. Despite the complete lack of wind, the tree's highest branches wavered and shook. Not the sort of movement the scurrying of a squirrel would cause; it was like something had just landed there.

In science class, Clark had learned that birds can sense the change in air pressure before a storm and either fill up on food (winter) or hunker down, roosting in trees to wait it out (summer). So maybe it would rain! A good rain or thunderstorm would certainly break the oppressive heat.

As Clark debated whether or not that was wishful thinking, what looked like a black wing fluttered and flapped into view as its owner balanced on the branch.

Clark stood on his tiptoes, trying to see.

The leaves were shifting and irksome, blocking his view.

It looked like there was something... *off* about the crow.

Was it hopping awkwardly on one leg?

Was it wounded?

It shambled forward and for a brief second Clark got what he thought was a clear view of its beak and face.

Of course it had eyes.

Just because Clark couldn't *see* them didn't mean they weren't there.

Or maybe they were closed. Or maybe the bird was blind in one eye, or maybe both, which was why its hopping was awkward.

Clark wasn't bothered by the term "murder," which meant a group of crows, and didn't think that ravens were spookier than any other kind of bird. When his mom had pointed out dozens and dozens of them straggling across the sky, he thought it was more fascinating than portentous.

(Anna, of course, loved them but really preferred vultures.)

For some reason *this* flailing and possibly damaged crow, which should have inspired pity from the normally kindhearted boy, evoked a strange sort of dread instead.

Clark shivered despite the heat and wondered what it all meant.

He wished he could see its eyes.

NINE

Monday Night

As if Clark had jinxed it or summoned it, dinner was shepherd's pie.

According to older campers, shepherd's pie was usually served toward the end of a session, to get rid of leftovers. So this was probably the work of the replacement staff: the new "nutrition" aide and mess hall workers.

Rumor spread from table to table faster than the salt about how one kid had found a whole bunch of plastic forks in his slice, in place of the filling.

(Which of course raised the question: Did it actually taste any worse?)

After dinner, Clark and D. A. decided to split up and arrive at the secret meeting place from different directions, to avoid suspicion. It was in the same spot as last year: behind the witch viburnum near the pine grove. The viburnum was a plant that looked to Clark like any other boring shrub at the edge of the woods—until it had been pointed out by Catherine-Lucille. Large heart-shaped green leaves, sprawling branches—*plantlike.* No pretty flowers, interesting spots, or tasty fruit to distinguish it.

Which is why it was perfect for a secret meeting spot. No one noticed it. Plus you could see all the main parts of camp from behind it—not quite a bird's-eye view, but good enough to make sure no one was coming.

When Clark got there, Catherine-Lucille was already hunkered down in the dust, Saneema and Scooter on either side of her. Three younger kids whom Clark didn't know sat silently near them, watching with big eyes.

James was there, too! He was a counselor this year; he wore the purple polo shirt of a CIT.

Which was perfect. Clark couldn't think of a better person to calmly and kindly take charge of kids.

"Put 'er there," James said, smiling broadly at Clark and shaking his hand like an adult.

"Hey," Saneema said with a little wave.

"Clark," Scooter mumbled.

"Private." Catherine-Lucille lifted her chin in acknowledgment.

Clark wondered where he should sit. He didn't want to offend anyone, or seem too grabby. He decided that on the other side of James was best. D. A. came a moment later, lifting his legs high over the scrub and immediately plopping himself down next to Saneema as if he had fallen out of the sky.

"Okay, I think we can skip roll call; all the third-sessioners are here," Catherine-Lucille began immediately. "Along with the leaders of our little network of spies who shall remain nameless in case we ever get caught or questioned. Gotta keep the young ones safe.

"We have a lot to talk about, so we'll start with Old Business— but let's keep the voluntary remarks to, like, three. How was every-one's school year?"

"I got a cat," Scooter said. "She's grey and I named her Edith."

"Excellent," Catherine-Lucille said. "Anyone else?"

"My brother started growing armpit hair and I got my own bathroom," Saneema said brightly.

"*Very* excellent," Catherine-Lucille said approvingly. "About the bathroom, I mean."

"I had a great year, that's all," James said. "Got accepted into this leadership program—gonna look a-mah-zing on the college apps—and took Shana Birenbaum to the spring formal. Life is good."

"Fantastic. All right, on to New Business. *Private Clark A. Smith.*"

There was no way to stand without being seen by the outside world, so Clark just straightened himself up, sitting as best he could. His heart began to race.

Catherine-Lucille cleared her throat and spoke solemnly.

"By the power vested in me as the leader of this motley crew, I hereby formally induct you into our secret club which has no name—"

"Which has no name," D. A., Saneema, Scooter, and James (and the three nameless kids) repeated.

"—and officially raise your rank. Welcome, *Corporal* Clark A. Smith. And congratulations."

She saluted him crisply.

Clark was so giddy he almost forgot to salute her back.

The three smaller campers clapped excitedly.

"Glad to have you with us, son," James said, tapping his knuckles. D. A. did the same. Saneema hugged him. Scooter gave a little thumbs-up.

"All right, sorry to rush this along, but we have dire things to discuss," Catherine-Lucille said briskly. "Namely, how camp *sucks* this year."

"It just isn't the same," D. A. agreed. "The food is terrible-er."

"Yeah, I've been coming here for eight years," James said. "I don't think I've ever tasted anything as bad as that shepherd's pie tonight. For real."

"Everything's off 'cause they're missing, like, half the people who work here," Saneema said, making a face. "My parents will totally not send me here next year if this keeps up. Especially if it's mono or the flu or norovirus or something that everyone's getting."

"At least Miz Shirley recovered and is still here," Scooter said. "I know she's just a secretary, but she's the one who really holds the camp together. Plus she's so nice. She's also the one who always hides the purple platypus," she added in an aside to Clark. "It's supposed to be a secret, but it's totally her."

"And what about all the slime?" D. A. asked.

"There's been a *third* slime sighting," Catherine-Lucille said. "In Sunfish."

"My old cabin!" Clark squeaked.

"So far the administration has said it's an unusual fungal bloom, or bat vomit, or—my favorite—*a prank.*"

"A prank that smells like butt and ruins your stuff? Seems a little hard-core," Saneema said with a frown.

"Okay, like, this should have been part of Old Business, I guess, but I think it's relevant," Scooter said. "Last session I found my Funko Pop Astrid and my stuffed *Anomalocaris canadensis* on the floor next to my bunk near a pile of—man, I don't know what it was. It wasn't slime, exactly, but it *was* weird. Dirt and little bits of things—none of it made sense. Sharp and ugly and gross and springy. And it smelled *bad.*"

"That definitely sounds like one of the lesser Monsters," Catherine-Lucille said. "A crowd of them, maybe. Like Feks. Did you see the photo I sent you guys from the Mo-fank forum? You can *almost* see the shine of their eyeballs from the flash. Usually their remains disappear, but not if, like, there were a ton of them. Your guys must have really taken an army out."

"Also? Scooter?" Saneema said. "You are really freaking weird. Why can't you just have a bear or a doll like everyone else?"

"Clark had a bunch of eyeballs fall on him," D. A. volunteered. "That's pretty weird."

"What Monster does that?" Scooter asked.

"So we *are* all thinking it's Monsters, right?" James said, sighing. "The slime, at least? I mean, the real slime. Not the food they've been serving."

"Unless you've got a better idea than *bat vomit*," Catherine-Lucille said.

"Okay, but if... if it *is* Monsters," Clark said slowly, trying to work out something that didn't feel right, "why would they choose cabins, and campers, with Stuffies? Which they did, for at least two of the slime incidents. And Scooter's, too. You would think they would stay *away* from kids who were protected by Stuffies. And attack someone else. Someone undefended."

"Hmm." Catherine-Lucille narrowed her eyes and tapped her tooth in thought. "That's an extremely good point."

"Maybe their methods and motives are changing. Like, I heard that some of the Monsters are *evolving*," James said. "Like they're figuring out how to get through phones and stuff. To travel to the other side."

"Nope." Saneema shook her head, refusing to believe.

Catherine-Lucille shrugged. "Kinda makes sense. Kids don't play with toys as much as they used to 'cause of video games. What a great place for Monsters to slip in, to take up the space left behind."

"Nothing wrong with video games," Scooter said. "There's room for both them *and* Stuffies."

"Amen," D. A. said with feeling. They tapped knuckles.

"Okay, but there's no video games here," Saneema pointed out. "What does that even have to do with anything?"

"I'm just saying," James said, "maybe the whole Monster situation is changing. Maybe they're getting clever, or sneaky. How much do we really *know* know, anyway?"

"We know that Monsters attack kids, and Stuffies keep them away," Catherine-Lucille said. "I mean, that's pretty basic. So why aren't these Stuffies keeping them away? Why are they . . . *attracting* them?"

"Well, what if their targets weren't the kids?" Clark asked. "What if it's the Stuffies themselves?"

Silence fell. Everyone looked at him.

"Why?" Catherine-Lucille asked. She wasn't saying it meanly or disagreeing; she was genuinely curious.

"I don't know," Clark admitted. "But no *campers* have gotten sick as far as we know, right? Or started acting weird? Just all those counselors and staff. *Adults.* Also not normal Monster targets."

"No campers have gotten sick because their Stuffies all killed the Monsters trying to attack them, right? Adults don't have Stuffies. Usually. So they're unprotected. Isn't all that slime dead Monster stuff? That's proof the Stuffies did their job." Saneema asked.

"Not necessarily; some Monsters leave traces. Like footprints, but disgusting. That's how you can track them sometimes," Catherine-Lucille said. "But listen: When the counselors were shown the slime, they found the Stuffies and took them away. No more Stuffies to guard that kid, or that cabin.

"So in a sense, the Monsters *did* accomplish something. If they were targeting Stuffies, I mean. They got them removed."

"Maybe they're also trying to poison us, with the food from the mess hall," Scooter said thoughtfully.

"*Great*," Saneema said, picking up a twig and throwing it down in disgust. "Camp is being invaded by Monsters. Clever ones."

"All right, all right, look, this is exactly what we're here for, soldiers," Catherine-Lucille said, seeing the fear and defeat on their faces. "Sure, we help protect the occasional vulnerable Stuffy-less camper by making Stuffies for them. And sometimes we lend a hand to complicated problems like Clark's last year.... But *this* is the real deal. Camp is being invaded, or Haunted.

"Worse yet, some of us are going home this Friday and the rest of us are going on the camping trip. Camp I Can will be completely abandoned and vulnerable over the weekend. When we get back, it's gonna be a total disaster—a total Monster fest. And totally unsafe."

"Don't the counselors stay here?" Clark asked.

James laughed. "Heck no. Everyone spends their paychecks in town, or goes to the movies, or the pizza place—some even go home, although that's frowned on. This place is like a ghost town. Even Miz Shirley disappears to take care of her gardens and bird feeders."

"So how do we stop the Monsters?" Saneema asked. "Especially if none of us will be here on Saturday and Sunday?"

"Well, we can start by figuring out how they're getting *into* camp," Catherine-Lucille said, pounding her hand into her fist. "We're in the middle of nowhere. Monsters usually *hate* that. They like being around people they can torture and feed on. There's no scary bedrooms here, and we keep all our stuff under the bunks. There's no basements or attics for them to hide in. So where are they, and how are they getting here?

"We need to keep our eyes and ears open, listen at doors when the counselors are talking. We need to make sure every weird incident is reported to *us*. First. So we can see if there's a pattern or something. We need to find every potentially scary location at the camp. Dark, deserted, dismal—Monster spots. We need to ID them and set up guards.

"And we need. To make. More. Stuffies."

TEN

The Circle of Fire

The call of the Moon was whisper-quiet, muted by clouds that smothered the hot and heavy earth.

But Foon heard.

His eyes snapped open and he leaped up, joyful. In two quick springs he was off the bunk and landing elegantly on the floor.

(With a spin of his trident as an unnecessary but skillful flourish.)

He looked around at the other Stuffies making their way out of their Boys' beds, sliding down sheets and tumbling softly to the ground like he did when he was New.

So much had happened since the last time Foon was in a camp cabin—and his movements reflected those changes. He stood taller, stepped more surely, and held himself both with more ease *and* more tension, always ready for a Monster attack.

He looked different, too.

There were some new and careful stitches sewn around his wounds. And resewn. There was a little puckering around the largest holes. His mouth pulled to one side when he talked—but it was a far better job than his Boy had originally done. Later operations were much more successful. Just as Foon had grown more accomplished in fighting, so too had his Boy improved his skill in repair.

Foon ached to be able to actually speak with him about it all. About the sewing, about his Boy's admirable patience, about the adventure itself in which he had saved his Boy's Family and the whole House.

Of course it was impossible.

Most Stuffies never even imagined such a thing. They lived at night, when their children slept, and slept while their children played in the light of the sun. Two worlds apart. Thus it had ever been.

But . . . just *once*. To be able to thank him for his care, and to hear from his Boy's own mouth about life in the House now that it was free of Monsters . . .

Foon shook his head. He wasn't a melancholy Stuffy. He didn't waste time dwelling on the impossible. Besides, there was the Circle of Fire to join!

"I AM AWAKE AND HERE!" DangerMaus cried from the top of the bunk. Foon gave him a friendly wave of his trident. The mouse jumped down and skittered in several bounces to join the other Stuffy, his needleteeth sparkling silver in the soft light.

Together they helped open the door. Foon lent a kind hand to a Baby Yoda—who was a babe in truth, having only recently opened his eyes.

Outside the air was thick and heavy. It brought its own sense of excitement and adventure, like the Stuffies were marching off to an exotic land. The clouds were bloated with deep crevasses and static wrinkles. No matter how hard the wind tried to move them along, no light from the Moon or stars pierced through.

Foon worried a little about what the night would bring. Would his comrades from last year be there? Would they accept him as easily and warmly as they had before? Had he made them proud with the battles he had won?

The scene at the Circle of Fire put his concerns to rest immediately.

To begin with, the Great Bear was there. Foon didn't know how the giant Stuffy managed to come, whether his child went to camp or not, or if his child was really a Grownedup. In the end it didn't matter—he had come.

And there, waving her paw delightedly, was the saber-toothed tiger. And next to her, waving one of his two—feet? Hands?—was the Stuffy whose name Foon had eventually learned was Baby Monster.

He strode over to them with gladness in his heart.

"Foon!" the saber-toothed tiger cried. Not caring about formalities, she wrapped him in a meaty, warm tiger hug.

"Well met," Baby Monster said with a grin.

"We have heard such stories about you," the saber-toothed tiger said, finally letting him go.

"We want to hear all about your year," Baby Monster said. "I've had some odd adventures of my own. Let us share them by the fire after the Great Bear has spoken!"

"I would love to hear them. Friends, this is DangerMaus," Foon said, introducing him politely.

"AT YOUR SERVICE!" the little mouse cried, giving a bow.

The bear was now making his way to his place at the top of the Circle of Fire. He lowered himself into a sitting position with the slow, heavy movements of an unthinkably powerful creature.

Then everyone else sat but waited a few more minutes for stragglers: tiny action figures and awkward things like a stingray who couldn't quite fly but didn't quite walk, either.

"By the Grace of the Velveteen, let us come to order," the bear finally began.

"By the Velveteen, let us begin," everyone else echoed back.

"I see many old and friendly faces tonight," the bear said, looking out over the assembly with kind brown eyes. "And many eager new ones. Welcome! You join us."

"You join us," everyone repeated.

"It is not a fit night to bestow the honors of first kills or grand quests," the bear continued, more gravely. "For the Moon's face is hidden and the stars won't see us celebrate. There will be time for that later. I fear we have more pressing matters to attend to. Something is . . . not right about this place of safety."

Everyone in the crowd made little sounds of surprise and wonder. Foon leaned forward and listened intently.

"I have seen no Monsters myself," the bear admitted. "And I have had no reports of anyone else actually seeing them defile this sacred space with their foul presence. But there have been strange traces in the wind. And the remains of what might be Monster spoor have been observed within the camp boundaries."

There were outraged hisses and murmurs of *no!* at this.

"Also, several of our compatriots have been unjustly locked up in the main cabin," the Great Bear added. "We will do our best to free them but must, as always, be sure none of the Grownedups suspect anything.

"So I will take the unprecedented step of assigning nightly watches and patrols. There is *something* Dark afoot here, and we must get to the bottom of it."

"I volunteer for the first guard!" a Barbie called out, tossing back her pink-and-black-striped hair.

"As do I!" Foon added immediately.

"It is well done," the bear said, nodding at them. "I shall assign the rest of the watches when we break. I do not know precisely what we are looking for—but keep your eyes and ears open and trust in the Light. For the Velveteen!"

"For the Velveteen!" the crowd chanted back.

The bear howled, his muzzle pointing where the Moon would be, hidden though she was by the clouds. It became the haunting, familiar chant all the Stuffies somehow knew.

When it was over he bowed his head.

"*By the Grace of the Velveteen, go in peace*—but prepare for war."

"*We go, with Love and Light,*" everyone responded.

The Stuffies immediately began to whisper among themselves about the strange and foreboding words of the bear—and rumors about what had been happening around camp. Foon looked for the Barbie he would be patrolling with, but his search was interrupted when a familiar reindeer approached. Behind her was an unfamiliar dog person and a *very* unfamiliar green thing with horns.

"Freya!" Foon cried in delight. He tapped his trident, Focus, twice on the ground in recognition and respect for her. "Sabertoothed tiger, Baby Monster, meet Freya. Freya, hail and well met."

"MIGHTY REINDEER, HELLO!" DangerMaus squeaked.

"Good Hunting to you," Freya said in greeting, lowering her antler rack. "This is Doris and Ren Faire Beast."

Freya was the Stuffy of a girlfriend close to his Boy. Freya, Foon, and some other Stuffies and action figures had hunted together many times when their children had playdates.

Foon liked Freya—she was tough like Winkum and mighty like Snow Killer. Together they had gleefully wiped out dozens of Tahks and a large flock of Cowbers and one particularly persistent Garloby.

Her body was that of a famous character from a movie or television show—a lot of Stuffies were like that—but she wasn't a boy, like that character was. And she was fiercely proud of being a girl.

(In this way she was a bit like Baby Monster, who was certainly not a baby, nor a Monster.)

"Ah, it's so nice for friends from the same village to meet in the sacred space!" the saber-toothed tiger said. "How lucky for you!"

"*Knight Foon!* Hail and well met!"

Foon turned, curious; he did not recognize the voice calling him. It belonged to a small but very serious-looking chartreuse cat who gazed at him adoringly.

"Well met, fellow Stuffy," Foon said formally. "I don't believe I know you...?"

"*IS THAT THE FOON?*"

A giraffe with indistinct features and a floppy neck (a baby's Stuffy originally, and obviously still very loved) came galloping over on its short and stubby legs.

"Yes, I am he," Foon replied awkwardly, looking back and forth between the cat and the giraffe. "May I just...Can I ask how do you know me? And..."

But more voices called out.

"*It's Foon!*"

"Foon!"

"*Mighty Foon!*"

"He's here!"

Suddenly Stuffies of all size and shape, age, and ability were surrounding him. Unaccustomed to crowds, Foon did his best not to back away—but moved his trident from one paw to the other nervously.

"Is it true you defeated a *King Derker* all by yourself? On your first battle night?" a crab—whose back unzipped to hold two smaller crabs—asked reverently.

"Absolutely not," Foon replied. "I would have died the final death had it not been for my brave companions. They finished off the Monster and kept watch over me until help came. I am eternally in their debt—as they are in mine, as we all are to each other, comrades in the fight against the Dark."

This brought sighs and murmurs of agreement from his—rapidly growing—audience.

"How modest you are!"

"And noble!"

"How big was the King Derker?"

"Did he have other Monsters working with him?"

"Did he lay eggs?"

"Can I see your mighty weapon?"

Foon started at this last request.

Not because he felt any harm would come to his silver trident, his trophy and "mighty weapon," but because it was a strange favor to ask. The trident was really just a tool, an extension of him; there was nothing magical or fabulous about it. He had named it Focus to remind him of his need to *focus* during fights and to not let battle rage take him over.

But he handed it over, deciding it would be rude not to.

The Easter chick who had asked now held it up, beak open in awe. Everyone oohed and aahed.

"Tell us more," an alien Stuffy begged, its tentacles waving earnestly. "What else happened that night?"

"There were other Monsters I dispatched along the way," Foon began slowly. "A school of Silver Fish, a particularly foul Lomer..."

This was met with exclamations of dismay and horror.

"Silver Fish *and* a Lomer?"

"*Two* Higher Monsters? On the same *night?*"

"Tell us the *whole* story!"

"Yes! Let us move to the Circle of Fire and tell us all!"

As Foon was gently pulled away by the crowd, he looked back helplessly at Freya, the saber-toothed tiger, and Baby Monster. The reindeer rolled her eyes. His other friends giggled with good nature. The Stuffies dragged him up onto the Telling Rock. The fire crackled before him and a sparkling sea of plastic, glass, and painted eyes looked upon him eagerly.

"Well," he began. "My Boy's house was haunted, and in most dire need of a Hero...."

ELEVEN

Tuesday:
Three Days until the
Cabin on the Mountain

Neither D. A. nor Catherine-Lucille (nor Jaylynn) was taking Fire Skills, but that was okay. Clark looked forward to it like an adventure, something he was tackling all by himself. He wished he could have brought his fire-making kit to use (and maybe show off). But it would still be pretty exciting to learn how to make a fire, even using matches.

And then he saw Kris. Lounging against the wooden sign that marked the path to Fire Skills.

Clark tried not to sigh, and his shoulders definitely didn't droop—this was not fourth grade, Kris was not Ben Eldritch.

(He kept telling himself.)

The other boy sort of perked up when he saw Clark. His eyes grew brighter and he straightened his lanky neck, swinging it around with interest like a potentially harmless elasmosaurus.

Potentially.

"Hey, you're D. A.'s little friend, right?"

"Yup," Clark said, choosing neutrality.

"Put 'er there, man!" Kris offered his hand to slap. Clark reached out and was not at all surprised when Kris quickly pulled his hand back and began to laugh—great, fake, gargling inbreaths that sounded like choking.

"Hilarious," Clark said, still neutrally, continuing down the path. Kris followed, laughing and telling other kids what he did. This wasn't Clark's first rodeo. Honestly, if he had to count all the times something like that had been pulled on him ... it would have been too high to count. Probably, like, a *googol* times, or googolplex.

On the official map of Camp I Can the class space was labeled *Fire Skills Pavilion*, inspiring an image of broad green fields, castles, knights with brightly painted coats of arms, and maybe dragons. In actuality it was a dingy, bare-dirt clearing a good hike from the center of camp. Well, actually not *bare dirt*: The ground was naturally paved with giant slabs of grey rock that might have been sparkly under sunnier conditions. Gneiss or granite. The boulders were so large and perfectly flat that they looked like they were set there by construction machinery of the gods.

On the north side of the clearing was a neat pile of logs stacked next against a green wooden supply bin. Near this was a bucket and tap, though the pipe looked like it merely diverted water from a nearby creek. The bucket was also green and had three friendly red licks of flame painted on it. A giant old garage broom leaned up against a tree; the ground was neatly swept.

All across the rocky "pavilion" were crude circles to contain fires, all made of pleasingly rounded stones. They looked like the ancient ceremonial ruins of a tiny but terrifying race. Several kids were already wandering around inspecting them, waiting for the session to begin. Some used old, charred sticks like pencils to etch games of tic-tac-toe on the ground like ominous black runes.

Clark began to get excited again, forgetting Kris.

The Fire Skills instructor—he guessed—was an older girl perched on top of the wooden supply bin with her arms dangling over her knees. Her straight black hair was gathered into a ponytail popping out the back of a Camp I Can baseball cap, and she had a whistle on a long lanyard around her neck. The lanyard was all different colors, made of odds and ends of craft supplies. Clark was pretty sure there was even a feather or two sticking out of it.

She watched the campers gather, eyes narrowed thoughtfully.

Suddenly she blew a long, shrill blast on her whistle.

Everyone covered their ears. It was a horribly painful noise.

"ALL RIGHT, CAMPERS, LISTEN UP!" she screamed.

James appeared—popping up out of the woods—silent and stolid beside her. Clark gave him a little wave. James smiled back . . . and then quickly reset his face to *blank.* He was staff now.

"WELCOME TO FIRE SKILLS. I'M FIRE SKILLS

INSTRUCTOR MAYA LIM. THIS IS JAMES. LET ME BEGIN WITH THE FIRST RULE OF FIRE SKILLS."

"There *is* no Fire Skills?" Kris asked, elbowing the camper on his right to get her to react to his joke. "Like *Fight Club*? The first rule of Fight Club is that there is no Fight Club?"

"Amusing," James said. "But zip it."

Clark watched with envy as the other boy, mollified by the compliment, settled down. James was always so good with people! Even the difficult ones.

"THE FIRST RULE IS THAT ANY CAMPER FOUND MAKING A FIRE OR HAVING FIRE-MAKING PARAPHERNALIA WITHOUT A COUNSELOR PRESENT WILL BE EXPELLED FROM CAMP IMMEDIATELY. THIS INCLUDES EVERYTHING FROM STRIKING A MATCH TO HAVING A ZIPPO LIGHTER IN YOUR BAG. AM I CLEAR?"

Everyone nodded or kicked their feet impatiently.

Maya the Fire Skills instructor leaped off the bin and blew her whistle again.

A couple campers actually fell down to the ground in agony from the terrible sound.

"AM.

"I.

"*CLEAR?*"

she asked again.

"Yes!" all the campers shouted desperately.

Kris was last to join in and trailed all the others so his voice could be heard by itself.

"...yeeessss."

"ALL RIGHT."

Maya nodded at James. He opened the big wooden bin and began taking out supplies. Clark couldn't help standing on his tiptoes, eager to see what was in there. It all seemed like magic.

"We will get to primitive fire-making skills by the end of the week, if all goes well." Although she switched to a normal voice, she gave them a smile white as death, her large black eyes bright with something like insanity. "Which may seem counterintuitive, but the whole point of this is to teach you to make *useful* fires. For camping, or in a fireplace, or a woodstove. None of which requires flint or a bow drill in this day and age. We want nice, well-burning, steady fires for cooking and warmth and marshmallows here. Got it?"

"GOT IT," all the campers shouted back immediately, terrified of the whistle.

"Excellent." Maya stood on the backs of her heels and put her hands on her hips, beaming at them. She was never not posing. Or—not *posing*, exactly, because she wasn't looking for a reaction. She was like a ball of lightning, or a million springs pushed down tight, a jittery fire imp forced to stay still within her human skin. Infinite energy that was just waiting for a release.

"There are three distinct ingredients to building a fire." She began pacing back and forth in front of them while James calmly divvied up the supplies into neat little piles. "In reverse order of application: your main fuel, which is wood…"

"*SHE SAID WOOD*," Kris said in a loud whisper, whacking the boy on the *left* side of him, which fortunately wasn't Clark.

"…kindling, and tinder." Maya narrowed her eyes at Kris but didn't say anything to him. "Now, most people get kindling and tinder confused…."

"Aren't those both dating apps?" Kris asked, lightly punching the first kid again. Clark realized he recognized the girl from last summer…. What was her name? *Pony Girl!* Well, actually Grace. *Grace* was wearing a pink tee with a sequin unicorn on it. She was taller and more sure of herself, but just as adorable and big-eyed as last time.

She whacked Kris right back.

"MAYA? JAMES?" the boy immediately whined, holding up his hand. "This camper right here hit me!"

☆　☆　☆

And that wasn't the end of Kris's interruptions. They got *worse* after the kids were split into groups and given their fire-making materials. Clark was, very fortunately, at a different circle—but that didn't stop Kris from wandering by and casually kicking several stones out of his ring. One of the other kids called him a bad word and Kris immediately ran off to tell a counselor.

Clark sighed and concentrated on repeating the day's lesson to himself.

Tinder was small and fuzzy and often oily and easily flamma-ble: pine needles, sawdust, or tiny bundles of twigs held together by wax (which they would learn how to make by the end of the week, to take home). Even certain brands of corn chips were so fatty they burst into flame when you lit them.

"And, bonus, you can make camping meals in the chips bag," Maya had said. "But that's Advanced Fire Skills: Cooking on an Open Flame."

Kindling was like super-tiny logs that the tinder helped to catch fire: larger twigs or small branches. They burned longer than the tinder and eventually lit the logs themselves.

For the *fuel,* logs were carefully placed on top of the kin-dling in such a way that there was room for airflow but nothing collapsed.

There were too many campers for them all to get a chance to try it on the first day, but Clark watched the others with the fixed concentration of a cat in front of a mouse hole. He saw Grace blow too hard, causing the tinder to go out. He watched Saul—a self-proclaimed firebug—put too much kindling under the logs; they burned quickly, collapsed, and crushed the baby fire out of existence. He cheered as Archer—a willowy goddess of a girl—stood back from her work and tiny flames began to lick the big logs, then finally envelop them in flame.

"Yahoo!" he cried, pounding her on the back. Archer smiled, and it was like liquid sunlight.

"Pretty neat, huh?" Fire Skills Instructor Maya said, crouch-ing down next to Clark, a single fingertip touching the ground for balance. "Fires are...amazing. You know? They cook and they warm.... They banish the shadows, but summon *more* shadows. Like magic..."

Clark tried to look at her without really looking at her. It didn't matter; her eyes were focused intently on the growing flames. Without looking at *him*, she put a hand on his shoulder and squeezed.

Fire Skills Instructor Maya was probably not altogether sane, Clark decided. But there was something weirdly comforting about her. *Safe.*

Then a grossly moist sound occurred above and to the right of Clark. A wet fizz and sizzle confirmed what he feared: Kris had come over and spat into the fire.

"I wonder if I could pee this thing out," he declared loudly.

"You can't," Maya informed him matter-of-factly. "Back to your own group, reprobate."

Yup. She was *definitely* safe.

TWELVE

Tuesday Night

After dinner ("spaghetti and meatballs"—not the worst, especially if you didn't actually eat the "meatballs" and used them as Ping-Pong balls instead), Clark went to meet Jaylynn on the other side of the pine grove. He was full of pasta and humming happily to himself when a terrible sight stopped him dead in his tracks.

The witch viburnum was shaking violently—but not because of a creepy bird.

The bright colors of a camp shirt stood out garishly against the dull green of the plant as the one who wore it kicked the ground and roots, shoved aside branches, and stripped leaves off the shrub.

Obviously it wasn't any member of the secret club.

It was Kris.

Again Kris.

What the heck? *Why* was he suddenly everywhere in Clark's life now? Wasn't there enough going on?

"What are you doing?" Clark tried not to demand. He also tried not to *stalk* or *stride* over to the other boy. Maybe there was still a chance to pretend it wasn't an important (and secret) spot.

"I'm looking for the mysterious Illuminati clubhouse where all the losers hang out," Kris said, roughly pulling a branch out of the way. "There's nothing here. No hidden candy, no stash of— Ohhhhhh."

He smiled with realization, and it was an ugly smile.

"You're *one* of them, of course. That totally makes sense. You're exactly the kind of dummy who needs a secret club to feel special. Isn't that right?"

Clark didn't like lying.

He didn't like Kris in what he considered private—no, *sacred*—space.

He paused too long.

"EXCLUSIVE little kids' club, isn't it?" Kris asked, immediately sensing weakness. He stepped over to Clark, kicking the bush—hard—as he went. "I want in."

"Why do you want to be in a *little kids'* club?" Clark asked as calmly as he could. "With *losers*?"

The bigger boy's face darkened. He stepped forward, looming over Clark.

There were, Clark realized, no counselors around. No one at all, in fact. Suddenly and stupidly he wished that he had Kevin or Pog or the newly made DangerMaus with him, in his pocket. Not that a Stuffy could do anything against a bully. But it would have made him feel better.

He tried not to back up, but fear—and Kris's unbrushed dinner breath—was making it hard.

"D. A. told me about it," the bully said. "I wanted to check it out."

Clark's fear quickly turned into rage.

D. A. had invited *this* cretin into their special place? True, as far as he could tell there were no hard-and-fast rules about who could join and who couldn't. And sometimes nonmembers came to the club with special requests, like Clark had once. But all who did were respectful.

And also—Clark noticed the very careful way Kris said everything. *D. A. told me about it*, not *D. A. invited me to join*. And *I wanted to check it out*, not *I want to join*. And he never answered Clark's question about why he even wanted to. Everything was worded to make it sound like Kris wasn't interested—but at the same time, he also made it all sound like a threat.

"Well, I guess no one's around now for you to check it out," Clark said. It was a statement of fact. He was neither confirming nor denying anything.

"No *kidding*, Sherlock," Kris said, rolling his eyes. "I'm gonna go find D. A."

He stalked off, pulling his hand along a branch of the viburnum, shredding the heart-shaped leaves as he went.

"You pick it, you eat it!" Clark yelled after him, unable to contain himself.

(This was a camp rule and saying to discourage the pointless hurting of harmless plant brothers and sisters.)

Kris bobbed his head back and forth, obviously mimicking him as he walked away.

Grinding his teeth with rage, Clark stomped off in the other direction.

But his fury quickly melted away when he saw Jaylynn sitting on one of the now-empty benches in the pine grove. She had a smile as wide as the best summer day and excitedly waved for him to come sit by her.

He had *so many things* to talk to her about.

"Okay, first your pins..." he said.

"...then *your* Geocaching..." she said.

"...and then Star Wars!" they finished together.

"These are from national parks," Jaylynn explained, pointing to the prettiest, most colorful badges. "State parks don't always have pins. They do have patches, though. But these are my favorite—my Junior Ranger pins!"

These were large and a little ungainly, too big to hang well on the lanyard. But they were made of wood and smelled like smoky campfires, and she sounded *so proud* of them.

"You have to earn them. Like, you do all the things in a booklet, answer questions, find stuff in the park...and then when you're done they swear you in! Like a real ranger!"

Clark was nearly consumed with excitement and envy. This

was *way* better than the Boy Scouts! He could earn badges with his family, on vacation!

"That's why I'm so jazzed to go on the intersession camping trip," she went on. "I've never actually camped out before—we always stayed in lodges and motels. Which my grandma said was *like* camping, because the beds were terrible, but it really wasn't. It's not camping when there are ice machines down the hall."

"Wait, you're going this weekend, too?" Clark interrupted. "So am I! And all my other friends!"

"That's great," Jaylynn said, grinning. "*Plus* it means we'll both be here next week, too. So tell me about Geocaching, in case I wind up loving Orienteering and want to take it."

"It's basically like a game of hide-and-seek with little hidden treasures—caches," he explained. "Normally you use a phone with GPS coordinates. Here at camp they use compass directions, the number of steps or paces you need to take to get to each position, and geographical clues. No electronics allowed. And probably no prizes? But who knows.

"So . . . speaking of *electronics* . . ."

From then until the first curfew horn blew, the rest of their talk was about Star Wars. Clark was sorely jealous that her dad watched all the movies and shows *with* her. He was the one who had given her the Rebellion symbol necklace for her birthday.

(Clark had to watch the TV shows alone, although sometimes Anna would keep him company on the couch while watching horror movies on her phone.)

As the two walked back through the gloaming together a

warm breeze blew...bringing with it a strange and sour smell. It was nothing Clark could immediately place: sort of sweet, like honey, but then fetid and rotten. Not exactly like garbage or the compost bin his mom kept on the counter (which he often forgot to deal with when taking out the actual garbage). Not even like the camp bathrooms at the end of a long day. This was way, way worse than both—and kept getting stronger as they walked.

Jaylynn gagged and covered her mouth.

"What the...? Oh my God, that's *disgusting!* Did a Porta-John get knocked over? With a decaying corpse inside?"

"It's like the dumpsters outside the mess hall. After it rains," Clark said, trying not to breathe.

"Everything at camp is so gross and off this year!"

"Definitely," Clark agreed. Wishing he could say more about... *things.* Wishing he could talk to her about Monsters.

"You know what else is weird? I'm missing, like, half my socks. I don't think anyone's taking them...they're *socks*. Gross old white socks. Who would do that?

"Also this weather is the worst. It's dark and hot like something terrible is coming."

"Maybe we'll get a thunderstorm that will clear it all up and get rid of this stink...and flood the fields."

"That would be the best! I love hiking, but I *hate* running laps," Jaylynn agreed.

Eventually they left the foul odor behind, but Clark remained unsettled. She was right: There *were* a lot of bad things at camp this year. Not all of it had to do with Monsters.

Most of it had to do with Kris.

All thoughts of him had been temporarily banished by talk of the Rebel Alliance and the Junior Ranger program. Now these worries demanded attention, rushing eagerly to the forefront of his brain like campers to the mess hall on Taco Night. Clark had to tell Catherine-Lucille about the boy and the vandalization of her secret meeting place.

If he *didn't* tell her about it and it came out later that he knew, she would be very, very angry. And feel hurt and betrayed.

(But most importantly be very, very angry.)

If he *didn't* tell her, but she found out about it later from someone else, and she never knew that Clark had known, it would all *seem* like it was okay—at first. But actually it would eat him up on the inside like a small, painful Monster that had decided to live in his stomach.

He had a hard enough time choosing between two ice-cream flavors. *This* was impossible.

But as it turned out it didn't matter.

He and Jaylynn arrived at the dorm cabins to find a small crowd gathered. Campers were watching and discussing and pointing at something Clark couldn't see.

And then, very much exactly like when you're playing a video game and it's the end of a level and the NPCs sort of nudge you to the boss monster because It's Time, Clark pushed through the gossipers and saw Catherine-Lucille and D. A.

Facing off.

Between the toothbrush and handwashing stations.

Catherine-Lucille wasn't screaming, and that was what terrified Clark most of all.

She was just standing there, hands on hips, face blank, dark eyes large and shooting fire.

"What's the big deal, C. L.?" D. A. was asking. Clark wondered if anyone else could hear the (tiny) note of nervousness in his voice. "I know it's not a democracy, but you're pretty open about who can come."

"Oh, please!" Catherine-Lucille shouted. Clark relaxed. Shouting was a *doing*. Not-shouting was a seething, a *planning-to-doing*. Something terrible, probably. "If he really wanted to join, he could have come like anyone else, with a request. He *didn't*, D. A.—he didn't respect the rules or the process."

"You didn't have this problem when I sent you Clark!"

"Clark was totally different!" Catherine-Lucille spat. "He needed help, and he made the effort to find me. And you—you didn't tell Clark where we met. You didn't tell him that he could just show up and stomp all over our bush and ruin everything. You told him to find *me*. And he did, and we helped him, and we became friends, and *then* he became a . . . you know."

"Please leave me out of this," Clark said.

But whether he was speaking extra quietly and no one heard, or no one *cared*—including both his friends—he wasn't sure. Either way, he was ignored.

"Wow, I wish I had popcorn," Jaylynn said. "This is kind of epic."

"Don't be such a snob," D. A. said accusingly to Catherine-Lucille. "Maybe *Kris* needs help, too. Just a different kind of help."

Reasonable, Clark thought.

He tried to imagine Kris in one of those guidance-counselor cartoons: a boy made into a bully because of Reasons, who could be Helped Out and turned into a Good Guy, an Ally.

…but he couldn't imagine it.

Clark was a bit of a connoisseur of bullies and didn't think that a single meaningful heart-to-heart or offer of friendship would change *this* boy's ways.

Or…was he being too hard on him?

"He doesn't act like someone who needs help. He acts like a jerk," Catherine-Lucille growled.

"Just get to know him! You'll see. He's really cool!"

"*How?* He didn't bother to get to know *me* or anyone else! And I don't think you know him half as well as you think you do anyway!"

"Ho darn!"

This was said by Scooter over by the Porta-Johns. She had one hand on the door, apparently too hypnotized by the fight to actually go in.

(On the other hand, finding a reason *not* to use the Porta-Johns wasn't really that hard.)

Clark wondered if he should step forward. If he could find something, some strength or brilliant insight, somewhere inside him that he could call upon. Maybe a stirring speech he could give that would fix the situation, calm his friends down, and impress the crowd. Like the hero does in movies.

He opened his mouth, hoping that something brilliant would come out.

And then Kris stepped forward.

"It's no big deal," the boy said unexpectedly. "Not worth fighting over. I was just curious about your little club. Don't want to break up a friendship over it."

Clark frowned.

The sort-of-bully *sounded* like he meant it.

Kris shrugged, *No big deal,* and looked back and forth from D. A. to Catherine-Lucille. "Come on, don't be weird. It's nothing. Sorry I kicked your bush or whatever."

Catherine-Lucille glared at him, as if expecting a trick or a laugh. "Apology accepted. Thank you. But this isn't really about *you.* It's about D. A."

Clark was very envious. Even in the midst of her fury Catherine-Lucille was able to state clearly what she was angry about. He wasn't very good at that himself. It always took him a long time to figure out exactly what he was feeling and then how to describe it.

"Oh, it's *always* about me," Kris said with a grin, stretching his hands up behind his head and pointing to himself with his thumbs. He spun around the crowd, his audience. "Me, me, me, meeeeeeeee! I'm da king of the worrrrrld, Ma!"

He bowed in every direction and waved his hands. He made a farting noise.

Everyone laughed or smiled. *Everyone.*

The tension was ... over?

Clark let his breath out cautiously.

Okay, Kris had done an actually kind of amazing thing. Now everything sort of felt stupid and less ... dramatic. It was all funny, not world-ending.

Even Catherine-Lucille relaxed, although she still looked suspicious.

Kris strolled away, his performance over.

At the last moment he called back, over his shoulder:

"I mean, for real? A secret club about *stuffed animals* and *monsters?* C'mon, guys ... why would I even *want* to join?"

He gave a nasty smile and disappeared down the path.

Catherine-Lucille's face turned bright red.

She swallowed—Clark saw her neck muscles move once, twice, like a snake on a nature show trying to deal with its lunch that was still alive and kicking.

"That boy's trouble," Jaylynn muttered, shaking her head.

Everyone in the crowd seemed to be following Kris while trying to look like they were *not* following him. But the clearing emptied out in his general direction. As if he were a drain sucking them all along with him—and down.

Clark wondered if he should go over to Catherine-Lucille.

Once again he was puzzled about where all of the counselors were.

They were always everywhere you didn't want them to be. Where were they now?

But before Clark could decide to do anything, Catherine-Lucille whirled and stalked off into the woods—the opposite direction of everyone else.

And D. A. was gone.

Just—gone, like he had vanished. Either with the crowd of kids behind Kris or his own way into the background. No apologies, no halfhearted attempts to make up, nothing.

Clark slumped and went back to his own cabin, alone and defeated.

And he hadn't even been one of the people fighting.

THIRTEEN

THE GREAT PLETICON SPEAKS

We are getting oh-so-close now, my dear Monstren!

The foul-smelling Vormonths have a definite lead on the boy.... And if the Chowgun haven't found him yet, they have still helped the cause. No less than *five* stupid Stuffies have been removed from their stupid children in the last two days!

(All Monsters currently in the World of Light for purposes of the Great Revenge Plan are, of course, welcome to feed on these now-unguarded children. At your discretion. Try not to leave obvious evidence like the Chowgun with their unfortunate slime.)

Just a few more nights and all our patience will be rewarded! (Deliciously!)

FOURTEEN

Tuesday Night, Late

Clark lay awake thinking about Monsters, and Kris, and D. A., and Catherine-Lucille.

Then he thought about other things.

Slime, counselors, and confiscated Stuffies.

He took Foon and carefully shoved him under his mattress, so that only the tip of one horn stuck out.

"Sorry, buddy," Clark whispered. "I just don't want anyone—Monsters *or* counselors—finding you and taking you."

Eventually he fell asleep, one arm dangling over the side of the bed so he could hold on to Foon's horn while he slept.

FIFTEEN

Patrol

With all the clouds it was hard to tell exactly when the sun set or the Moon rose. The strange weather made all minutes seem the same.

Even the children were troubled by this. It took a long time for them to fall asleep deeply enough for the magic of the Moon to ease them into that stillness beyond dream.

And rather than popping up fully awake as Foon was used to, he got up slowly, almost groggily. Only the urgency of his task reached clearly through the confusion of his mind, to slap him upright.

And then—when he *couldn't* sit upright—he suddenly realized why the air felt so heavy and dark.

He had been stuffed under his Boy's mattress.

By his Boy—if the hand grasping his horn was any indication.

"Strange," Foon said. Then he carefully pushed himself out and climbed up on top of the bed.

He checked his Boy with concern, but everything seemed all right. He looked peaceful with his eyes gently shut and rosy cheeks—still a child, once the falseness of daylight hours had dropped away. All the words and screens and bags and food and running were shaken off, leaving him the pure core of himself. Foon laid a paw between his Boy's eyebrows and murmured a little song he had learned from Winkum.

Sleep and rest and heal and dream
Peace and strength and light and love

"Is there a Calling?" DangerMaus asked a little sleepily. He was tucked under the Boy's pillow. Only his nose stuck out, and it twitched as if he could smell fun or threat.

"No, I am on patrol. The Great Bear is correct. There is something wrong...something not right about this place."

"That's for sure," DangerMaus said, nodding his slightly misshapen head. "And I don't just mean the stink of these kids' feet. I think some of them have been wearing the same socks all week."

"Keep an eye out here, keep our Boy safe."

"I'll keep *all* the Boys safe!" DangerMaus promised, saluting.

Foon privately doubted that the little mouse could do much good against a Lomer or a Derker, or even a clique of Garsts, but he appreciated the Stuffy's enthusiasm and confidence. He saluted back and slipped out into the night.

The Barbie was waiting for him on the path outside. A breeze tried its hardest to break apart the clouds but only succeeded a little. The Moon shone off and on through holes in the ivory thickness, as if an old worn sheet covered the sky. Its occasional beams glittered in the Barbie's black-and-pink hair.

"Well met, Stuffy Foon!" she declared, raising a weapon above her head. It was, he saw, a plastic microphone stand. She wielded it like a bō staff.

"Well met, Doll Barbie," he answered, raising his own weapon.

(A real one. A silver one. A prize he had won for beating a school of Silver Fish, and to help him in his quest against the King Derker.)

He hopped down the wooden steps to join her on the path. Despite the dullness of his colors, together the two still stood out, twin small things who didn't belong there under the tall trees and open sky.

"Normally I would see no reason to waste our time around the empty buildings," the Barbie said, immediately getting down to business, "as our main goal is to protect the children. However, since we don't know exactly what manner of danger we're looking for, perhaps we should investigate any lonely-seeming places for Monster activity."

"Agreed. Well thought, Barbie."

She made a noise through pursed lips. Foon wondered if he had somehow offended her, if maybe he had implied that a Barbie couldn't think well in general.

They fell into step, only a little awkwardly, marching through patches of moonlight and shadow. Despite the ragged clouds—or perhaps because of them—the night was beautiful. The edges of everything were outlined in pale silver, brighter and duller as the light changed. The middles of everything were ebon black.

Foon wondered if this was what it was like to be Outside during a stormy afternoon—but with sunlight and bright colors instead of the black-and-white world of night.

"Have you ever been Awake during the day?" he asked the Barbie curiously.

"Sure. Bunches of times. When they're away—at school, usually."

The casualness with which she spoke, her familiarity with the world of children and their lives away from home, was bewildering. Maybe it was because the Doll looked like one of them. Was dressed, more or less, like a person. Had accessories and props that were made for purely person things, and not just weapons for protecting the world from the Dark.

They were quiet for a while as he pondered this.

"I have never worked with a Doll before," he admitted.

The Barbie gave him a look. It was hard to read with the giant triangles of blue paint above her eyes.

"First time for everything" was all she said.

"The Dolls in my House are not—friendly."

He did not add that they were fiercely loyal to their Girl but completely untrustworthy as comrades. That they even threatened Stuffies whenever they came too close.

"Well, we're not usually welcome in places where Stuffies rule," she said. "Different worlds."

"The Dolls in my House are vampires," Foon explained.

The Barbie guffawed: an ugly, pleasing sound.

After she stopped there was another noise, so slight it barely tickled the tip of Foon's horns. But the Barbie suddenly whirled around, bō staff twirling dangerously over her head and body. She crouched, prepared to strike.

Foon dropped into his ready stance.

There was a flicker of not-quite-shadow, another shade of grey different from all the others shapes around them.

Faster than his eyes could follow, the Barbie started to bring her staff down on it—

—but faster still, Foon put a paw out to stop her.

Immediately she froze. Like the very best soldier, sensing that her comrade knew something she didn't.

Floating just above them, barely a Foon's-height high, was something that looked like smoke which hadn't quite dissipated. Or a tissue not quite dissolved in a bowl of water. Or the idea of a gentle wave made real.

It was longer than the Barbie and as wide as Foon. It

undulated a little like a caterpillar, but instead of feet it had ragged edges, not quite tentacles, not quite wisps. Two long feelers flew back like feathers from what might have been a head.

"What *is* that?" the Barbie asked in wonder.

"Some say it is a child's dream," Foon said, watching it with a smile. "Some say it is another thing entirely—not Stuffy nor Monster, not of the Light or the Dark. Something that just *is*."

"It's so strange, and beautiful!"

"I saw one once outside when my Boy was having a sleepover," Foon recalled. "An old and wise leader, Dredful Duck, stayed my hand from attacking, just as I have yours. She said no one knows what they are, but they are harmless. Just another one of the thousand mysteries of the night."

They watched for a long moment as the gossamer thing held steady against unseen breezes in the night sky. Then it moved on, to parts unknown, and so did they.

"If it's a dream, I wonder what it's of," the Barbie mused.

"Us, maybe?"

She smiled and tapped her staff against her shoulder. He had no idea what that meant. But it didn't seem to be disagreement.

The dusty path was silent, the night dark, the trees peaceful.

(The woods were of course devoid of Monsters; they clung to human habitations and remains like sickly shadows, leaving the wilds alone.)

So far nothing had seemed especially unusual or unfriendly. They passed the tiny plastic bathrooms the people used here, but didn't look too closely; the only Monsters likely to haunt them were Vormonths, and though unbearably stinky, they were pitifully frail—a Defense of a quarter of a point or less.

So the two warriors patrolled, alert, but not alarmed. The mood felt thoughtful and gave rise to things Foon often considered when he patrolled alone.

"I wish—" he began.

"There are no wishing stars," the Barbie interrupted.

"What I mean to say is *I would like*, or . . ." Foon stopped, frustrated. "Don't you ever want to be able to talk to your child?"

The Barbie stopped and stared at him.

"It's impossible," she said. "We walk different rays of the Light; our paths don't cross but in sideways smiles."

She was quoting something, Foon was certain, a hymn or poem he didn't know. But it sounded right.

"Yes, but—I want to hear about my Boy's day. I want to comfort him when he is sad," Foon persisted. He would never have mentioned this to other Stuffies. There was something about the night and the strangeness of the Doll that made saying such ideas aloud less embarrassing. She didn't know him or admire him and her mind was utterly alien. He didn't feel like he would be judged. "I want to discuss the games he plans."

The Barbie pursed her plastic lips.

Foon wondered if he had said too much.

"I'd like to be able to answer my Girl's questions," she finally said. "She has so many, and she only asks me and my comrades. And we can't answer."

The two looked at each other for a long moment.

"You're a strange Stuffy," the Barbie said, but not unkindly.

"I am handmade," Foon said with great dignity.

"That's not what I meant. Wait—look!" Suddenly she pointed with her bō staff, giant eyes widening even further.

Foon slowly approached the spot that she indicated.

There was a footprint.

A series of little footprints actually, smaller than a Foon paw but larger than a Barbie toe. Two ugly claws forward, two raggedy ones back.

Even as they watched, the telltale spoor of the Monster bubbled and roiled, malodorous grey ooze filling and seeping into the ground where the heel of the foot had been.

Foon and the Barbie looked at each other.

They had circled the camp on their walk and were back right where they started.

The footprints led away from Fishercat Cabin.

SIXTEEN

Wednesday:
Two Days until the
Cabin on the Mountain

That night Clark had strange but beautiful dreams of things he couldn't quite remember. But when he woke up and saw the rounded shape of D. A.'s butt pushing the mattress down above him he remembered how everything at camp was actually mixed up and a little rotten.

As if simply being thought about was enough to wake him, D. A. leaped down like a jack-in the-box whose crank had just hit the release trigger.

"Up and at 'em, Clarkyboy," he said cheerfully, swatting him in the face with his baseball cap before putting it on for the day.

Was his cheer a little forced?

Or was Clark looking for things where there wasn't anything? Monsters where there were only shadows?

For breakfast there were aspirationally named "griddle cakes."

"Griddle cakes" made Clark think of an old-fashioned three-layer iced chocolate cake out of some nostalgic dream of a birthday—or a farm breakfast involving aprons, black iron pans, nutty grains, and chores involving chickens.

Of course Camp I Can griddle cakes were neither. They were giant canary-yellow pancakes whose centers weren't cooked at all. No one ate them; a few kids actually started gagging when they tried.

(Saneema tore two eyes and a mouth out of hers and applied it like a facial mask at a spa, like on TV shows.)

(It dried there—other campers swore they saw her at the nurse's tent later getting it chiseled off.)

As Clark dumped his own raw and gross breakfast into the garbage, a tiny camper sidled up to him and whispered a message while looking the other way.

"*Emergency Meeting. Quiet Time.* Ask for *James* in the main office. Tell them you have an in-tra-person-alish shoe."

Clark regarded the eight-year-old curiously, but she scampered off once the message was delivered and her own breakfast—entirely uneaten—was dumped in the trash.

Whatever had happened the night before, Catherine-Lucille still had the power to command her strange camp network.

But first: Fire Skills! Clark was super excited for it.

The focus that day was going to be *banking* fires: taking the flames and sort of slowing them down so they gave off less heat but more evenly and lasted longer. This was better for cooking, warmth throughout the night, and eventually charcoal production.

(Charcoal production was in the Super Advanced Fire Skills class—Teens Only, in conjunction with Primitive Clay Pot Production and Firing.)

It was an interesting but difficult class. Despite there being no wind, the fires refused to light or stay lit—banking them was nearly impossible without healthy flames to begin with.

Maya squatted down and grumpily poked at the smoldering logs that Clark's group had managed to light.

Clark tried looking away, but he couldn't avoid staring. There was just no way to ignore Fire Skills Instructor Maya's mismatched socks.

Like, *glaringly* mismatched socks.

One outrageous fat purple sock was scrunched down and jammed into her left boot. One thin turquoise sock exploded out of her right boot and reached up to her knee, tightly hugging her calf.

Everything Fire Skills Instructor Maya did was deliberate; it might be sudden, quick, and random-seeming at the time—but it was never without cause.

"Your socks don't match," Clark's mouth said before his brain could stop it.

Maya gave him a quick sideways look under a glowering brow, like a bear not ready to strike *just* yet.

"Half of my socks are missing," she grumbled. "Everything's—*off* this week. My coffee tasted like there was salt in it. And before you ask—I *always* check to make sure no one has switched it out with the sugar as some dumb camp prank."

"My sister Anna sometimes puts a tiny bit of salt in her coffee," Clark said, hopefully helpfully. "She says it's Italian."

Maya narrowed her eyes until only little tiny sparks could be seen glinting from her black pupils.

"Are you saying the talentless creep they subbed in for the missing mess hall guy—the one responsible for this morning's breakfast tragedy—is making *fancy Italian coffee?*"

James swallowed loudly. Apparently they were treading on very thin ice here.

"I'm saying that some people who are fancy, like my sister, like coffee with salt," Clark said very carefully.

Maya thought about it for a moment.

"Okay. I can live with that. I'll say it's fancy. *Italian.*"

She beamed, blew an enthusiastic breath into the fire, and the flames leaped up eagerly.

James and Clark both relaxed.

"Hey, I hear you're on the intersession camping trip," the Fire Skills instructor said, giving Clark a second look—a more appreciative, thoughtful one. "Good deal. I'm the senior counselor on it. Should be fun."

"Hey, that's great! Me and my friends are—"

"FIRE IN THE HOLLLLLLLE!"

Kris was screaming, running through the pavilion. He carried the emergency bucket of water over his head and of course it sloshed and spilled on everyone he passed.

Clark couldn't see exactly what happened next. He could have predicted it, though.

There was a loud *SPLASH* and then silence.

And then some very ominous dripping.

The crowd parted and Clark saw that Kris was—as expected—standing over a now-very-extinguished campfire. Three mostly sodden girls (including Grace) looked up at him with incredulous eyes. Little rivulets of water dribbled through the ash, making a muddy, ugly mess.

"THEIR FIRE WAS OUT OF CONTROL," Kris cried triumphantly, pointing with his non-bucket hand.

"It wasn't—" one of the girls began.

"I SAW IT!" Kris shouted down into her face. Then, modestly, facing the counselors: "I saw it. I saved everyone. I should get a medal."

"I should get more Italian coffee," Fire Skills Instructor Maya said through gritted teeth. She pulled up uselessly on her purple sock. It stayed scrunched down.

☆   ☆   ☆

The afternoon was bleak and grey; perfect for solving the Mystery of the Missing Golden Idol in Geocaching. Everything felt spooky and Counselor Tyler really got into it, preparing seven different cache locations to find and wearing a monocle and everything. Clark's team came in third and he didn't even mind. They learned lots of things, including a valuable lesson about how moss doesn't really always grow on the north side of trees. And while the reasons why were fascinating, so were the plants themselves: tiny fairy forests of dark green plants like pine trees that loved moisture. Clark could see Anna grabbing some and doing something weird with them, like putting them in a jar with tiny figurines. Maybe pebble headstones.

Even the Golden Idol they found at the end of the session was kind of cool. It was really just a brass keychain with the head of a famous statue or something, but it looked old and valuable.

Plus it was a Traveling Geocache, a treasure that once you found and logged you then hid somewhere else for someone else to find.

Canoeing, on the other hand, was terrible. It was strangely cold out over the lake and their paddles seemed to do nothing, dipping into water like thick honey. Their usual instructor had been replaced by a pale man with a mustache who shouted a lot without any actual instructions.

"Where's Scalybutt?" Clark whispered to his partner, Shannon.

(Their usual instructor wiggled her butt weirdly when she came out of the water to dry off—not properly like a person or even a dog. Everyone assumed she was part slimy fish.)

"I heard she got an infection from the lake and now has a flesh-eating virus," Shannon whispered back.

Clark glanced at the water in alarm. It probably wasn't true, but those black depths could have hidden anything.

Then someone did something wrong—no one was sure what—and as a result they *all* had to "practice survival swimming."

This meant throwing themselves into the cold water, T-shirts and everything still on, and swimming to shore.

Which would have been bad enough.

But that's when the screaming began.

"Leech!" a girl shrieked, panicking and kicking her legs. "Oh my God, leech!!!"

"There's no leeches in here," a boy said disgustedly, treading water and splashing some at her.

"I know what leeches are and one just tried to get me!"

Clark sucked in his stomach and anxiously scanned the murky depths (while also protecting his privates).

Was that…that wasn't something black and sinuous gliding down there, was it? Undulating, thin as a shadow, drifting over his legs?

Clark tried very, very hard not to scream.

"One's on me!" another boy cried out. *"It's on me!"*

Immediately there was frenzied splashing and screaming as everyone all at once forgot how to swim and tried to make a mad dash to the shore—abandoning their canoes.

"get back here" the instructor ordered, but quietly and without real conviction.

Crying and hyperventilating and generally freaking out, the campers all somehow made it to the beach, like a very confused flock of animals.

There was no blood, and despite a couple of kids running to the nurse—life jackets still on—there did not seem to be any actual leeches.

What there *was*, well...Clark would not have believed it if he hadn't seen it with his own eyes.

There was indeed a long, black, slimy, shadowy thing flowing down the back of one girl's leg, unnoticed by her. But it didn't stick there like a real leech. It trickled down along with the water as it dripped off her, not seeming to move on its own.

It dissolved into a pool of clay-colored ick that hissed and steamed as it settled into the sand.

Clark stood on the beach, freezing, speechless, and wet. Terrified by what he just saw.

He wanted nothing more than to run back to the Fire Skills Pavilion—Maya would definitely have some sort of fire going somewhere. He felt like he would never get warm again without one.

Also, he wanted to be near a grown-up. Even an insane one like Maya.

But instead he dutifully (and drippily) went to go find James and the secret meeting. Boy, would he have a lot to report.

Clark had never actually been to the Hobbit House—the main administrative cabin—before. It was made of logs and had a cheery sign hanging next to the window that said ALL WHO WANDER ARE NOT LOST. Inside was a giant desk and comfy old chairs covered in moose-y fabric. Behind the desk sat the kindly, large old lady with the purple glasses whom Scooter had told him about: Miz Shirley.

Although...she didn't *look* that kindly. Despite her kooky glasses and the duck pins on her Camp I Can shirt, she gave

Clark—not a *frosty* look, exactly, but a sort of blank one. Blank and slightly evil.

Actually, she didn't seem too different from Miss Nugganoth, the creepy secretary at Warnock Elementary and Middle School.

"Um, hello?" Clark said uncomfortably. He couldn't tell if she was looking at him or not; the glare of the light on her glasses hid her eyes. "Is James in? I have some, um, *intrapersonal issues* I need to talk about with someone."

There was a long pause.

The loudest thing in the room was the lake water slowly dripping off him and onto the foor.

Then the woman s-l-o-w-l-y turned her head and tipped it toward Clark.

"open counseling hours are on in the c.i.t. day cabin out back make a right when you leave here follow the path c.i.t. james is seeing campers now you may go in want a butterscotch"

It took Clark a moment to realize she had said two, maybe three, distinct things.

There *was* a giant basket of old-fashioned butterscotch candies on the desk in front of her, yellow and unwelcoming.

"Uh, no thank you, but thank you anyway," Clark said.

They were both quiet.

Miz Shirley continued to stare down at the basket.

(Probably? He still couldn't see her eyes.)

"So, um, have you hidden the purple platypus anywhere really good this time?" he asked, trying to be polite.

Her head swung up to stare at him.

"what platypus"

Clark swallowed.

Had Scooter been playing a joke on him? Was it all a lie?

"Uh, never mind. Thank you, Miz Shirley. See you later, I guess."

He had to resist the urge to back away from the scary woman (so he could keep an eye on her). He sort of sashayed sideways awkwardly toward the door—and then hit his head on the frame. He clawed it open a little more desperately than he meant to.

Outside he took a deep breath of air, which, while moist and hot, was still fresher than in the administrative cabin. He felt like he had barely escaped something terrible. He practically ran down the path away from it (and Miz Shirley).

The Counselor-In-Training Day Cabin was an astonishment. It was an entirely open structure on one side, as if a normal cabin had been sliced in two by an alien beam and half had been removed for further study.

It still had "indoor" furniture: a desk and several chairs and a beanbag chair and a floor lamp. But you could sit on the edge of the cabin, one foot in the grass, one tucked up under you on the wooden floor. An in-between place.

James was doing that right now, sitting on the edge, sewing something.

Catherine-Lucille and Saneema were hanging out a little farther inside . . . *also* sewing. C. L. was hunched over, feet tucked up under her, a little tense like she always was, stabbing quickly at what she held.

"Welcome to the new hideout, Corporal," she said, looking up at him with a wry smile.

"*This* is the new hideout?" Clark asked in wonder. "*Our* new hangout?"

James laughed quietly. "Yup. We won't be bothered here. Don't even worry about it."

"Nice," Clark said appreciatively.

But he realized he was clenching his teeth and scrunching his toes. Usually he only did that when they had to visit Great-Aunt Cassie or some parent was commenting about how cute he and some girlfriend looked together.

"Please don't tell me not to tell D. A. about this," he finally blurted out.

"No need," Catherine-Lucille replied coolly. Meaning she had already thought of it. "Kris gets within a hundred feet of this place and Miz Shirley out there gets him. If he somehow manages to bypass her, James can just pull rank and . . . 'schedule a better time for some Real Talk.'"

"He *could* use some Real Talk, though," James said thoughtfully. "That boy has issues."

"D. A. could use some Real Talk, too," Catherine-Lucille growled. "Corporal, you're dripping."

"Yeah, um . . . yeah . . . about that . . ." Clark sat down next to her, a little awkwardly because of how the skin on his arms and legs rubbed, still wet from the lake. He smelled like copper and wasn't sure whether or not to be embarrassed by this. "Something really, really weird just happened in Canoeing. Our regular instructor, from, like, *Monday*, was gone . . . and the new guy made us all dive in with our clothes on. . . ."

"Lakebait!" Saneema said, laughing.

"Yeah, but then everyone began freaking out because of leeches. . . ."

"There's no leeches in Lake Wantastiquet," James said, frowning. "The trout eat 'em all, and the flow from the streams around is too high."

". . . but they weren't really leeches," Clark finished. "The one I saw was more like . . . um, I dunno . . . a leech-like shape if it was made out of oil? Or old coffee with some grounds still in it? It sort of dissolved when it flowed down this kid's leg and hit the sand."

The three other club members stared at him, smiles gone.

"When it hit the *sand*," Catherine-Lucille demanded, "or when it came out of the water on the kid's leg and was exposed to sunlight?"

"Oh, I don't . . ." Clark thought about it. "Maybe, yeah. It was cloudy though, no actual sunlight. . . ."

"It was enough, I'll bet. Especially for Crellans. They're delicate—except for their needle straw mouths."

"How could it be *Crellans*?" Saneema demanded. "I thought they only came out of faucets and bathtub taps and stuff like that!"

Clark's body had a hard time deciding whether to shiver or throw up. Those . . . icky things . . . usually flowed out of *faucets*?

He pictured himself alone in the house, about to wash his hands, and one slithering out...too quickly and black and slimy....

Or in the tub...no way to move away from it...

"Yeah, but it's, like, the only water Monster I really know of," Catherine-Lucille said thoughtfully. "And look, that lake is so gross and dark they could live at the bottom for a while without getting hurt by the sun."

"WHY ARE THEY HERE?" Clark practically shrieked.

"They're part of the invasion, obviously," James said. "Like with all the other Monsters."

"Hey, y'all!" Scooter appeared at the door/giant opening of the cabin, holding a box of sugar-free, gluten-free vegan crackers (swiped from the Special Diets section of the cafeteria).

"Nice!" Catherine-Lucille said, brightening. "I'm *starving!*"

Scooter scooted herself down into the middle of the others, opened the box, and handed them out.

Camp taught you things you didn't even know you didn't know, Clark reflected. Before, he never would have dreamed that sugar-free, gluten-free vegan crackers would taste as good as Oreos to his rumbling stomach.

"So, latest development: We have a definite Crellan sighting," Catherine-Lucille informed Scooter, jerking her head at Clark. "You can ask him later about that. And the Canoe instructor is missing."

"That's the sixth counselor this summer," the other girl said, frowning.

"What's weird is that none of the junior counselors or CITs like me have gotten 'sick,'" James said. "Only people in charge—like in charge of other counselors or units, you know—people with decision-making powers."

"That's ominous," Catherine-Lucille said, tapping her tooth. "So...all the folks at the top, including Park, are being replaced. I wonder if, or how, the Monsters managed that."

"Hey, speaking of people in charge," Clark said, giving Scooter an injured look. "Your Miz Shirley was *not* nice. She was creepy and weird and cold and didn't know anything about the platypus. Were you just pranking me?"

"No," Scooter said, eyes wide with shock. "No—she really *is* the nicest person. She hugs a little too much, and she's the one who came *up* with the whole hiding platypus thing!"

"Scooter, I just talked to her. It was weird," Clark said. "And her candy looked gross."

"I mean, her candy *is* gross," James said with a shrug. "But she really likes it herself. Maybe I'll go have a little talk with her later, see what's up."

"Maybe she's been taken over, too. By a Shawgrath. Or Ghellish, I'm told, can also do it on occasion," Catherine-Lucille said.

"Also Fire Skills Instructor Maya keeps losing her socks. And so does Jaylynn," Clark added.

The others stared at him doubtfully.

"I thought it might be important!" he said defensively.

"It might be," Saneema allowed, patting him on the hand.

"Maybe it's good y'all are going away from the camp for the intersession camping trip," James said with a sigh. "And you two are going home. Maybe it's safer."

"In the meantime, *here*." Catherine-Lucille picked up something fuzzy and cloth-y and threw it at Clark.

"Hey! It's DangerMaus!" he said in surprise.

It was indeed a version of the little Stuffy he had made himself, but with blue fur and felt ears and eyes and no tail.

He looked around at what everyone else was sewing.

"You're all…making…DangerMauses. DangerMice. Danger…um, my guy," he said slowly.

Catherine-Lucille gave him a grin. "Brilliant simple and fast design, Corporal. So we borrowed it. Gather round, y'all…."

She pulled a piece of paper out of her back pocket and carefully unfolded it. Everyone bent over to look.

It was a map of the camp. But it had been drawn on and written over, just like the one Clark had been given to find the illegal cell phone the year before. This time there were Xs on camp buildings and arrows pointing to corners that didn't make sense (at first).

"Okay, I've been working with our tiny spies to find all the most abandoned, dark, lonely, and scary places in camp. Spoiler alert: There aren't many. When it's not cloudy, this place is all sunshine and dumb freaking songs. But there are a few! Like here, here, and here. That's where I figure the Monsters hang out—when they're not bothering us." She pointed to several places with Xs drawn on them.

"So. The plan is to make as many DangerMauses—"

"DangerMoose," James suggested.

"As many Danger*Moose* as possible," Catherine-Lucille conceded. "We'll hide them in the scary places. To watch and guard them."

"Wow, smart," Clark said appreciatively.

"So. I've already assigned James to deploy his DangerMoose in the places around the administrative cabins. Scooter will take the periphery: the old shed back behind the fields and the bird blind on the east side of the lake. Saneema will do this section of the campers' cabins here. I'll do the other section. And some of our unnamed tiny spies will be doing the low-hidey-crouchy places, like under the steps near the nice guest outhouse. Which only leaves the basement of the mess hall."

"That place is freaking terrifying, man," Saneema said.

The mess hall itself was always loud and cheery and full of smells.

The mess hall *basement*, on the other hand . . .

The one time Clark had looked down there it was . . . scary. Like the basement of every school, church, or grown-up gathering place ever. Deserted and silent. But even *more* deserted and silent than it should have been.

"I'll do it," he heard himself saying.

"You sure, Corporal?" Catherine-Lucille asked. "It's a doozy."

Clark swallowed and nodded.

"All right, well, here's another one for good luck," Saneema said, handing him a second, bright pink DangerMaus she had just finished.

What had he just done? What had he just volunteered himself for?

But... they had promoted him to corporal. He had to prove he deserved it.

He looked at the two little Stuffies in his hand.

He could do this.

He *had* to.

SEVENTEEN

DangerMaus

I AM MIGHTYYYYYY! I AM LEGION! SEE HOW MY MINIONS, MY ARMY OF MIGHTY MICE, SCAMPER OUT ACROSS THE LAND TO DEFEND INNOCENT SLEEPING CHILDREN!

MONSTERS, BEWARE!

WE ARE AN ARMY OF LIMITLESS MOUSY DOOM!

EIGHTEEN

The Circle of Fire

Foon woke instantly, called not by the Moon but by other Stuffies.

He ran as fast as his paws—and the giant door—let him, hearing urgency in the summons.

At the Circle of Fire the Great Bear stood over a small crowd. Foon could hear the murmurs and mutters of wonder even before he got close. Everyone—Doris, the Ren Faire Beast, Baby Monster, the saber-toothed tiger—was there.

"Knight Foon! They caught the Monster!" a tiny creature with big eyes said. A beanbag Stuffy; his solemn look was greatly enhanced by the thick ring of eyelashes around each giant blue eye.

As politely as possible, Foon pushed his way through the crowd. At the front Freya and a cat guarded a tied-up Chowgun.

There was no question that it was the Monster whose trail Foon and the Barbie had found. The ugly little thing had two long skinny legs like a nightmarish bird's, and each foot ended in four claws: two forward, two back—just like the footprint from the other night.

It was hideous to behold and a little terrifying despite its size. A sort of human neck and head rose up from a baby chick's body. And no matter how hard Foon looked, there was no way to focus on the details of the face. The eyes and nose and mouth just sort of blurred away.

It scratched the ground with its claws and chuffed and peeped piteously.

"Foon, well met," the Great Bear boomed. "As you can see, Freya and Boppy brought in the prey whose spoor you tracked."

"Well done, Freya, Boppy," Foon said, bowing to each. Freya lowered her giant rack of antlers in return.

Boppy was a bright red floppy kitten who looked under-Stuffed and very soft to touch. She meowed in response but her eyes remained murky.

(Probably a Berserker, Foon decided. These were quiet, quiet, quiet warriors who would suddenly and insanely go violent on the battlefield. Good comrades—but you needed to know how to manage them.)

"If I may, why didn't you kill it?" Foon asked curiously.

"It was on my orders," the Great Bear said. "So we could question the foul thing. Its presence here in this place of peace and respite is beyond strange."

Foon nodded, struck once again by the bear's wisdom. Such a thing would never have occurred to him—Monsters were for slaying, not getting information from. Perhaps there was a place for that in emergencies. It was something to remember for the future.

"We have learned little as yet," Freya added. "It is not the smartest member of its disgusting kind."

Indeed, the way the thing was peeping and scratching, it looked like it barely had a thought in its head—more like a Tahk or a Fek, not a middle-order Monster with a Defense Six.

"Loathsome beast," the bear growled, looming over it threateningly. "Tell us! What brings your cowardly self into this sanctuary of Light?"

"*SANCTUARY SANCTUARY SANCTUARY!*" the thing spat. Its voice was deeper than it should have been, considering its size.

Foon gripped his trident tightly, wanting more than anything to eliminate this stygian monstrosity.

"NOBODY CARES ABOUT YOUR DUMB *SANCTUARY!*" it continued. "SOON WE WILL HAVE REVENGE. SOON WE SHALL FIND THE ONE WE SEEK. SOON WE WILL DESTROY YOUR WORST MIGHTIEST. WE SHALL SPREAD OUR DARKNESS LIKE BLACK OIL ACROSS THE GROUND ON WHICH YOU TREAD AND YOUR ENTIRE WORLD. ALL SHALL BE SWALLOWED, ALL DARKNESS HALLOWED!"

"Answer the question," Freya said impatiently. It was obvious that she, too, was itching to impale the thing on her antlers. "Why—particularly—are *you* here?"

"*I OBEY THE LOMER WHO WATCHES US WITH ITS UNEYES. IT SENDS ME WHERE I NEED TO GO. IT TELLS ME WHAT I NEED TO KNOW!*"

A Lomer...? *Here?*

Lomers were Higher Monsters, rare and cunning—and cowards. They only showed up when an even *Higher* Monster had already infested a place, making it safer for creatures of the Dark. The one Foon had defeated was haunting his Boy's House because there was a King Derker in the basement.

(And it was only finally destroyed with the help of the friendly Ap-Lions in the kitchen. Lomers were fiendish opponents.)

So why was one *here*? And ordering *other* Monsters around?

Foon's thoughts were interrupted by someone tugging at his ankle. He looked down; it was the big-eyed beanbag from before.

"Mighty Foon—*you* were tracking the Monster. To you goes the right of First Kill, or capture. Are you mad at Freya?"

"No," Foon answered patiently. "We *all* work together to defeat the Dark. My patrol was over. Freya and Boppy continued what I and the Barbie had begun.

"I am *glad* they found the enemy and captured it; now the Great Bear will find out why Monsters foul this place with their presence. Quickly, I hope—I would like to be there for any battle, and soon I join my Boy on a mighty camping adventure in the mountains. But while I am gone I trust my comrades will complete the task without me."

The little beanbag Stuffy looked chastened and lowered his eyes. "You are so wise and bighearted, Knight Foon. Forgive me. I am newly made. Someday maybe I will be as good and brave and wise as you, if I listen and learn."

Foon patted the furry thing on his shoulder and gave him a kind smile.

But he was still thinking about what the Monster had said. *We shall find the one we seek.* Who—or what—were they looking for? Another Monster? A child? A Stuffy? A Stuffy made more sense, especially because the Chowgun had promised to *destroy your worst mightiest.* Did it mean the Great Bear? He was the mightiest of all the Stuffies.

But didn't the Monster recognize that the bear was standing right in front of it? Possible; the thing looked insane and had limited intelligence. Which might explain why it needed to be given orders by a Lomer . . .

But that was *also* strange. Monsters did not organize themselves like this. They were chaotic and anarchic and served no one but themselves and the Dark.

Something very big, and very bad, was up.

Something . . . *new.*

NINETEEN

Thursday:
One Day until the
Cabin on the Mountain

The day passed in a blur, the two Not-DangerMauses (DangerMoose) stuffed into Clark's pockets.

(Feeling a little silly, he had introduced them to the real DangerMaus the night before. He thought about calling them Maus Two and Maus Three, after the graphic novel, but decided that would be weird.)

Quiet Time seemed like the best time to hide them at their assigned post. But when would the mess hall—and its basement—be emptiest? How long would he have to wait after lunch? How much time did it take for everyone working there to clean up and take a break before beginning dinner prep?

Also there was an urn of coffee and a bowl of (tiny, sour, possibly unwashed, "healthy") apples set out in the entrance that were refilled occasionally . . . He had to be careful about that, too.

Clark idly wondered what scared him more: being caught by

an adult in a potentially illegal situation, or alone in a potentially Monstrous situation. He decided they both stank.

Then he got an idea.

An *amazing*, brilliant idea.

An idea that fixed two birds with one stone. Or whatever.

He would ask D. A. to come along.

Clark got almost dizzy with excitement. First of all (and possibly most importantly) he wouldn't have to go into the basement alone! Second, it might smooth over any hurt feelings or lingering anger. *Come help out with this secret club mission!* How could that not appeal to D. A.? Maybe Clark could even get him and Catherine-Lucille talking again.

Also it would just be way more fun if it was the two of them. More like shenanigans, as his dad would say, and less like a terrifying, kind of hard-to-explain thing to do.

It was another hot but cloudy day. Muggy. But like Jaylynn, D. A. wasn't a huge fan of swimming. So Clark searched the shady pine-gnarled hills that separated the cabins, instead of the lake. He bet correctly: D. A. was lounging in a cool ravine between two ridges, seated on a nice mound of moss.

He was alone, which was weird for D. A. Then again, things had been kind of weird for the last twenty-four hours. But he was also tossing a baseball up into the air and catching it, which was not weird at all for D. A.

"Hey!" Clark said.

"Hey," the other boy said, brightening at seeing his friend. "What's going on?"

"Not much," Clark said, trying to remain calm while feeling a dandelion puff of hope. Should he sit down next to D. A.? That would be more friendly. But it looked so comfy and green and soft and magical, he was afraid he wouldn't get up again. "I'm going on a dangerous secret mission—want to come?"

Immediately he felt stupid about how he sounded. Too much, too fast.

D. A. pushed back his baseball cap to get a better look at Clark.

"Is this a secret club thing?"

"Yes."

"Did C. L. send you to me?"

"No…"

Clark wasn't sure if this answer was a good or bad thing. He wasn't Catherine-Lucille's messenger boy. On the other hand, maybe D. A. would have liked it if she were trying to send a peace offering.

"Mmm," D. A. said, showing neither interest nor disappointment.

"It's just a fun thing I thought we could do. We're hiding these little mice all over camp…." He held up the two Not-DangerMauses (Not-DangerMoose). He didn't say *why* they were doing it. "I got the mess hall basement. I always kind of wanted to know what goes on down there….I thought maybe you'd wanna check it out, too."

"Huh." D. A. scratched a bite on his elbow. "Sneaking around places we're not supposed to be *does* sound kinda interesting."

"Yeah, I can't believe I'm actually doing it. Breaking camp rules." Okay, maybe that sounded a little forced, but it wasn't *not* the truth. "We can check out all the secret rooms down there. Like where they store the food that's actually edible."

"Well," his friend said, sitting up. "I *was* thinking about going over and grabbing one of those nasty apples they leave out in that bowl. I'm stashing it for when we canoe across Lake Wantastiquet tomorrow to go camping... in case we see a beaver. Turns out beavers *love* them."

Clark waited for what seemed like millions of seconds.

"All right, I'm in." D. A. made the decision the same way he did everything: firmly, no thinking twice, no regrets. Clark wished he could be that sure of himself. That quick to decide.

"Great!"

They tapped knuckles and did the squid thing. D. A. leaped up with the casual grace of a lesser sports god and the two walked down the path together. It was exactly like old times—okay, with a *little* tension. They passed Pony Girl (Grace) and Clark waved. She waved back with a giant wand she was blowing even giant-er bubbles with. These sparkled and changed colors in the sun like something out of a fantasy movie. D. A. waved at someone Clark didn't know. Clark wondered if college would be like this: hanging out with friends, going places by themselves, relaxed and chill...

"Hey, how come you weren't at the meeting yesterday?" he suddenly asked, unable to stop himself.

What was *wrong* with him? It was a perfect moment. Why did he have to spoil it?

But he had to know.

"I had Field Sports—we organized a special game of kickball and one of the counselors agreed to ref."

"Oh. Cool."

Clark felt a wave of relief. It was a real reason for D. A. to not be at the meeting, not because he was uninvited or refused to show up.

Clark's heart felt so light it was like it was going to explode out of his chest.

They passed the administration offices—Clark shuddered at the memory of Miz Shirley—and the canteen. The mess hall, squat and ugly, was last.

Clark tried not to slow his step or hesitate, but he felt fear rising up from his stomach to his throat. It was of course much better *with* D. A., but still terrifying. What if they were caught? Or eaten?

D. A. put out his hand to stop Clark.

"We should totally case the joint first," he said.

Maybe his friend was also nervous, trying to delay things . . . but it *was* a good strategy.

They crouched down across the way, behind a bush with a good view of the front of the building. And they did observe some interesting things.

The new "nutritionist"/"executive chef" came out with the stiff movements and blank stare of a *not* friendly robot. Very, very similar to the behavior of Miz Shirley and the weird new canoe instructor. He walked with jerking steps to the parking lot.

Then another person came out, a guy Clark recognized from last year. He slouched and looked around sneakily...and slipped far too *casually* behind a tree.

The two friends exchanged knowing looks.

Clark pointed at a different tree that would give them an even better view of what was going on. D. A. nodded and they quickly tiptoed to it.

The mess hall guy was definitely up to something.

He took one last quick look around, stuck a hand into his pocket, and...

...pulled out a cigarette.

With a sigh of contentment he lit it and took a deep drag.

D. A. shook his head in disappointment.

"Well," Clark whispered, "at least that explains the ashes we find in the eggs sometimes."

Nothing Monstrous about that.

"We should get in there now," D. A. whispered. "It looks like most of the staff is gone on break."

Clark nodded. He steeled himself.

The two friends bent low and snuck around to the tree where the cook was just leaving, stubbing out his cigarette butt and shoving it into his pocket. They threw themselves flat against the wall as he hurried to catch up with another cafeteria worker—a pretty girl.

The boys rolled their eyes and prepared to tiptoe inside.

And then.

"Hey, D. A., whatcha doin'?"

Clark's shoulders drooped.

Kris.

Kris and two henchmen—friends—were wandering insolently down the main drag of the camp, very obviously looking for trouble.

And here, Clark thought, they had found it.

Lucky them.

"We're gonna sneak into the basement of the cafeteria, see what's what," D. A. said, slapping hands with the other boy. "Want in?"

Clark gritted his teeth. He did *not* want the other boy "in." On the other hand, the idiot probably wouldn't even notice if Clark quickly hid the mice somewhere. There was no way Monsters were going to attack with the three of them together. Five, if the others came, too.

"Nah, me and Alphonse and Raph here are gonna head over to Snowshoe Hare Cabin and eat some illegal candy we got and toss around a ball. Wanna come?"

"I love candy," D. A. said. "Can my bro tag along?"

Bro? Tag along? Who was this suddenly next to Clark? Had he been taken over by a Monster?

"*This* guy? I guess, if he's with you," Kris said, shrugging.

"No, I'm going to sneak into the basement," Clark said. "C'mon, D. A. You said you'd come."

"'C'mon, D. A., you said you'd come,'" Kris mimicked. "Geez, what's up with the girlfriend routine?"

Clark tried very, very hard to ignore him.

"Let's just run down, count to ten to say we did it, and come back up," he suggested, keeping his voice light. "Then you can go off with these guys. Fair?"

"Fair," D. A. agreed. "But you should come, too. *Candy*. And ball! It's living the dream."

"'Fair,'" Alphonse or Raph mimicked, mimicking Kris. The two boys laughed and tapped knuckles, but Kris turned to go.

"Do what you want," he said. "I can't promise we won't eat it all by the time you get there."

"Nooooo!" D. A. cried, pulling his baseball cap down in mock anguish. "C'mon, Clark. We can do the basement thing later."

Clark desperately wanted D. A. to come with him. He wanted things back how they were.

But...he didn't want to compete with Kris. Or beg. Kris was a bully, and manipulative, and there was no winning that game.

"I'm doing it now, D. A.," Clark said. "It's the only time I have. It would be more fun if you came."

Kris was now walking—no, *striding*—away, the two others close behind him.

"I'll catch up with you later," D. A. promised. "*Candy*, Clark. I'm dying here. Haven't had a decent bite in days. I'll save some for you."

And then he also turned and walked away.

Clark watched the four of them go. He shook his head, trying to get angry rather than allow the sudden painful stinging in his stomach to settle there.

Without even thinking, he marched over to the mess hall, walked straight to the basement entrance, and began going down the stairs.

The rage kept him going until about halfway down. Then, stupidly, he stopped.

It was silent.

Like *silent* silent.

The Bad Silent, the kind where no grown-ups or anyone else is around and the evil things can slip in. Death and loneliness and empty halls.

Catherine-Lucille was right when she called this one a doozy.

This wasn't like when Clark was in the woods by himself looking for the cell phone the summer before. That had been scary, but he knew Monsters didn't roam the wild. Here he was *specifically* going to a place they were pretty certain might be haunted by Monsters.

And he was still by himself.

Clark felt like he was suffocating, trapped between the layers of upstairs and downstairs. Determined to move on but too terrified to do so.

Was it his imagination, or was it suddenly a little darker?

Think of D. A., Clark told himself. *Stupid D. A.! Get* angry!

Slowly, too slowly, he slid the toes of his left foot down to the next step.

Think of Scooter. The crackers she brought. I'll bet she got them down here somewhere.

He managed to inch the rest of his foot down, heel finally also touching.

Think of Saneema, whose smile is so pretty.

When she smiles.

He picked up his right foot. It paused there, hovering.

With great effort he forced it along to the step below.

Think of James, who's so calm and always knows what to say.

Another step.

Think of Catherine-Lucille. She's not afraid of anything.

Another step.

Almost at the bottom.

The silence was deafening.

The sunlight failed.

Clark was completely cut off from the upstairs world now, submerged in the fecund atmosphere of this underground level.

Think of Foon. Who saved your dad and your entire home. Mostly by himself.

He clenched his teeth and forced himself to take the last three steps all at once.

Tap.

Tap.

Pitter-pat.

He was down.

He stood at the end of a long, narrow hall whose floor was ugly cracked linoleum. The only light was provided by an old flickering bulb that looked like it was screwed directly into the ceiling. At the far end of the hall was a door. It was tall and narrow, probably a broom closet. Before this were several more sketchy-looking doors (all painted brown) on both sides of the hall, and one open doorway.

Clark made himself slide his feet along the floor, listening, fearfully and hopefully, for the sounds of another person down there.

(There were none.)

He passed the open doorway after what seemed like an hour. It was double wide, probably to let in a delivery cart or something. The room beyond was fascinating, and Clark sorely wished D. A. were there with him to explore it. Ancient wooden shelves were stacked with all sorts of strange and out-of-proportion things. Unmarked cans the size of dogs. Giant sacks of grain or coffee with no words printed on them, just a giant red slash across the front. Jars as big as toilets filled with unrecognizable pickled vegetables, which Clark was pretty sure—and desperately hoped—hadn't been in any of the meals he had eaten so far.

Something scuffled.

Clark nearly choked in fear.

He had heard that exact sound once before—late at night, in his room. Before Foon arrived. Like something was slurping or moving or squinching along the floor that couldn't quite pick its feet up.

This time it sounded like it was on a carpet.

There were no carpets in the basement, as far as Clark could see.

Sweating and breathing shallowly through his mouth, he forced himself past the storage room the rest of the way down to the end of the hall.

There.

That's where he would put his Not-DangerMoose.

A foot away from the broom closet (or bathroom). Where the silence was the loudest. Where Clark could imagine them eventually finding his broken body, pale, without blood or emotion.

With less respect than he meant, Clark pitched the two stuffed mice at the door.

The poor things hit it with a soft thump-*thump* and fell to the floor.

Then Clark turned and ran upstairs two steps at a time, feet slamming loudly, not caring who heard him this time. As long as it was a *who*, and not a *what*.

But he had done it.

He had done what no one else wanted to do—no one else *dared* to do.

And he hadn't been caught.

That was a win.

TWENTY

Thursday Night

Clark chose to spend dinner going from table to table—when the counselors weren't looking—to hang out with those who weren't coming back for the next session: Archer from Fire Skills; Grace (Pony Girl); his Canoeing partner Shannon; and Small Boy Who Was Crying.

(SBWWC was giggling and had a french fry up each nostril. He seemed just fine.)

Finally Clark joined Saneema and Scooter and Catherine-Lucille at their unofficial club table. He and C. L. discussed his adventure in the very public, very crowded dining area like this:

She looked at him questioningly.

He gave a thumbs-up.

She nodded. Once.

(That was it.)

When dinner was over, the four friends walked out together.

Only once they were far away from the rest of the campers did they relax.

"You did good, Corporal," Catherine-Lucille said.

"It was terrifying," he said.

"Bravery isn't *not being afraid,* it's keeping on when you *are* afraid," Saneema quoted from somewhere.

"Then I am *super* brave," Clark decided.

Scooter laughed. "Saneema and I are going to go divvy up our perishables among those who are staying through Session Four. Come by before it's all gone!"

The two girls ran off to their cabin together, trying to whack each other on the head as they went.

"Hey," Clark said when they were gone. "I'm going to go through all my stuff for the camping trip tonight. Want to come to Fishercat with me before heading over to their place?"

"Oh, um, no, thanks," Catherine-Lucille said, strangely nervous. Indirect.

"Okay," he said suspiciously.

"I think maybe I'll go pack up, myself," she added, looking to the side.

Clark frowned at her.

"Catherine-*Lucille,*" he said sternly, drawing out her full name.

"Okay, okay! If I see D. A.—or Kris—right now, I'm gonna deck him! Them!" she finally admitted, tightening her fists at her sides angrily.

Her eyes told a slightly different story.

What Clark read in them—large, a little wetter than usual—was *I feel betrayed and hurt by D. A. and what he did.*

Or maybe that was what *he* was feeling.

"You going to stay mad at him forever?" Clark asked her—or maybe himself.

"We'll see if he apologizes and stops being a jerk," Catherine-Lucille said, setting her jaw. "But that's not important. The *important* thing is that we've protected the camp as best we can while we're gone, and we can finish this Monster business when we get back. And since no one is going to be around this weekend, no one else can get hurt."

"Yeah, I guess that's true. All right, g'night, then."

He saluted her, a little tiredly.

"See you bright and early," she said.

He watched her go. For a moment she was just a girl walking down a path, kicking a satisfying-looking rock out of her way.

Beneath her capable, leader-y exterior she was still a kid and could be hurt like one.

Clark sighed and headed to his cabin.

It was full of kids packing up to go home, or getting ready for the trip tomorrow—but D. A. wasn't one of them.

Spirits were high (even with Amos or Amir). Campers who were leaving the next day were giving out illicit snacks and treats to those staying. Illegal games of cards—*with betting*—were being played. Clark joined in a round of Magic with someone else's deck.

First, and then second, curfew horn sounded out.

Still no D. A.

When Clark was getting ready for bed—fluffing his pillow, getting his pj's, moving the slightly scratchy embroidered fake pee stain out of the way—he found something brown and shapeless on his pillow.

He jumped back, horrified, trying not to breathe.

He had been slimed! They had hit *him*! Was Foon okay? What about DangerMaus? Clark's heart began to pound in panic.

And then he smelled...

...chocolate?

Cautiously he crept back up to his bed.

What he had mistaken for slime—or poop—revealed itself to be a half-melted half a candy bar. A Krackel, by the looks of the nubbly bits that were sticking out of the ooze.

A gift from D. A. Half-eaten, staining his pillowcase.

Whatever was going on in Clark's mind, his hands had different thoughts and the bar was in his mouth before he could reasonably decide what to think of the whole situation.

Delicious.

It finished melting on his tongue and Clark had to work very, very hard not to lick the pillow.

He got into bed—after turning over the pillow.

He stared at the smooth, uniform shape of the mattress above him. D. A.'s butt wasn't pressing down into it. He wasn't there.

Clark woke when D. A. squeakily clambered up into his bunk an hour later—and at least fifteen minutes after final, *final* curfew.

TWENTY-ONE
THE GREAT PLETICON SPEAKS

Are you ready, my Monstren?

The time of our revenge is at hand!

TWENTY-TWO

Friday:
Six Hours until the
Cabin on the Mountain

Friday morning Clark woke up with only one thought on his mind.

How was he going to spend the next few days hiking and camping with his two best friends—who weren't speaking to each other?

(And what kind of friend *was* D. A., anyway?)

Everyone going on the trip spent the morning packing their backpacks. . . . A sleepy D. A. just threw all his stuff in a jumbled mess and zipped it shut while Clark spent time carefully arranging his own gear and supplies.

He kept hoping Catherine-Lucille would stop by and see how they were doing—but of course she didn't.

When he was done, Clark brought his pack over to the

van that was going to truck all the campers' stuff the long way around the lake so they could pick it up on the other side after canoeing across.

(Apparently the camp *used* to just put all the gear in the canoes, until one year a splash fight got out of hand and everyone's packs got soaked.)

Fire Skills Instructor Maya was checking off everything as it was stowed. She was so angry that Clark was pretty sure he could see smoke coming out of her ears.

"Here's my pack," he said as politely and quietly as possible.

"Cool," she said flatly, grabbing and throwing it into the back of the van a little harder than was strictly necessary.

"Um … are you okay?" Clark asked, resisting the urge to step away from the obviously upset girl.

"Yeah, Clark, sorry." She huffed and crossed her arms. "I just … They just told me I'm not coming on the trip."

"*What?*"

"Yeah, I know, right?"

She dug in her hoodie pockets, found nothing, dug in her shorts pockets, found nothing. Then she reached up under her baseball cap and found, like a magician, a fresh piece of gum there. She unwrapped it and popped it into her mouth in a quick, desperate gesture. "I. Aah'm so. *Issed.*" It was hard to understand her with a mouthful of what looked like Dubble Bubble.

"But why?" Clark asked, feeling his stomach sink.

"I don't know!" She threw her hands in the air. "I keep

asking *who* is going to be the senior counselor on the trip, and they won't tell me! Administrative jerks!"

"That stinks," Clark said. "I really...wish you were coming."

More than he could say. She was safe crazy, like his sister. And with D. A. and Catherine-Lucille fighting, and the Monster situation at camp, she was one of the things he was looking forward to being "normal" on the trip.

"Aww, Clark, that's so sweet of you." Maya suddenly froze all her movements and gazed at him intently, her eyes as large as skateboard wheels. It was a little frightening to be the focus of that much insane energy. "But you'll be fine. You're a steady pacer. You have a good head on your shoulders. You just need to amplify yourself when you have something to say. People will learn to listen."

That was a lot of words to take in, and some of them didn't sound nice. "'Steady pacer'?" What was that, like a horse?

Kris slouched up to the van and threw his frame pack at the counselor's feet.

Of *course* he was coming. His family probably signed him up for the whole summer so they wouldn't have to deal with him until fall.

(And then send him to boarding school.)

Without missing a beat Maya reached down, picked up his bag, opened it, and began rifling through the contents.

"Hey, what are you doing? That's my private stuff!" Kris wailed with all the indignation of someone who is often caught doing something wrong.

"I am looking for contraband," the Fire Skills instructor said carefully through gritted teeth.

Clark tiptoed away, trying not to giggle.

☆　☆　☆

The Camp I Can staff did a very good job of making sure the intersession campers were far away from the main camp when families came to take their kids home. Just in case there was homesickness or jealousy.

So after lunch the intersession-ers put on their life jackets and canoed across the lake in a solemn procession. It was supposed to be gloriously ceremonial, like a grand flotilla crossing into the unknown, but the happy cries of arriving families could still be heard drifting across the water. It made the whole thing a little bittersweet.

Clark wished he could say something to the girl with the long curtain of brown hair who hunched in the stern of her boat, hiding her face. He recognized all the classic signs of secret crying: shivering shoulders, tense arms, head turned sideways. As an expert secret crier himself he knew that the *last* thing she wanted was someone noticing.

So he very carefully splashed her—and only her—using just the tip of his paddle.

She spun around, furious.

He waved and smiled.

She shook her head and rolled her eyes in disgust . . . but

when she turned back around it looked like she was also beginning to smile (or plot revenge).

Two canoes over from her was Jaylynn, who saw Clark and waved her paddle at him. He happily waved back.

His spirits were already soaring when they docked on the far side of the lake. The weird weather created a heavy mist that rolled down from the mountains and spread across the water, like the cover of a fantasy book. It was just the sort of place a cloaked figure with a grave face but ultimately helpful advice would hide out, waiting for the right hero to make himself known.

Clark sighed in contentment, feeling adventure approach, and strapped on his pack.

"Hey." Catherine-Lucille trotted up to him, wearing a green canvas army backpack that was far too big for her height. She saw him staring at it and shrugged. "Yeah, yeah. It's my uncle's. My parents refused to buy me a new one until I proved this was something I was gonna really get into. But look, I made some super-cool patches for it!"

She turned around so he could see: The dull olive color of the pack was broken up by five outrageously colored circles of embroidered fabric. He leaned close, frowning, trying to figure out the symbols.

"Boy Scouts are stupid," she said, as if reading his thoughts. "But their whole system is cool. Earning ranks and patches and stuff? So I made my own badges for the things I've achieved in my life. Advanced Needle Skills, Tree Watching, Expert TV

Remote Operation, Stuffy Troop Number Twenty-Eight, and Zombie Killing."

Now the tiny pictures all made sense. The last one was of a pale screaming head lying sideways on the ground.

"'Zombie Killing'?" he asked.

She shrugged. "A little premature, I admit. But if it ever came up, I think I'd be pretty awesome at it."

Clark couldn't disagree. If it ever came to a Zombiepocalypse, he would definitely want to be in Catherine-Lucille's survivalist bunker.

Off to the side he saw D. A. getting his own pack on, with "help" from Kris. The taller boy kept on holding out the pack for him to slip his arms into—and then yanking it away at the last minute. D. A. was cracking up and didn't seem to really mind. But he finally said something—Clark couldn't hear what it was—and Kris relented. Then D. A. glanced over to Catherine-Lucille but looked away quickly, as if it was a mistake.

Clark sighed, the weight of his pack suddenly feeling twice as heavy as it had a minute ago.

☆　☆　☆

The actual hiking didn't get any more fun, either.

There wasn't a lot of extra breath left for chatting, but sometimes when the path was wide enough Catherine-Lucille and D. A. would wind up on either side of Clark. And talk *at* him. While ignoring the other friend.

170

"Okay, so, the Crellans and Chowgun we're pretty sure about," Catherine-Lucille was saying, frowning at the ground as she walked. "You've *seen* a Crellan. And the slime was either left by living Chowgun, or dead...anything else."

"Hey, look at that bird," Clark said. Monsters were of course super cool to discuss. But he kind of wanted to forget about them right then.

Catherine-Lucille looked up to where he pointed. "Huh. Cute. Looks like he's wearing a hat. Chowguns are supposed to be, like, half bird, you know...."

Clark rolled his eyes good-naturedly.

"Hey, did you get the little present I left you last night?" D. A. asked. Not even acknowledging C. L.'s presence.

Her expression darkened, but otherwise she didn't react.

"Um, yeah, thanks. It was great," Clark said. "Although it sort of stained my pillowcase."

"I'm just lucky I managed to save you anything. Man, they tore through the bag like animals. It was crazy! And then we snuck out to the dock and dared each other to go in and get leeches. You should have come! It was amazing."

"I never properly thanked you for helping out with deploying the Stuffies in the basement, Corporal," Catherine-Lucille said out of nowhere. "I know how hard it was. But it was kind of fun, wasn't it?"

D. A. shook his head and rolled *his* eyes but not good-naturedly.

"Hey, Clark, did you know Kris plays junior league baseball? He's got over a three hundred average!"

"Wow. That's amazing. I wonder why you aren't hanging out with him *right now*," Catherine-Lucille muttered.

D. A. shrugged. "They're talking about girls. It's kind of boring."

"There's a girl right here. Does that bore you, too?"

And this went on.

They never said obvious and stupid stuff like people on TV did, like *Well, I hope Catherine-Lucille knows I'd forgive her if she just said sorry* or *I wonder if D. A. even knows what an idiot he's being.*

But still.

Clark found himself wishing he could walk on alone. Which was weird; he used to wish he *had* a close friend—even one! Now he had *two* best friends...and they were both being annoying. Plus, if they just left him alone he could concentrate on the quiet world around them. The deepening shadows, the richly scented air. The way water was drawing itself out of the sky and into little drops on everything: the tips of leaves, moss, and the alien puffs and strands of whitish-bluish stuff that hung from tree branches like strange drifts of snow or bones or something from a fairy garden.

"*Usnea*, old-man's beard," one of the counselors said, noticing his interest (he thought her name might be Robin—a midlevel counselor with no decision-making powers). "It's a lichen, a weird marriage of fungus and algae. Mushroom and photosynthesizing plant. Not a moss. It's really susceptible to pollution—what they call a bioindicator. You can see really big healthy clumps growing here, so that means the air you're breathing is super pure and good for you."

And while the extended explanation broke Clark's imagined fantasy world a little, it was extremely interesting. He would have to write a letter to Anna about it; she would love such a pretty-ugly thing. It would be great to send her a tiny piece of it, too, but Clark didn't want to hurt the little fungus-algae weirdo.

Behind him, Kris broke off a long vine that hung over the path, whacked a perfectly nice tree with a stick he had found, and threw baby pinecones at other hikers.

And somehow, once again, he managed to do it without any of the counselors seeing. It was a special power—he was like Superman that way.

Or, Clark grumpily thought, a *Monster.*

TWENTY-THREE

Back at Camp

Miz Shirley stood statue-still outside the administrative cabin. Fire Skills Instructor Maya also stood nearby, but *she* swayed and paced and moved, hands wrapped around a steaming cup of coffee. Senior Counselor Stan (in charge of the boys' cabins) walked jerkily up the path carrying a lumpy-looking sack with suspicious bulges.

"I have ... checked all the backpacks and frame packs ... and removed the ... contraband items," he said, shaking the sack.

"What are you talking about? I already did that," Maya snapped. "For the campers with potential problems."

Stan and Miz Shirley slowly turned to stare at her.

"You didn't need to check them all, is all I'm saying," Maya continued peevishly. "And if *you're* still here, who is the senior counselor going along the trip? I didn't see anyone else."

"That is not a concern of yours," Miz Shirley said.

"What is *up* with everyone today?" Maya demanded. "Okay, whatever. Just give me my check and get me a ride into town. Everything stinks this session. Including this coffee."

For some reason, both Miz Shirley and Stan found that very amusing.

Sort of.

"Ha. Ha ha. Ha," Stan said.

"Ha. Ha ha. Ha," Miz Shirley said.

And for just a moment, Fire Skills Instructor Maya felt an icy hint of fear.

TWENTY-FOUR

The Cabin

As the afternoon drew on it began to rain.

At first it was soft and almost pleasant, more like they were climbing into a low cloud that had plumped up nicely. Clark enjoyed the way it felt on his hot brow. He imagined how, when it grew chilly later, he and his companions (who, in his story, were *not* fighting with each other) would be eager to get out of the Misty Mountains and hunker down in front of a campfire. Or maybe they would spend the night at the Prancing Pony in Bree—an inn just outside of the Shire, where hobbits and heroes of all sizes stayed. D. A. would take out his lute and Catherine-Lucille would have the other travelers on the edge of their seats as she told stories about their adventures and quests...

...and then the rain got worse.

Like, *bad* worse. Slowing-down-the-hiking worse.

Campers tripped over slippery roots and rocks. Some tried

to get off the path—which was rapidly turning into a tiny stream—only to be yelled at by counselors to get back *onto* the path and to look out for poison ivy.

Someone would suddenly stop to adjust a hat or put on a poncho and cause a twelve-person pileup.

Not everyone had brought a high-end waterproof hiking jacket.

Plastic bags were found and distributed.

The counselors were ... not that great. Clark overheard the trio (probably Robin, possibly Kai, and maybe Evan) muttering to one another about how there was supposed to be at least one senior counselor along, or even an administrator. They were junior counselors and not prepared to deal with so many of the younger campers by themselves.

Still, they tried. Without complaint they comforted every wilting soul, pointed out interesting forest trivia to distract, found unsoggy snacks for those dangerously low on blood sugar. Clark could have sworn he saw an M&M or two but didn't feel like he had a right to ask. He was doing okay.

"THIS STINKS," Kris swore, his face glowering and wet.

Clark couldn't disagree. He didn't see how stating the obvious helped anything, however.

Catherine-Lucille glowered at the sky as if she could bully it into behaving. Rain trickled down her forehead and onto her nose and cheeks, but she didn't seem to notice or care, which was absolutely Catherine-Lucille and also absolutely freaky.

"Man, doesn't this beat all," D. A. said cheerfully, standing with his back to her so his pack was in her face. "It couldn't have waited to do this until next week?"

Clark's beautiful vision of an inn with a roaring fire like the Prancing Pony was quickly given up for the much more banal hope of an only *slightly* damp tent. Anything was better than hiking through the storm.

Because that's what it was now: a storm.

Somehow the rain grew even worse. It was as if the weird clouds had been saving their rain all week, like pee, and were letting it all out *now*. In huge, hard drops that hurt when they hit.

The wind picked up. Although the worst of it was broken by the thick trees and their branches, icy hands snuck through and managed to find where socks were too short, the back of a neck was exposed, a hat could easily be knocked off.

There was water inside Clark's boots now.

When he caught a break from the rain—and his friends' complaints—Clark took out the compass his mother had given him and checked it. He knew the mountain peak was almost directly due west from their starting point on the lake. He had tried to keep track of the switchbacks and approximate number of steps. So he was pretty sure they were approaching the summit, and it was just to the north of them.

Probably.

But water must have gotten into his compass.... The pointer twirled and swung back and forth meaninglessly.

Disappointed, Clark put it away.

The trees were changing; on the higher elevations they were

smaller, gnarled, and cramped. The hikers looked the same: hunched over, taking careful, tiny steps. With a cry and a crash someone up ahead fell hard on the path.

Clark winced for her, then breathed a sigh of relief that it wasn't him. And then felt bad for that sigh. He hurried over to see if she was okay and offered a hand up.

It was Jaylynn. She had slipped off a slick rock and landed on her butt in a muddy puddle of gravel and leaves.

Her face was swollen and it looked like she was close to sobbing. Angry sobs, like she was generally done with everything.

"This is the worst," she said, swallowing. Trying not to cry.

She was wearing shorts despite the camp's strict instructions to wear long light pants the day of the hike. Grit and blood flowed off her knee, dissolving into the rain.

She gave him a look: Neither one of them was going to tell the counselor, right? It wouldn't be worth it.

Then she turned around and began walking again. Clark considered running after her and walking beside her—but she really looked like she wanted to be left alone.

And then they were at the top. The rain was so fierce it became a thick grey sheet that hid almost everything from view. The wind made it even worse; the landscape around them flickered in monochrome stripes like a scary old TV. Every time Clark thought he got a glimpse of something real—a large rock, an old and abandoned cabin, an ancient dead tree—the wind blew between him and it, erasing it like a dream.

This was how people got lost and died in the White

Mountains. Clark had never been to them but had read about the deceptively familiar range in New Hampshire. Easy to lose the path in a sudden storm, easy to die of exposure.

The campers stopped and huddled uncertainly like a herd of confused buffalo.

"Hey. Hey, Counselor," D. A. shouted. "How we gonna set up the tents in this? We didn't even practice it dry!"

Catherine-Lucille gave him a grudging look of respect.

Well, it was the truth.

It seemed like the dumbest idea in the world to begin taking out the soggy tent bags in the wet, unrolling their contents in the wet, putting together cold tent poles in the wet with cold wet fingers, stomping mud all over the ground tarps and even the tents themselves in the wet—doing anything at all in the wet, wet, wet.

They weren't Boy Scouts; they weren't even in the army. This would be Clark's—and many others'—first overnight in the woods.

The counselor D. A. was questioning (Evan? They were all alike, with slightly different accessories) looked as defeated as Clark felt. He wasn't even that old. A cold droplet ran down the sharp arc of his nose and dangled at its tip.

"HEY! What about *that*? What is it?" Catherine-Lucille yelled, pointing at the cabin as the wind blew the rain away for a second.

"An old Civilian Conservation Corps–era permanent base camp," Evan (?) yelled back. "The workers stayed there while they built the trails. Now it's a shelter for through-hikers.... Huh. Be cool for a sec, I'm going to go talk this over with the other counselors."

"*THIS IS* STUPID!" Kris screamed, stomping his feet in the muck. "I'm going to have my parents sue you! I'm going to get sick!"

He looked particularly pink and hale—hardly a potential victim of pneumonia.

"I'm going to go stand under the pine trees over there, where it's dry," Catherine-Lucille announced.

"You will absolutely not!" snapped one of the other counselors, Robin or Kai. "Wind could knock a tree over onto you, and lightning could start any minute."

C. L. groaned but didn't object. She was like that, all bully and bluster until she saw a good point. Angry but logical.

Clark watched the counselors bend toward one another, discussing things, as if they were figures in an old etching on a museum wall that he was trying to understand. There was something ominous and foreboding about their hunkered-down demeanors.

"Awright!" The other boy counselor, Kai maybe, came stomping and sloshing back to the campers. "There is *no way* we can secure the tents against the weather safely out here. So we're going to go bivouac in the old cabin."

"'Bivouac'?" Clark asked.

"Bivvy, bed down in, spend the night," Catherine-Lucille explained.

The campers who could hear this cheered.

(The rest murmured and demanded an explanation. Then they cheered, too.)

Clark and Catherine-Lucille looked at each other—and at D. A.

There was nothing, *nothing* more inviting than a sturdy, dry cabin in a storm, no matter how decrepit and stinky it was. Drips in the corners and wind shrieking through drafty holes would be a blessing compared to whatever sleeping with just a layer of cloth between you and the rain would be like.

But...

The wind in question swept the rain and fog away from the expanse of the flat mountaintop, laying the scene bare for a moment.

The cabin they were going to stay in was small. Old. Worn. Made from stones that reminded Clark of teeth. Its windows looked exactly like eyes.

Hanging over it like a witch's hand was an ugly dead tree with a gaping black hole in its trunk, rotten to the core.

If a popular horror writer had come down from the sky and tried to design a scarier-looking abandoned cabin in the woods, she would have utterly failed.

"Yay," Catherine-Lucille said faintly.

BOOK II:

INTO DARKNESS

TWENTY-FIVE

Foon

He opened his eyes and stretched, feeling a little luxurious, a little lazy and slow.

He rolled himself over for one last cuddle next to his Boy's sleeping form—

—but there was nothing there, just a pile of leaves.

Foon leaped up immediately, readying his trident.

He was in...the woods!

The dark, cold, damp woods.

All by himself.

"Hello? Comrades?" Foon called out.

There was no response.

Where was everyone? Where was his Boy?

Foon saw with his hunter's eyes the tracks through the woods left by large feet. *Human* feet. He immediately followed them backward, running and leaping over twigs and duff. After only a few Grownedup paces, he came out onto the main path that cut through camp.

Strange...It was like someone had entered the woods carrying the Stuffy and purposefully left him there....

Quickly orienting himself, Foon ran to the cabin where he and his Boy had been staying.

"DangerMaus!" he cried, slamming on the door with his soft paw. There was no way he could open it from the outside by himself. "DangerMaus, let me in! Help me!"

He heard the near-silent patter of tiny, sustainably imagined feet approaching the door.

"On three! You push, I pull!" Foon ordered. Working together—with a bit of shouting—they managed to get the door open a crack. The bigger Stuffy stuck a hind paw in to keep it from closing, then squished himself down as thinly as possible and thrust himself through.

"Foon, is the camping trip over so soon?" DangerMaus asked curiously. "You need not worry about the cabin—I have been guarding it, awaiting your return!"

"Camping trip? Over?" Foon asked in confusion. He looked around the cabin.

It was empty.

The children had all left on the special camping trip the Boy had been talking about for weeks.

Without him.

Foon's horns drooped.

Clark had been *so excited.* His Mother had bought him a

compass so he wouldn't get lost. His Father had reminisced about his days camping with other boys in a troop like a Stuffy fellowship. His Sister had talked about pooping in the woods. And Clark had repeated it all to Foon, going over every detail and how much fun it would be to have his friends all to himself and far away from *theligthtsofcivilization*.

Foon had been excited, too. He couldn't wait to join Clark on this adventure.

But...

He had been left behind somehow.... Tossed, unwanted, into the woods. Like garbage.

He felt funny.

Something, like a scratchy piece of thread but made of feelings, poked its way stabbingly through his belly. Or maybe his heart. His body felt heavy and lopsided and painful.

"But...what happened?" Foon asked helplessly. "I was supposed to go with him."

"I don't know," DangerMaus said. "Did you fall out of his bag somehow?"

Wouldn't his Boy have noticed? Wouldn't he have felt it happen, or come back, running, to grab him?

"I...I have to go talk to the Great Bear," Foon said.

"Of course! I shall continue to keep guard until your return!"

DangerMaus saluted him as best he could without any real paws; he stood up straight and cocked his whiskers back. But Foon was already gone.

Outside the sky was watery with quick whisper clouds,

and there was a haze in the air. Everything looked blurry and formidable.

His Boy was out there, somewhere, sleeping in that weather—in the rain that hadn't come down into the valley yet. *Without him.* Without Foon to comfort him when the wind screamed or the other campers whimpered and cried in their sleep. When it sounded like the whole world was collapsing into the storm and he would never be dry or warm or safe again.

How could Clark have forgotten Foon? How could he not have noticed he was missing?

Foon ran. His cloth nearly tore with the effort as he leaped over stones and used his trident to vault over logs. He left the path and cut through the tiny forest, ignoring curious and unusual nighttime creatures.

He burst into the pine grove and almost tumbled into the Circle of Fire. Quite a few sewn and painted eyebrows rose with interest at his entrance.

"Great Bear!" he cried.

This was no formal gathering; most of the camp's children were gone in between the two sessions, as were their Stuffies. Bear was speaking casually to a few of his top advisors.

"Is something the matter, little one?" the bear asked, looking alarmed. "Has there been another Monster?"

"What? Oh no." Foon skidded to a halt, suddenly realizing how alarming his arrival must have seemed. He immediately knelt. "Apologies, this is nothing to do with Monsters—but it *is* an emergency!"

"What has happened?"

"Today is the day of the big camping trip and—my Boy has left me behind!"

The bear's face—didn't *fall*, exactly. It *relaxed* into something like a sad smile, or relief, or worry. He murmured a few words to those Stuffies around him and they nodded and immediately made themselves scarce.

"Or...I fell out of his bag, and he did not notice," Foon continued helplessly. "He did not come back for me. And now he is alone on that mountain, and I am alone here. Unable to protect him."

"Come here, little one," the Great Bear said kindly, holding his paw out. Foon obeyed. While the larger Stuffy was doing nothing more than putting a companionable arm around his shoulder, because of his size it was like Foon was entering a sheltering embrace, a warm home protected from the world.

"There is a moment in every Stuffy's life...You have no idea when it will come. It could be when your child is two, or when he is grown and about to be married. You know this in your Stuffing, Foon: At some point, your Boy won't need you to protect him anymore."

Foon swallowed. Of course he knew this. He wasn't newly made. He was over a year old now. It just wasn't worth thinking about.

It was so...far off....

"But remember." The bear turned Foon to face him. "That is what we *want*. That is what we live for—for our children to grow and grow up, to gather what they need to protect themselves. To do more than protect themselves—to go out into the world bravely and fiercely. Like warriors.

"If they do this, then we have done our job, and we have done it well. And we will have helped raise another force for the Light: good humans who will make the world a better place, with love and power."

"I know this to be true," Foon answered, measuring his words carefully. He had a strange urge to scuff his hind paws in the dirt, to tap his trident nervously. He was facing feelings he didn't want to think about. "But...it was so sudden. We were going to go on this great adventure together. And I was tossed aside. Even if it was an accident, it is like he just... *forgot*...about me."

The bear sighed and gave Foon a gentle squeeze.

"It very well could have been accidental. A onetime mistake. But, Foon—no matter what happens—your Boy will never forget you. Not completely. Not forever. And someday he may need you again, more than ever before."

Foon tried to still his traitor toes. He felt so small and foolish next to the bear.

"You are a mighty fighter," the leader of the Stuffies said softly. "And a formidable hero. But there are things you have yet to learn, understanding yet to come to you, to round out your already impressive skills. *Acceptance* is one of them."

"I'm just—" Foon stopped. He started again.

"It's only that—

"But I—"

A big sigh came out over his tusks; he wasn't sure from where. He didn't think he had that much space in his stuffed body. His breath whooshed out in great clouds, emptying his cloth and filling the air around them with silence.

He felt quieter—not exactly better, but a little calmer when it was done.

"Thank you, Great Bear," he murmured. "I will think about all you have said."

"Excellent," the bear said, clapping him on the shoulder. "But you should also spend time with your friends. You needn't be alone right now. A laugh with friends is better than all the medicine in the forest—or the bathroom cabinet—as they say."

"A laugh with my *comrades*, you mean?" Foon asked, a little confused.

The Great Bear himself laughed at that, throwing his head back and opening his muzzle wide. It wasn't mean; it was like all of the good nature in the world. Echoes of his laughter bounded off the hills that surrounded the camp and the bottoms of the clouds above them.

"I am going to see how our prisoner interrogation gets on," he said when he had finished. "We still haven't learned anything useful. Come join me when you have visited with your . . . *comrades*. Perhaps some work and fight will relieve your current mood."

Foon nodded glumly.

As he wandered over to the Circle of Fire, a few other Stuffies looked at him with interest—Doris and Ren Faire Beast among them. At first Foon stared right back, a little defensively. What were they thinking? Were they wondering what the Great Bear was saying to him? Did he look like a child being yelled at by his parent?

Or—maybe they thought the bear was consulting with the mighty warrior Foon on some tactical plan against the Monsters.

Foon sighed. He was being stupid.

He would think upon what Bear had said: He would stay at the Circle of Fire, dance, maybe find someone else who had been left behind. Maybe he would talk to a Newly Made, like that seal—he would give good advice the way others had when he was young. That would be useful *and* take his mind off things. And then he would go on patrol.

And maybe he could stop thinking about his Boy for a moment.

He would be fine without Foon for two nights.

TWENTY-SIX

The Cabin in the Woods

On the other side of the weirdly heavy door Clark was immediately hit with a musty, slightly sour smell. It was unsettling, but he couldn't have said why.

"Rats," Catherine-Lucille said grimly. "Or mice. My grandfather's garage smells like this."

"I'm going to go with *squirrels*," D. A. said from behind them, trying to sound cheerful.

It wasn't as dirty as it could have been: there were little breeze-gathered eddies of crumbled leaves and twigs, but nothing obviously animal or terrifying. The floorboards, thick and warped, were that ancient greyish-brown color old wood became. The roof was mostly intact. There were some drips in the corners, that was all. The wind howled miserably through holes between the stones in the walls, but it wasn't enough to make the place really freezing.

It was *just* enough to drive you batty from the whines and squeals in different pitches around the room.

There was also, Clark was heartened to see, a giant open hearth in the middle of the cabin. Like cabins from forever ago used to have. A partially protected hole in the roof right above it allowed smoke to exit—and not much rain to enter. And though Fire Skills Instructor Maya was not along, maybe one of the other counselors could be convinced into building a nice, cheery campfire.

Once inside, the campers all made sort of relieved and kind of happy noises. The quicker ones, the ones who had a friend or two on the trip with them, grabbed the driest corners. Clark looked at his own friends sadly; a week ago they could have been one of those tight-knit units, thinking as one and bent on survival.

D. A. still had his pack on and was laughing with Kris, who was shaking himself off like a dog and getting everyone around him wet. Clark, normally not a tidy kid, winced when he saw water pool on the floor, turning previously dry patches of dust into muddy puddles. It was going to get super gross super quick in the cabin.

"C'mon—looks like that wall over there might be okay," Catherine-Lucille said. The two of them rushed to claim it before anyone else noticed that it was mostly wind- and drip-free.

"AWRIGHT, EVERYONE, JUST QUIT MOVING AROUND AND BE COOL," one of the boy counselors—Kai?—shouted.

"LET'S KEEP THINGS DECENT IN HERE. WE DON'T HAVE PRIVATE TENTS, SO GIRLS ON THIS SIDE, BOYS ON THAT."

"Ignoring," Catherine-Lucille said, continuing toward the area they had picked out.

D. A. had of course gone with Kris and his two friends, Rafe and Algernon or whatever. Clark tried not to think about that. It was pretty easy, considering he was too wet and cold and tired to think of anything besides how wet and cold and tired he was.

He and Catherine-Lucille took off their packs and leaned them up against the wall, where the water could run off into the corner away from where they would sleep.

"Hey, um, can I join you?"

It was Jaylynn. Her knee had stopped bleeding but hadn't begun to scab up yet.

"You guys...actually look like you know what you're doing," she added.

"We don't," Catherine-Lucille said cheerfully. "It's sort of like playing house, but with sleeping bags."

"Yeah, and a whole lot more wet. I'm Jaylynn." She gave a tired little wave of her hand.

"We were in Canoeing together last year," Clark explained to C. L. "And she loves Star Wars."

"Nice to meet you. I'm—"

"Catherine-Lucille. Yeah, everyone knows who you are. Nice to meet you, too." The other girl didn't say it meanly; she said it matter-of-factly. Catherine-Lucille smiled.

The three of them began to arrange their sleeping bags. They discussed whether it should be in a defensive U with the wall and their packs as the back side and all their gear in the middle, or the other way around, with their stuff as a bulwark protecting them.

"Come on, campers," Counselor Robin (probably) said with a *very* forced cheerful tone in her voice. She approached the three friends, keeping her hands on her hips, trying to look in charge but cool. "This is the girls' side of the cabin. Clark, get to the other side."

"Nope," Catherine-Lucille said, not even bothering to look at her as she fluffed out her inflatable pillow. "Everyone's staying right here."

"Okay, Catherine-Lucille. There are rules just like back at camp, and…"

"Hey, Counselor Robin?" Jaylynn spoke up, pointing across the cabin. "I think some boy over there on the *boys' side* is pretending to pee in the corner. At least I *think* he's pretending…."

"What? Where the— *KRIS! GET AWAY FROM THE WALL!*" Robin stomped off.

Catherine-Lucille nodded approvingly at Jaylynn. "Well done, Private!"

At least Kris is good for something, Clark thought.

He watched the counselor try to deal with the situation. She soothed and chatted—a little desperately—her way through the unsettled campers. Some of whose spirits, rather than having been dampened by the, well, *damp*, were rising a little too high for the confined space of the cabin.

She confiscated illegal cell phones that the less sneaky kids didn't hide in time. Clark wasn't sure if he should be amused or worried; more phones meant more of a chance to call for help if things went south.

Evan and Kai set up the cookstoves and then went around collecting the communal cooking gear that had been divvied up among the campers (Clark had carried a—now useless—tent). They made a little impromptu kitchen on the corner of the hearth.

Clark saw his opening and approached them. "Hey! It would be great if we could build a fire here later."

"Too dangerous, camper, the whole place could burn down."

"This hearth is solid stone—it's, like, six feet across," he protested. "A small fire in the middle of it wouldn't be dangerous at all. We could set up watches, and there's more than enough water around to make sure it's out for good at the end of the night."

"We don't have any fuel," Evan or Kai said.

(This one wore a necklace so tight it was really more of a dog collar. The bright blue-and-green glass "earth" stone in the middle must have made an indentation on the skin beneath.)

"I saw an old woodpile stacked next to the cabin outside," Clark pointed out. "The bottom pieces will probably be dry."

"We don't have a Fire Skills instructor here with us."

"But it's the most basic human skill! Aren't you guys all experienced backpackers? Can't you do it?"

They looked at him blankly.

"I can help," he pleaded. "I was taking Fire Skills. Please. The hike was terrible. We're all wet and alone on this mountain and this cabin is *scary*. A fire would cheer everyone up. We could even sing dumb—um, I mean fun—songs around it. Whatever you want."

The two counselors looked at each other. Clark wondered if they were communicating in a frequency only they could receive.

"Let's have dinner; that will cheer everyone up," the first counselor said (maybe Kai; the one without the collar but *with* a tattoo of a pine tree on his arm). It could have been the answer to any question or suggestion—or the start of an entirely different conversation.

Clark exhaled heavily in a cross between a sigh and an attempt to get rid of his breath before he said something he shouldn't. Something about the dumb counselors with their dumb rules about girls and boys and fires and just how dumb they all were.

He stomped back his friends.

"They won't even *consider* lighting a fire," he grumbled, sitting down on the ground next to his sleeping bag.

"Easy there, Corporal," Catherine-Lucille said with a look of amusement. "I think I just heard you *growl*. Let's get all our stuff arranged for sleeping or whatever while it's still light enough to see. We should save our flashlights for the night—the *real* night."

"I can't *even* about how spooky this place is," Jaylynn muttered, wrapping her arms around her knees. Her nails were painted with little flowers in glitter shades. "Is it just me, or is it somehow getting *quieter* in here despite all those idiots over there?"

She wasn't wrong. Somehow things seemed . . . not subdued exactly, but weirdly echoing and off. Like everyone was farther away from one another than they actually were. In pitch-dark it would have been terrifying.

"Yeah. Definitely feels like Monsters—er, or ghosts or something," Catherine-Lucille agreed. "We'll set up watches so one of us is always awake with a flashlight."

"See, I knew you guys knew what you were doing," the other girl said smugly. "In a haunted house situation, you always stick with the people who are the most competent."

Clark flipped open the top of his pack, flinching as it splashed large, cold droplets onto him. He shoved his hand in, feeling around. He would need his flashlight—and the second flashlight, *and* the LED ring one Anna had given him that was really for raves.

He grabbed his pj's to change into in his sleeping bag—he was good at that—and tried to remember if he had anything else that lit up. Also maybe an extra pair of socks in case it got cold and . . .

"Wait a minute," he whispered, mouth going dry.

"Where's Foon?"

TWENTY-SEVEN

Foon

The little Stuffy drifted sadly over to the fire, remembering a particularly wonderful spring day when his Boy had strapped him to the handlebars of the bike he was finally allowed to ride around the block. Things that happened in the day were strange and dreamy and not quite real for the otherwise frozen Foon, but he remembered the joy on his Boy's face. He felt the freedom Clark felt as they wheeled around and around the same twelve Houses.

After finally being exhausted by this, they flopped on the ground in front of the House and watched the clouds. The Boy told Foon what he thought it would be like to live in a stratocumulus palace.

Foon sighed and swallowed, wondering if that would be the last of their good times together.

A tiny Stuffy whiskered by him on the path, interrupting his thoughts.

Foon jumped, thinking it was DangerMaus—what was he doing out of the cabin?

"Mighty Foon! Sir! Foon!" The mouse saw him, stopped and saluted. On closer inspection Foon realized that this was a girl mouse. Similar color and build, with different eyes and a longer tail. Otherwise a dead ringer for his friend. Odd.

"As you were," Foon said, straightening up and saluting back.

The other Stuffy saluted one more time, then hurried on in a frenetic ball of blue-and-brown felty determination.

As soon as she was out of sight, Foon slumped again. He watched a few Stuffies who were laughing and singing.

How could they, knowing what was to come? For every single one of them? Abandonment? Loneliness?

Maybe they knew something he didn't.

Maybe they had a different sort of strength, or weapon, or tactic for dealing with it. For continuing on when their children were growing up.

The last thing Foon really wanted right then was to be around other Stuffies and loud happiness. But perhaps they did have wisdom to impart. To help him grow wiser—and maybe lift his spirits.

He walked by the stockade where the Chowgun was being kept, nodded at the guards there.

The Monster was, as usual, screaming nonsense.

"*FUR AND CLOTH AND PLASTIC YOU ARE USELESS AND MEATY AND TOO LATE. IT HAS BEGUN. YOU CANNOT HELP NOW! OUR PLAN HAS WORKED! KEE-HAW, KEE-HAW!*"

No one paid much attention to the horrid thing; it cried out obscenities constantly, and all were equally meaningless.

Foon kept walking.

The Moon passed behind a thick cloud.

Suddenly the Monster's insane head snapped up, its unblinking eyes focused on the sky.

"*OUR KING DERKER SHALL FINALLY BE AVENGED! FOON SHALL DIE OF SORROW AND SHAME WHEN HIS BOY IS GONE!*"

TWENTY-EIGHT

The Cabin in the Woods

"Where's Foon?!"

Clark began to panic.

He grabbed everything out of his pack as fast as he could and threw it all into a pile on top of his sleeping bag. Clothes, toiletries, a secret stash of candy, illegal hand sanitizer, pack of cards, journal, pencil, change of clothes...

Nothing.

At each moment he expected his fingers to close around the familiar sock-y cloth of his stuffed animal, anticipated the sigh of relief that almost feels like when you finally get to pee.

It didn't happen.

"Get control of yourself, Corporal," Catherine-Lucile said calmly. "I'm sure he's in there. I mean, you packed him, right? Really deeply in there, so no one could see, right?"

"Yes!"

"Let me look." She turned on her ridiculously oversize floodlight/flashlight. She had to hold it with both hands while he held open the sides of his pack.

Every corner, every seam, every rivet was revealed.

There was no Foon.

"Here, you can hold Freya while we get to the bottom of this," Catherine-Lucille said in a soothing voice, and turned to her own bag.

Clark *hated* being treated like a baby.

But he didn't object.

"What the..." she said softly.

Her next words were in Spanish, and, Clark guessed, not very nice.

"Freya's gone! She's gone, *too*! I *totally* packed her!"

Jaylynn nervously looked from one friend to the other while they freaked out.

"I'm just... I'm just gonna..."

Clark assumed she was "just gonna" move away, embarrassed by what was going on: him almost crying, Catherine-Lucille swearing, both very upset because of their missing *stuffed animals.*

They really were acting like babies.

He didn't care; all he could think about was Foon wet and muddy on the trail somewhere, maybe grabbed by a coyote, stepped on by another hiker, *stolen by Kris....*

But Jaylynn wasn't backing away. She was opening her own backpack and looking through it.

"My, uh, Barbie," she whispered, scrabbling desperately in the black depths of her bag. "I have a Barbie, I packed her.... *No* one knows about her. I hid her under my shirt on the drive up and stuffed her under my mattress every day that I was here. *She's gone.*"

She looked up at Catherine-Lucille and Clark, face full of dread.

"Why are all of our guys missing?"

TWENTY-NINE

THE GREAT PLETICON SPEAKS

Trapped! Trapped on that mountain like a Gnabird in the fungal nets of a Dark Larvacean!

We have him now, my Monstren.

Foon's stupid Boy.

Trapped with his other child friends, all without their stupid Stuffy protectors. Unable to escape! Unable to defend themselves! The boy is as good as ours!

And if we grab a few of the others to nibble on, well, that's just a bonus, isn't it?

THIRTY

Foon

Foon froze, not believing that he had just heard his own name.

The guards and other Stuffies blinked with astonishment. Even the Great Bear looked up in surprise.

Foon stomped over to the Chowgun.

"*What* did you say?"

The Monster just stared at him—maybe. It was hard to tell with its blank and blurry face.

With a strangled cry of rage Foon shoved his trident, Focus, in between the bars of the stockade and caught it round the Monster's neck, pinning the creature against the back wall.

"What.

Did you.

Say.

About

My.

Boy?"

"Don't hurt the prisoner," one of the Stuffy guards warned.

"Why not?" the other one asked curiously.

The Chowgun was having trouble breathing, its throat slowly being crushed.

"EVEN NOW WE ARE HAVING OUR REVENGE ON 'YOUR BOY.' EVEN NOW. HE IS ALL ALONE WITHOUT YOU OR ANYONE TO SAVE HIM. THERE, ON THE MOUNTAIN…"

Foon twisted his trident hard against the Monster's neck but not as hard as his stuffed heart squeezed itself.

"Speak plainly, foul creature of the Dark," the Great Bear said, growling a real bear-growl. He loomed over both the Monster and Foon, paws extended. Each of his claws was as long as the Monster's head. Anger flashed like lightning deep in his plastic eyes.

"YOU WILL NOT WIN," the Monster whined. It sounded a little less triumphant now. *"DO WHAT YOU WILL TO ME, BUT WE HAVE THE BOY. WE HAVE PLANNED THIS FOR SEASONS. WE ROBBED NATURE OF HER WEATHER AND REPLACED IT WITH OUR OWN STORMS. WE SAPPED THE ADULT HUMANS OF THEIR HEALTH AND REPLACED THEIR WILL WITH OURS. IT WAS THEY WHO MADE SURE FOON AND HIS DISGUSTING STUFFY FRIENDS WERE LEFT BEHIND.*

"NOW YOUR BOY IS ALONE AND HELPLESS. THE MOUNTAINTOP IS OURS—IT HAS ALWAYS BEEN OURS, QUIET AND WAITING TO FEED.

"AND THERE IS NOTHING YOU CAN DO."

Silence fell over everyone for a moment.

Foon swallowed and tightened his grip on the weapon.

The Chowgun gripped the bars of his prison, pushing its ugly, squamous head as far through them as he could. It gibbered at Foon.

"THE MIGHTY FOON, THE ONE WHO KILLED OUR DEAR KING DERKER—MOST BELOVED FOUL OFFSPRING OF THE PLETICON'S HORDE. DID YOU THINK SUCH A THING WOULDN'T EARN OUR REVENGE?

"ALL WILL SEE HOW THE ACTIONS OF THE ONCE-MIGHTY FOON BROUGHT DEATH TO HIS OWN BOY!"

THIRTY-ONE

The Cabin in the Woods

"Wait...you're missing your doll, too?" Catherine-Lucille demanded.

"Yeah. Okay, this is weird. I don't think they *all* just fell out, *all* of them, out of our packs," Jaylynn said.

"Is it just Freya?" Clark asked. "What about...?"

"I left Doris behind. And Ren Faire Beast. Thought it would be pushing my luck to pack all of them. But Freya comes with me everywhere. I *never* leave her behind."

"What the *what*," the other girl swore, stomping her foot to hide the brightening wetness of her eyes. "Is this some dumb Camp I Can thing? They go through our stuff and take out all the contraband without even telling us?"

"No...Because I still have my candy, and my hand sanitizer," Clark said. "Those're totally illegal."

He and Catherine-Lucille looked at each other.

"All of the senior counselors who got 'sick' and were replaced..." Catherine-Lucille began, thinking out loud.

"The weird weather..." Clark continued. "The Crellan, the slime, the food, the smells..."

"Our Stuffies mysteriously disappearing..."

"The missing socks..."

C. L. rolled her eyes at that but let it go.

"This was all planned," she said grimly. "We've been brought up to this deserted, stormy mountaintop with the wrong counselors and no Stuffies for some—nefarious—reason."

"We were spending all this time trying to make sure *camp* was safe," Clark added in realization. "But it had nothing to do with camp at all! It's been to get us *here*. In...this...cabin!"

"Away from adults," Catherine-Lucille said, nodding. "And lights and all the usual protections from Monsters. We're cut off and vulnerable—perfect victims."

"What? Come on, what are you guys talking about?" Jaylynn demanded. "I was joking about the haunted house. Sort of. *Monsters?* There's no such thing."

"Yeah, if there's no such thing as Monsters, why did you bring your Barbie to camp and sleep with her every night—and why are you upset she's gone?" Catherine-Lucille asked reasonably.

"Because...come on...she's just..." The other girl trailed off.

"I'm going to go around and see who all tried to bring Stuffies or action figures or dolls or whatever," Catherine-Lucille said. "And if they're missing. If we have *any* protection at all. Oh—D. A. probably brought his action figures! I'll go ask him!"

She said this without thinking, brightening.

Then she glowered, remembering how things were.

"*I'll* go check with him," Clark offered quickly.

C. L. crossed her arms and remained silent, obviously angry at everything. Jaylynn slumped down onto her sleeping bag, looking defeated.

☆　☆　☆

The counselors had finished making dinner and were setting it out on the stone hearth—it looked like some sort of rice-and-unidentifiable-protein soupy stew thing. *It can't be any worse than the recent mess hall food,* Clark decided.

All the campers were loud and a little hysterical. He couldn't imagine what it would be like after they ate. Huddled around the door were several kids who had to "use the facilities." They watched the horizontally blown rain out the window in fear and desperation, waiting for a break so they could run outside.

D. A. was with Kris and a few of the rowdier boys, one of whom had a pair of underwear on his head. Actually it was kind of funny because they were *PAW Patrol* underwear and the boy was laughing, not embarrassed at all. For a moment Clark wished he could join in.

"Hey, D. A.," he said.

His friend saw him and grinned.

"Hey, Clark! Totally not what we signed up for, huh?"

"Yeah, no. This stinks. So...you didn't happen to bring any of your action figures, did you?"

"Yeah, of course, I always do. Especially the Ahsoka special edition, don't want her stolen." D. A. pointed to a pile of things he had laid out on his sleeping bag. It may all have looked thoughtlessly thrown there, but Clark noticed how carefully the action figures rested on top.

Still...interesting! It was like whoever removed the dolls and Stuffies missed these guys, or didn't think to remove something as small as action figures.

"I was just checking 'cause all of our Stuffies are gone. Foon and Freya," Clark said. "And Jaylynn's doll. Like someone took them out of our bags."

"Oh man, that sucks!" D. A. said with feeling. "Who would do that? *Jerks.* You want to take my guys? I know how...important this is to you."

Clark was surprised. It was an amazing thing for D. A. to offer. Especially the limited-edition Ahsoka, and the Ultron with the two easily lost, fire-able missiles.

And...it was kind of weird. Or sad. Or something.

D. A. was obviously worried about Clark not *feeling* safe without his Stuffy.

But he wasn't worried that Clark wasn't *actually* safe. He wasn't worried about...Monsters.

He also wasn't worried about not having his own guys nearby. It was more important to him that Clark have them.

D. A. was in a strange place, Clark realized. In-between.

Not quite grown up enough to *not* have guys, but maybe he no longer exactly believed in them. Or Monsters.

But maybe he did, a little?

In other words, D. A. was actually in more danger than Clark. Not old enough to be completely immune to Monsters, not young enough to believe in the things that would protect him anymore.

Now Clark was less concerned about Catherine-Lucille, Jaylynn, and himself—and *more* worried about D. A.

"Wow, that's totally great of you. But…maybe *you* could come sleep over with us tonight?" he asked. "Like we were all kind of planning, originally?"

D. A. made a funny face. Not disappointed. Not really resigned. Maybe a little bit touched.

"Dude, that's the girls' side—and I already told Kris I'd hang with him tonight."

"Please?" Clark begged. He really didn't want D. A. to be alone. Even with his action figures. Not with all the ominous things happening. "I'd feel…um…*better*…if you were there."

D. A. rolled his eyes. "Okay, *fine.*"

Clark let out a sigh of relief.

"But you gotta play cards with us tonight," D. A. added, a twinkle in his eye. "You and Kris need to get along. You'll like him! Once you get to know him!"

Clark nodded, reluctantly.

If this was the price of protecting his friend, so be it.

THIRTY-TWO

Foon

It took all of Foon's willpower to not kill the Chowgun right there and then.

"*Do not. Threaten. My Boy!*" he hissed.

The Great Bear gently pulled Foon away.

"This is a serious matter indeed," he said gravely. "Let us discuss it...over here."

"The Monsters planned all this," one Stuffy guard said in wonder.

"For many Moons!" the other guard added.

All the Stuffies began to murmur among themselves in dismay.

"The Lomer! The Crellans!"

"It is all part of the same thing! Their revenge plan!"

"How did the Stuffies get taken from their children?"

"Monsters? Monster-controlled Grownedups? How did they do all this?"

"It matters little," the Great Bear said, his voice rising above everyone else's. "What is important now is figuring out what to do."

"It's all my fault," Foon whispered, falling back against a tree. "All my fault. The Monsters are seeking revenge on my Boy for what *I* did. I killed the King Derker, not he. They should come after *me*, not my Boy."

"They *are* coming after you," the bear said with a growl. "Through your Boy. This is not at all your fault. The King Derker had to be killed. All Monsters have to be taken care of. You were doing your duty, and saving your House. Pull yourself together. You need to be strong."

Foon knew the bear was right. He could feel guilt later—after his Boy was safe.

He shook his head, resettled his Stuffing, and tried to clear his thoughts. To decide what was the most important thing to do *right now*.

"I must save him," he said, taking a deep breath. "Where are the children now? Where is this camping trip?"

"I know!" a voice called out from the crowd.

"Purple Platypus, Guardian of the Camp, approach!" the Great Bear commanded.

"Sorry," she apologized, waddling forward. "If I smell bad it's because they hid me behind the compost bins this time."

"Be not concerned," the bear said graciously—although his nose may have twitched a little.

"They are on the Mountain of the Lost River, Mount Wantastiquet," the platypus said. "They go there every year."

"And how far is that from here?" Foon demanded.

"About two man-miles, if you go straight across the lake. Four otherwise. And one man-mile up to the top."

Foon's horns crumpled in dismay. "Even if I ran straight—through day as well as night, if it were possible—I would never make it on my small Stuffy feet!"

All the Stuffies muttered and moaned among themselves.

Foon sank down until he was sitting on the cold ground, his head in his hands. Stupid Monsters...stupid revenge plan...plotting in the depths of their Dark World for months...And then just appearing like magic wherever they wanted to do their evil deeds. While the Stuffies only had their own paws to run on and...

Foon suddenly looked up, a thought occurring to him.

"How did the Monsters get into the camp?" he demanded.

The platypus bowed her head, blushing. "It is usually a place of safety and peace. We do not normally post patrols..."

"No, that's not what I mean," he said, getting excited. "How does *any* Monster get anywhere? How do they suddenly appear here and there? In closets and under beds?"

The Great Bear looked thoughtful. "They have their own secret ways from their world. I think I see where you're headed with this. Lorekeeper Brush-Tailed Phascogale!"

A furry, adorable little creature came up and bowed, blinking its black eyes.

"I am here!"

"Lorekeeper, as I understand it, the Monsters have a way of...cutting through distances. They can enter almost anywhere in our world from theirs. Is this so?"

"Not entirely," the creature said, bowing again. "It seems as though they must stick to particular spots they use again and again—doorways, if you will. And these don't always work, and sometimes these doorways come and go. All lead *back* to their world from this side, however."

Foon felt a stirring of hope. "And if I went through one of those doors—into the Darkness? Once I'm in their world, I could take one of these doorways back out again? To someplace else?"

The Lorekeeper blinked. "*Their world?* Why would you ever choose to go there?"

"So that I may come out again near my Boy to rescue him," Foon said, a little impatiently. "Please keep up."

"Oh." The phascogale blinked some more, thinking. "I... suppose it's possible. But no Stuffy has ever successfully gone into and returned from the Darkness in *ages*. The Great Song Cycles speak of Juanita the Brave Bunny who entered the Dark Realms and came back out alive...if changed. But she returned the way she went in. Through the same laundry chute. No one has traveled from one place in the World of Light to another *from within* the World of Darkness."

"Well, one is about to," Foon said, standing up. He threw back his shoulders and stuck out his jaw. "Where is the closest doorway around here that you know of?"

"It's whatever one the Chowgun came from," the Lorekeeper said. "Ask *it.*"

"Gladly," Foon said with a grim smile.

And in the stockade, the Monster actually quivered in fear.

THIRTY-THREE

The Cabin in the Woods

"One five."

"One six."

"Two sevens."

"BS!"

Kris flipped over Raph's cards. One nine, one eight.

"Aw man," the other boy said good-naturedly, scooping up the entire pile and adding it to his own.

The game wasn't actually as bad as Clark had imagined. Sometimes several whole minutes went by in between Kris's dumb jokes or mean comments or rude gestures. He concentrated on winning and once even laughed at something Clark had said. In some ways he was like the annoying cousin you had to put up with once or twice a year. Just barely bearable for a little while and then you were super glad you never had to see him again (until the next holiday).

Maybe Kris was sort of almost okay in small quantities. But Clark still couldn't understand D. A.'s constant loyalty to him, although sometimes flashes of the other boy's allure became clear.

"Ha! Dig my bold move," Kris said. "Of course, not as bold as that steal Ohtani made in that game against the Cubs."

"Did you *see* that?" D. A. said, whistling. "Man, I was glued to the TV the whole time. Didn't even break for snacks."

"I saw it *in person*. My dad took me. We saw the entire series."

"Whoaaaa."

Not only were they both into sportsball, Kris was *seriously* into it. And maybe his parents were rich or something.

"My dad took me to a football game once," Clark said, as casually as he could manage. "At the local college. It was a lot of fun."

Kris threw down his cards in a fit of forced, hysterical laughter. His two cronies fell over themselves.

D. A. just shook his head.

"Buddy, the Cubs and the Angels are *baseball*."

"Yeah," Clark said, not quite lying. "I just meant my dad took me to a game, too. That's all."

"'My dad took me to a game, too,'" Kris cackled. "You sure it wasn't tiddlywinks?"

It took two more rounds before Clark realized he should have rolled with it; he should have said something like *No, we only go to* semipro *tiddlywinks games* or *Absolutely not; it was Nerf darts.* He wished he was cleverer.

When it was time to go to sleep, D. A. stretched and threw down his cards and said, "Awright, well, I promised to hang with my old buddy Clark here *weeks* ago—but I'll see you all in the morning."

"That's what his sister said," Kris said, pointing at Clark and guffawing.

It didn't even make any sense.

(And Kris was very, very lucky Anna couldn't actually hear him. In the morning he would have found his head was shaved, rude things were tattooed permanently into his skin, and an animal skeleton had been hidden in his underwear.)

The energy in the cabin was that of tense, forced merriment as everyone got ready for bed. Even the campers who claimed they didn't believe in Monsters weren't looking forward to spending the night in what was very obviously a haunted old mountaintop cabin. The three counselors had a hard time quieting everyone down.

On the girls' side Catherine-Lucille and D. A. sized each other up warily.

"Guess I'm bunking over here tonight," D. A. said.

"Guess so," Catherine-Lucille said. "Make yourself at home."

"What's going on with those two?" Jaylynn whispered to Clark.

"Uh, long story. Nothing romantic," Clark promised.

Catherine-Lucille took first watch, of course.

She sat crisscross-applesauce, back straight as a knife's blade, hands resting on her knees like some ancient yogi. Jaylynn conked out immediately; she sprawled with her mouth wide open and made little snoring noises. Clark wondered how many spiders a year she ate in her sleep. He had read somewhere that the average American ate three, but wasn't sure if that meant averaged across those who kept their mouths shut tight and ate none (hopefully him) as well as those who welcomed in dozens of dry and thirsty arthropods with their wide-open jaws (probably Jaylynn).

D. A. didn't fall asleep immediately; he sat up on his elbow, once or twice looking over to where Kris and the others were. They, of course, were scrumbling around in their sleeping bags, pretending to be caterpillars, making lots of gross noises.

Then he fiddled with his fancy watch for a while. Clark had no idea what he was doing—playing games, setting something, maybe checking texts? And D. A. didn't offer him an explanation. He was there with them, like old times. But not *really* there, not like old times at all.

Clark twisted back and forth, trying to get comfortable.

He watched dust fall through the somehow not-that-comforting glare of the flashlights that were set up in a triangle, beams crossing. Their light was too white and cold. In movies and TV shows they were friendly yellow, like dumbed-down versions of the sun.

Beyond the flashlights were the five pathetically tiny and plastic action figures carefully placed like the points in a pentagram when someone had forgotten to bring candles.

"Five guys, three flashlights, four friends," Clark murmured to himself. Would that work? Somehow it didn't seem like it would work. And Jaylynn was new, and she and D. A. weren't even friends at all.

The cabin was strangely dark for all the flashlights and things the kids held in secret: contraband phones, forbidden video games, Cyalume light sticks and glowing toys that some slept with for fears they could not name. No light from these made it to the peaked ceiling of the drafty cabin.

The windows looked out on a dark that was somehow even darker, like dead eyes on a head they were all inside of.

"Five guys, three flashlights, four friends," Clark said again. "Five times three is fifteen. Fifteen times four is sixty."

He wasn't sure what it meant, but it sounded round and powerful.

"Sixty. Sixty seconds in a minute, sixty minutes in an hour...Seven hours until morning.

"Sixty times seven is...um...four hundred and twenty.

"Good night, Mom and Dad and Anna. Good night, Grandma Machen. Good night..."

He fell asleep sometime after the forty-third good night.

THIRTY-FOUR

Foon

The Chowgun did not give up information very easily.

Mostly because it didn't have any.

Anything it did know it had already said, gloating and peeping hideously:

1. The Monsters had a plan for revenge (against Foon).
2. There were many different Monsters involved in this plan.
3. Some took over Adults and made them remove the Stuffies from their children.

(Clark had *not* left Foon behind! Or forgotten him! On hearing this, Foon's Stuffing swelled with happiness.)

4. This plan had been in the works for a while.
5. The goal was to capture Foon's Boy on the mountaintop and hurt him or eat him—the details weren't clear.

(Nor, maybe, were they necessary.)

The Chowgun only vaguely remembered being ushered from the World of Darkness to the Bright Lands. The plan actually sounded like a mess, and crowded with many small Monsters sent out to help search out Foon's Boy . . . or just to wreak havoc on the camp.

The prisoner also didn't know words for colors (pink, blue); words for things that weren't from its world (wood, stairs, tree); or basic directions (north, right, uphill).

All the Stuffies could really get out of it was that it had maybe come from a basement somewhere. Damp and dark and close and empty.

"We will mount a grand search," the Great Bear said. "I shall call all the remaining Stuffies in camp to me. Our numbers are—surprisingly—larger than they were before. We had quite a few new members newly made this very week. Almost all mice. We will blanket the entire property and search every nook and cranny for this Dark doorway. When it is found, report back to me at once!"

But Foon didn't want to wait for the rest of the Stuffies to assemble; time was passing too quickly. He ran off to search on his own.

"Wait up, Foon, we will join you!" Baby Monster cried, puffing along on his two legs. Behind him were the saber-toothed tiger and Doris (and Ren Faire Beast).

Foon was pleased; together they would make short work of the search.

"The Monsters took you from your Girl as well?" Foon asked Doris as they set out.

"No, my Girl left me behind on purpose. I think she was worried about the safety of the camp while she was gone. But she took Freya for protection," the coyote/fox/girl/thing said. "We should find her if she is here as well...."

A mouse suddenly zoomed out of the bushes, speeding around in nonsensical zigzags.

Foon couldn't believe it. This newly made Stuffy *also* looked like his companion, DangerMaus. Same shape and whiskers and eyes. But this one was hastily sewn and one of his eyes was falling off.

"whereistheGreatBearwhereistheCircleofFire" the mouse muttered to himself, sniffing trees and pausing to balance on his hind legs for half a second before running again.

"Hold!" Foon said, putting his trident out to stop him. The thing immediately paused and looked at him lopsidedly. "The Circle of Fire is that way—but what is the matter?"

"DangerMaus Number Twelve reporting for duty, sir!" The mouse saluted, whiskers whisking back just like Foon's DangerMaus and the other DangerMaus. "I have news for the Great Bear but must not abandon my post for long!"

"What is this news?" Foon asked.

"Sir, the place I was assigned for my watch duty, sir," the mouse said. "*It* is the place everyone is looking for. The door to the Dark World."

"How do you know this?" Foon asked.

"Sirs." The mouse saluted again. "And ma'ams. I was created for the sole purpose of guarding against Monsters in Dark places. And not a single Monster came by on my watch or my twin's watch—until tonight!

"A *Lomer*, sirs. And ma'ams. It flew down the stairs and tried to get through the door to something on the other side. I believe it was trying to head back to its foul home. I and my twin, Number Fourteen, fought it off!"

Foon and the other Stuffies looked at each other uncertainly. It was obvious no one wanted to say anything. Lomers had high Defenses. . . .

"Well, we *scared* it off," the mouse admitted, seeing their looks. "We are not short on courage! Only size. And Attack."

"Of course not, you're a good mouse," Baby Monster said soothingly. "You and your twin both. Mighty mousy warriors indeed!"

"Where is this door?" Foon demanded.

"It's in the basement of the cafeteria, sir."

"Makes sense," the saber-toothed tiger said thoughtfully. "That's an especially scary, deserted place."

"I must go there immediately," Foon said, turning back to run.

"But, Foon, the Great Bear said to report to him first," Doris pointed out.

"My Boy's life is in danger! Because of *me*!" Foon cried. "You may go tell the bear—I will go save my Boy!"

And with that he turned and ran.

THIRTY-FIVE

The Cabin in the Woods

It felt like Clark had just closed his eyes when Catherine-Lucille's strangely warm hand grabbed his shoulder and shook it. Somehow he was neither scared nor surprised. He immediately knew it was her and where he was and what was going on.

"You're up, Corporal," she whispered.

Clark looked around. Most of the glows and lights scattered throughout the cabin that he had fallen asleep watching were gone: switched off or burned out. The blackness contained only snores and whiffles and sighs.

Outside the wind screamed and moaned like every evil metaphor Clark had ever read in scary stories.

"I sort of have to pee," he said, testing the words out.

"I wouldn't" was all Catherine-Lucille answered.

She was right, of course.

She was wearing, Clark noticed, a matching top-and-bottom

pajama set whose shirt had big blue plastic buttons. There were little sort-of-manga characters all over it, black-eyed smiling monsters and kittens and unicorns.

Weird.

She stepped into her sleeping bag and snuggled down almost like a normal girl.

And fell asleep instantly.

Also weird.

And disappointing. Clark had hoped they could talk a bit before she passed out.

Now it was just him...and the night.

THIRTY-SIX

Into Darkness

"This is the door," DangerMaus Number Twelve whispered solemnly. DangerMaus Number Fourteen was marching back and forth in front of it and didn't stop until the saber-toothed tiger gently put a paw on his head.

It looked like the door to an ordinary broom closet.

An ordinary broom closet in an ordinary basement. Ordinary dark, ordinary silent, ordinary scary. Not a place any child would choose to go willingly, except maybe to creep in and jump out to scare *other* children.

All the Stuffies peered suspiciously at it; they were bright and soft and out of place in the eldritch hall. Tahks skittered just out of sight in the shadows along with their sort-of-opposites, the Dust Bunnies.

(Basement Dust Bunnies were not as friendly as their upstairs counterparts. They were often studded with sharp bits like glass and nails. But they did not actively bother the Stuffies on their business.)

Foon opened the closet door with the tip of his trident.

The door creaked—of course it did—and swung aside.

What should have happened:

A clumsily leaned broom should have fallen with a clatter.

An ugly grey pail, metal and crusted with loathsome deposits, should have stood there proudly. Left over from an earlier, darker century.

A spider should have scuttled out.

A cloud of dust should have blown in the Stuffies' faces, causing them to sneeze adorably.

Instead...

Nothing happened.

Very black nothing.

Long tendrils of *black nothing* curled and reached out questing fingers to the rest of the basement. *But stopped short of the doorway itself.* As if the three boards making up the frame were a magical barrier. Garbage and bits of *nothing* hit up against this invisible wall from the other side and disappeared like soot before pouring down to the floor.

The silence from beyond the doorway was so heavy and complete it could be felt, a presence louder than any shriek or terrifying siren.

"How do I find my Boy once I am in there? How do I find the right way back out to him?" Foon wondered aloud.

He wanted to say so much more: *I am scared. This is impossible.*

I wish there was another way. But these were foolish thoughts. *Of course* he was scared, it *must* not be impossible, there *was* no other way; if there were, he would be doing that instead.

"No one knows, Foon," Baby Monster said. "That is why we should wait until the Great Bear comes. He'll know what to do—and maybe send along a team to help you."

"There is no time," Foon said impatiently. "It's my fault this happened, and my fault alone. *I* must do it. If I am indeed 'the mighty Foon.' There is no sense in anyone else putting him- or herself in danger."

"Let me come," said DangerMaus Number Twelve.

"I am mighty, too—and can assist you!" said DangerMaus Number Fourteen.

"Continue to guard this door," Foon told them. "Let no more Monsters try to escape back to where they came from—or come *out* and befoul this place of peace. That is the best thing you can do. Keep it safe—until I return."

Doris shook her head but didn't object.

Foon turned once to salute his friends—then, without a second thought, leaped in.

THIRTY-SEVEN
The Cabin in the Woods

The night was long.

Clark tried to sit as Catherine-Lucille had, spine straight, knees touching the floor...but his back hurt pretty quickly.

He tried kneeling, and then lying on the floor with his head propped up on his arm. He watched cobwebs—or Cowbers—slowly undulate in the upper reaches of the ceiling.

He sat up again.

He tried making little shadow-puppets with his fingers in the beam of Catherine-Lucille's giant floodlight...but just creeped himself out even more.

He decided to try and peek out a window, see what the night was like. He got up and carefully stepped over the triangle of light made by the flashlights, anchored by the action figures—and that's when he heard it.

Come outside

What?

Did someone say something?

Actually, why *didn't* he go outside?

Why didn't he go before? What was stopping him? Didn't he have to pee? He should go now. It looked like the weather had let up for a moment. Everything was still and quiet. The dead tree looked almost pretty standing there against the quiet sky. Its branches curled up protectively. *Safe.*

Outside was definitely less scary than the shadowy corners of the cabin.

Come outside

It's nice out finally and

safe

The wind and rain *had* stopped. A cold mountaintop was definitely safer than a haunted cabin. Clark reached for the cabin door.

"*GO TO SLEEP, CAMPER!*" a voice hiss-whispered across the cabin.

Clark spun around. Evan—probably—was sitting up in his sleeping bag. He made a V with his fingers and pointed them at his own eyes, and then at Clark. *I'm looking at you.*

Clark sighed, went back into the circle of protection, and settled down into his own bag.

All thoughts of going outside disappeared immediately.

Well, it was a dumb idea anyway. At least it was warm inside. He propped his head up on the edge of a book (*Half Magic*), letting its sharpness cut through any urge to drift off.

But…those shadows on the ceiling? Behind the cobwebs? How could they be there? There was almost no light in the cabin now. So there was nothing to make shadows with.

And actually, with the wind and rain stopped, it was *too* still. Too silent. Just the noise of everyone breathing…the cabin breathing…

Clark thought about the windows, how they looked like eyes. How the campers were *inside* the haunted house's brain, looking out. Maybe being the brains themselves.

Were they new thoughts in the old building's head? New ideas?

Or would they just be quietly absorbed, forced into its old way of thinking? Ancient crimes, grisly old plots, hidden bodies, erosion and decay…

Clark swallowed—despite his throat being bone-dry—and looked at Catherine-Lucille's watch, which she had left out for him and Jaylynn.

1:36 a.m. Two and a half hours to go.

THIRTY-EIGHT

The World of Darkness

Foon tumbled end over end until he landed with a quiet *fwoomp* on the hard, rocky ground.

The very first thing he noticed was the light.

It was not right *at all.*

When he looked down at his feet, it seemed like a normal cloudy day, maybe near dawn or after dusk. Everything was sharply outlined and clear—but also dull and grey. There were no shadows. Not of Foon or anything else. Which was strange: He would have thought a place called the *Darkness* would have been full of shadows.

He looked up at the sky, which was blindingly bright.

Sort of.

Half of it was a deep, unbroken black. No stars.

The other half was an ugly, unbearable whiteness with scattered black spots that *might* have been stars.

In between these two extremes the sky was a smeary red like the sunset above an old factory or garbage fire.

"Shining" in the middle of it all was what passed for the sun in this world: a dead, coal-colored disk. There were no rays or halo or anything coming off it to indicate heat or light. It hung, motionless in the upper air, like the rotting eye of a fish in a polluted lake.

All around Foon, jagged and unlikely mountains reached vainly for that sun. Their harsh edges scratched the sky as if erosion never occurred, weather didn't happen, time didn't change anything. Instead of normal peaks they were topped with gigantic, slick bulbs or stony scythes, blades aimed into the strange emptiness above.

There were colors to these cliffs and ranges, but only barely: grey, bad-medicine orange, ugly-makeup lavender, and old-pudding white. Foon had little knowledge of geology but was pretty sure that none of the processes that formed these mountains were natural, at least in the earthly sense.

In the far distance, and taller than everything else, was what appeared to be an artificial structure: a skinny, ill-built tower that rose higher than seemed possible. It was topped with an uneven cube. On each side of the cube was a clock face—which should *not* have been visible considering how far away Foon was. But the faces were as clear as if he was just a few feet from it. Each of the maggoty-pale dials had a single crooked hand that hung brokenly, pointed at nothing.

Foon felt a wave of vertigo—or maybe it was nausea. Everything here was so *wrong*. The colors were wrong, the light was wrong, the distances and buildings were wrong. It was as if someone had set about to make something completely opposite from—and far uglier than—the real world.

He turned to look back where he had come from.

The door was closing.

It took all of Foon's willpower to stop himself from lunging through the "broom closet" before it shut entirely. Back to the lovely, safe World of Light.

But he could see (even after the door was shut) where the door was: a strangely even cleft in the rock that mimicked the shape of a door. Within that crack floated black and corrupt glints of un-light—whatever the opposite of sparkles were. Darkles?

Foon marked the spot in his mind: a misshapen tree thing hanging on a ledge above, a path leading away below, the rust-colored plateau where it all stood.

He would be able to find it again.

Provided, of course, that places stayed put—like they were supposed to—in this land of awful things that didn't make sense.

Foon saluted the friends who could no longer see him and set off into the World of Darkness.

THIRTY-NINE

The Cabin in the Woods

When it was time for Clark to wake Jaylynn for her watch, she snapped out of unconsciousness immediately—but weirdly. Long-lashed eyes wide, staring at nothing, blinking a little like a hideous Monster in wait. She had been sleeping very lightly.

"The wind won't stop," she moaned.

"It did for a while. Sometimes it does," Clark said. "And believe me, it's better when it doesn't."

By unspoken agreement they all decided not to ask D. A. to stand watch. Even Jaylynn somehow sensed it wasn't right.

She and Clark reversed positions: She slowly pulled her legs up in her sleeping bag and corkscrewed herself around into a sitting position. He got back into his bag and stretched into a giant Y.

And then it was his turn to try to sleep but lie mostly awake, listening to the storm rage around them.

FORTY

The World of Darkness

The trail widened as Foon wandered down through the dead canyons. Soft sand replaced bare rock underfoot. Foon knelt down and tried to identify the prints and tracks that were now visible, but it was impossible even with his mighty hunting skills. They could have been from the soft susurrus of a snake thing, the multiple pitters of a many-legged Srocha, or even the wide, tail-dragging pace of something larger. But who could say? The tiny grains of sand rounded out and blurred everything.

And what if there were creatures native to this realm that weren't Monsters?

What a strange thought! An alternate world with a complete ecology, unique to itself...

Foon suddenly jumped up and pushed his back against a rock, his trident at the ready.

There was the faintest noise from somewhere up ahead. Around the corner.

fshwoost

Once and then gone.

Barely a sound at all.

Foon waited.

He counted.

The moments dragged out.

Finally he *leaped.*

"Halt, foul Monster!" he cried, landing in a perfect warrior stance: crouched, his weapon, Focus, aimed at the enemy.

The Monster he had *known* would be there made a strange whistling noise like it had sucked in air the wrong way. It rolled back over itself in fear and confusion, legs and long body knotting around and around.

"*BE STILL*, that I may face you with honor!" Foon demanded.

The thing quickly untangled itself.

It had the sinuous, soft, ugly white body of a worm. Its neck and tail were long. Sticking straight out from its sides were three pairs of chubby legs. Overall it seemed a little moist.

Its head was…also moist. It was not out of proportion with the body, unlike most of the worst Monsters. The face was spade-shaped and split by a wet mouth; there were two sunken patches above the nostrils where maybe some ancient ancestor once had eyes. Now there were none; the thing was blind. It had giant feathery fans behind where its ears would have been—well, less feathery than *fleshy.*

(If Foon had known anything about biology he would have noticed a striking similarity between this Monster and an axolotl, a reasonably normal, if weird-looking, amphibian from his own world. And then he would have been surprised. The harsh, dry mountain environment was exactly the wrong sort of place for such a delicate creature with gills.)

(Then again, maybe he *wouldn't* have been surprised. After all, this was a Monster, not a normal amphibian.)

"Don't hurt me!" the creature begged, backing up on its four hind legs and clasping its front two together, pleading.

"Silence! You are evil, a Monster of the Darkness, put here only to destroy the Light. Your very existence is a mockery of all that is good!"

The Monster swayed back and forth in confusion. It didn't deny what Foon had said; it didn't whine or beg, either. It really seemed more dismayed than anything else.

A little confused by this behavior—which was less Monster-like than he expected—Foon continued: "Though you do not deserve it, I shall spare your miserable life on one condition: Lead me through this accursed land on my quest."

Still the creature swayed meaninglessly. The pits where its eyes would have been furrowed a little, as if it was frowning in thought.

"All right. But where is it you need to go?"

Foon was once again brought up short. There were no threats, no pleading, no whining, no begging. The only Monsters who could talk—really talk, like sensibly—were higher level; Derkers and Lomers and the like. They used their mastery of language to confuse and entrap their opponents. Lesser Monsters couldn't talk at all. Midlevel ones like the Chowgun barely made sense when they spoke. It was as if an accident of nature—or unnature—had gifted them with words but without the brains to make sense of them.

This Monster could speak, and spoke simply.

Odd.

Perhaps it was a trick.

Foon straightened himself up, throwing his shoulders back. "I am seeking my Boy, who has been captured by one of your evil kind. He is being held on a mountain far from me. I must travel as you Monsters do—cutting through space unnaturally to make short work of my trip. I must find a way out of the Darkness to him through one of your doorways."

"Oh."

The Monster rolled and unrolled the belly flesh in between its forelegs and middle legs in a gesture that could have meant nervousness or thoughtfulness; Foon couldn't tell. But it definitely wasn't rearing up for an attack.

"I've never heard of such a thing before, a Stuffy traveling by Dark Seconds," the Monster added.

"I care not whether you have *heard* of such a thing," Foon snapped. "I will do it. You will help me. Or I will end your miserable existence."

"I don't know where your Boy is," the Monster pointed

out. "But your being here is weird. Everyone's talking about the Great Plan—'revenge on the mighty Foon.' Are *you* the mighty Foon?"

The little Stuffy was shocked to hear his name once again from the mouth of a Monster.

He wondered if it was giving the creature too much information to admit who he was—then again, maybe it would force the Monster's hand.

(Or claw, or whatever.)

Foon nodded modestly.

The Monster swallowed in fear.

"Then I'll definitely take you to the Lowlands. Because otherwise you will *definitely* kill me—the stories of your murder and violence are legend."

Foon didn't think the word "murder" was appropriate— these were *Monsters* he dispatched, after all. Not Stuffies or humans or cats. But he couldn't help feeling the slightest bit of a glow. His reputation in the Dark was legend—literally! His very name struck terror into the unhearts of Monsters who had never even met him!

"Why the Lowlands?" he demanded, getting back to the point. "Do not try to trick me, Monster!"

He jabbed the trident threateningly at its midsection. The creature wailed and sucked its belly in like a Father at a pool.

"I don't know for certain! But there are more Dark Seconds down there, near the City, where the Great Pleticon rules and all the Higher Monstren live. That's where they do all their Dark business. But if you let me, I'll talk to my neighbors now and try to find out."

Foon frowned. Little of what it said made sense. Dark Seconds? Great Pleticon? Was this a trick? A way to plan a surprise attack?

He considered his enemy.

All soft—no tentacles, teeth, hard edges, or weapons any-where. Poison *was* a possibility, but as long as Foon avoided direct skin-to-skin contact it wouldn't be a problem. Unless the creature spat (which Foon also had experience with—some Zagtraphs at a sleepover). He just needed to be wary. He could probably defeat this one and *all* of its cousins if he had to.

"Very well," Foon said (fairly graciously, he thought, given the circumstances). "Lead on. But remember—I and my trident are right behind you."

"Hard to forget," the Monster said, eyeing the weapon's sharp tips.

FORTY-ONE

The Cabin in the Woods

Clark had terrible dreams.

Star-shaped things that weren't pretty. That weren't *natural.*

Cold, rubbery tentacle arms reaching out. A perfectly round mouth with teeth rimming it, pointy, white, and sharp.

Suckers that groped onto his body and *stuck.*

Pulling him, pulling him in…

Were there stars in the ugly mouth? Was there the blackness of space?

Was Clark about to be eaten—

Or something *worse?*

FORTY-TWO

The World of Darkness

The Monster didn't slink along as Foon expected, as a lizard or a snake might—or even a normal Monster, for that matter. Its six little hands/feet moved deliberately, one after the other, and none too quickly. Its rear set of hips swayed left and right, its first set of shoulders worked in the opposite directions. It all seemed a little awkward. *Plodding*, like every inch gained was a triumph. The small creature didn't seem tired or put-upon by its own laborious movements; it almost seemed jaunty. Which was odd, considering the pointy trident behind it.

"What manner of Monster are you?" Foon asked, trying not to sound curious. "I have never encountered your kind in the World of Light before."

"My people are called Phlebbish," the thing answered.

"People!" Foon snorted. As if they were ... *people.*

"We don't go to the Bright Lands very often, except under the cover of night when all is quiet and lonesome. And then only to add to our collections."

"I *have* heard about you, then! Or something like you, in stories at the Circle of Fire. I thought you were just that: stories. Little Monster thieves who scurry and hide. You do not *feed* on children or Grownedups, but you steal from their Houses?"

"We do not *steal!*"

The thing turned around and gave Foon what was probably an offended look. It was hard to tell on a being without eyes. Its fan-tentacle-gill-things waved forward and back in a way that was most repulsive.

The Stuffy warrior wasn't used to subtleties of emotions in Monsters. They were either raving or raging. Sometimes whining and cringing and begging. But that was all.

"We *Collect*," it said with great dignity. "And only the things that are Lost. Dropped, forgotten, unwanted, unneeded, rejected. Left behind and evicted from the sunny world of humans.

"Socks, mostly."

"Even worse!" Foon leveled his trident, Focus, at its head. "Cold-blooded stealers of socks! You are the ones who slink around in secret and shadows and take half a pair, leaving confusion and desolation in your wake, especially on laundry day!"

The thing stared—or, really, just faced Foon silently. Maybe in confusion.

"We—only—take—what—is—forgotten—and—unneeded,"

it repeated slowly, as if the little Stuffy were stupid. "It's our way. Anything with . . . *ties*, we can't touch. Children shed things; we take them in. If a child loves something, we can't take it."

"But the Mothers and the Fathers—and sometimes elder siblings—are responsible for those objects! They must be washed, dried, put away, and worn. Your stealing them leads to anger and chaos!"

"Then why don't they keep better track of their socks?" the Phlebbish asked. As if it was curious—not like it was trying to make a point. "We find them in the places where only useless things gather. Under beds, in basement corners, behind piles of old magazines . . ."

"Yes, but . . ." Foon trailed off, unable to figure out a way to explain it.

"We're near my village, it's just over there," the Phlebbish said, either bored with waiting for an answer or having decided that the conversation was over. "I'll go ask about the Plan and revenge and where you should go."

"Won't they grow suspicious with you asking so many questions?" Foon demanded.

"If they do, I'll just tell them there's an insane, violent Stuffy waiting outside who will kill us all if we don't do what he wants."

And while once again Foon didn't like "insane" or "violent"—he was a skilled warrior, not a berserker—he decided not to mention that. It might seem a bit self-centered.

And besides, the Phlebbish was right. If any of them *did* try to prevent his rescuing the Boy, he would destroy them all.

☆　☆　☆

The Phlebbish lived in a dry valley, in what would have been constant shadow if this were the normal world (it was a little darker than the surrounding area, but that was all). High mountains around the village blocked out the sky, the strange sun, and the clock tower.

It seemed . . . *safe.* From the rest of the Dark World.

Strange.

Foon wondered why this would be important. Weren't all Monsters the same? All evil? Why would some hide from others?

The valley was filled with the soft sand that Foon was beginning to realize was what the Phlebbish, with their delicate skin, preferred to wallow in. Erupting randomly from the ground were narrow branches of stone that reached up from the ground uncomfortably like arms. In clearings free of these were . . . "houses."

They looked like the forts the Boy made in his Room (or sometimes in front of the television) out of whatever lengths of cloth he found. Sheets and blankets tied to chairs and table legs, belts and scarves used to stretch from the corner of a tablecloth to someplace where it could be fastened tight. Sometimes he and Foon had picnics inside them, pretending it was snowy and disastrous in the living room beyond their fabric walls.

These tents were made out of socks.

Higgledy-piggledy but carefully overlapping each other like tiles, in dome shapes. Mostly the socks were dirty white—some were actually dirty. Some dusty, others downright filthy. But there were a few colored ones, too, black dress socks and bright ones with fun designs. These were draped over doorways and windows for decoration.

"I'll go ahead and ask around. Wait for me on the other side," Foon's Phlebbish said.

"You live in buildings made out of socks," the Stuffy warrior said, feeling strange. He rubbed his paw over his belly; he, too, was made out of socks. Slightly more colorful ones—and Adult ones, not children's. Chosen, not stolen.

"Only the left ones in *my* home," the Phlebbish said with a sniff. Then it leaned and whispered in disgust: "Some are less choosy. And some even choose ... *right.*"

It scuttled off in its swishy, tail-lash-y way.

Foon hid behind a rock and watched closely to see if there were any tricks. But there were only Phlebbish.

Awkwardly, mostly using their mouths despite all their handsfeet, some worked on their tents, pulling a fresh (well, stinky) sock into place. Others nosed trinkets and bits of junk into neat little piles next to their houses: rubber bands, paper clips, SD cards, buttons, pennies....

Hideous, wormy white Monsters performing useless labor over and over again in the dark light of the dead sky.

Or...

A bunch of harmless and weird creatures doing harmless and weird things quietly in their own neighborhood, bothering nobody.

Foon shook his head, not liking where the thoughts in his Stuffing were going. It was uncomfortable. These were Monsters, this was like the End of the World, he had a Boy to save from them. There were only two sides: Light and Dark. Nothing in between. And he was a warrior for the Light.

And so he waited and sharpened his trident.

FORTY-THREE

The Cabin in the Woods

Morning.

Clark cracked open an eye and should have felt overwhelming relief—the Monsters didn't get him!—but didn't.

Something felt *wrong*. Unfinished. Like the other shoe was about to drop.

There were little noises all over the cabin of people getting up, stretching, gossiping. Nobody looked well rested. Even the heartiest members of the group were pale and tired. The counselors were straight-up strung out and screechy.

One of the boy counselors (Evan maybe? Not-Kai; the one with the Earth necklace) was grimly getting the little stoves going, making coffee and oatmeal. Clark hoped there was brown sugar. It was the only way he could stomach the beige-and-healthy glop his mom sometimes served. Lots of brown sugar, lots of cinnamon, lots of butter.

He didn't think there would be butter this morning.

Clark glanced out the window. The sky was as angry as ever, a mean series of grey stripes that looked apocalyptic. He jumped back as the wind sent a large branch—with leaves still on it—smashing into the side of the cabin. It nearly hit the window and would have broken it.

He wanted to go home. Even back to camp. Very badly.

But not through that.

"Okay, well, that was fun," D. A. said, stretching and running a hand through his scruffed-up dark brown hair. It was weird seeing him without his hat. "I'm going to go say hey to Kris and the others and see if I can get this taste out of my mouth."

Catherine-Lucille sat up, yawned, and immediately began to methodically undo her braid. Then, using only the tips of her fingers, she re-straightened her locks, divided them, and plaited them back up again. It was strange seeing his friend do this sort of thing. Kind of girly and private. But it was also so Catherine-Lucille: precise and without comment.

Clark ran a hand through his own hair, unconsciously imitating D. A. He wondered how badly he needed the Brush.

D. A. grabbed his sleeping bag and went to scoop up his action figures—as if it were just the end of a playdate, as if everything was normal.

"Hey, where's my Hondo?" he demanded. "There's Ultron and Ahsoka.... I'm missing a clone trooper, too."

Clark felt his heart turn into an icy, tiny nugget of ice. He and Catherine-Lucille and Jaylynn looked at each other.

"Someone must have grabbed them by mistake," D. A. muttered.

But the closest pod of campers was several feet away and—although Clark could feel his sister glowering at him for even thinking this—they really weren't the sort of girls who would collect action figures, even an Ahsoka. He didn't remember any other camper looking with finger-grabby envy at the toys, either. If someone from Kris's terrible crew had wanted to, he surely would have stolen it at a more convenient time. Not at night, which could involve the shameful embarrassment of getting caught *on the girls' side of the cabin.*

No, the figurines were *gone* gone. It was pretty obvious.

"We'll keep an eye out for them," Jaylynn promised unsteadily. But she kept her gaze very obviously *off* the floor, as if refusing to check for popped-off accessories, tiny feet, heads.

"Cool, thanks," D. A. said. Clark wondered if any of it was an act.

"Oh man," Catherine-Lucille said the moment he was gone. "I hope they're all right somewhere."

"*I* hope we get the heck out of this place today," Jaylynn countered.

Clark didn't say anything. He occupied himself with not panicking. He tried to be mindful (as his mother would say) about the small steps that would lead to the rest of the day. He changed in his sleeping bag. He carefully rolled up the bag and packed it away. He went to get some Morning Glop, as the counselors cheerfully called it.

(There *was* brown sugar, but only two spoonfuls per camper, except for Darren, because he had insulin problems.)

Catherine-Lucille somehow managed to get a mug of coffee from the counselors, which she split with Jaylynn. Clark politely declined—he hated the stuff, even his sister's *un*-Italian super-sugary chocolate creations.

When a giant *thump* hit the cabin like an entire tree had been knocked into it, everyone shrieked. Clark jumped like a bomb had gone off.

"Hey, Corporal, you okay?" Catherine-Lucille asked. "Relax. It's day. We made it. The action figures—well, we'll look for them. And if we don't find them... well, it's a shame. And a tragedy. We'll have a ceremony for them back at base camp. But they did their job. They kept us safe. Nothing left for us to do now but hike home and blow all our allowance on candy at the canteen to forget about this."

"But can't you *feel* it?" Clark asked. "The... whatever it is? It... the Monsters... they didn't get what they want. They're not done with us yet."

His friend gave him an odd look. Not like she didn't believe him; more like she was surprised, impressed, or... *thoughtful* about his concerns.

"DUNDERBUCKETS!" Counselor (probably) Evan swore, throwing a small black piece of tech onto the stone hearth. "First the phones, and now the radios aren't working."

With perfect timing, the wind began to scream, filling the silence that was left by the campers processing Evan's outburst.

(Some were quietly checking their illegal, and as yet unfound, phones.)

"Maybe you're right," Catherine-Lucille murmured. "Maybe we're *not* making it out of here today."

"It's exactly like the beginning of every horror movie ever," Jaylynn whispered.

No, Clark thought.

It's exactly like when you're a quarter of the way in, when the heroes realize they can't get out.

FORTY-FOUR

The World of Darkness

Long minutes passed.

The Phlebbish did not reappear.

Foon grew impatient.

He tried to calm himself by meditating on what it meant to be a warrior.

One of the greatest Stuffy Heroes of legend was Tomtom the Wookah: He waited without moving for three days outside a seemingly innocent mouse hole. On the fourth day a clever Defense Six Thrangle stuck its head out to look around, and Tomtom immediately lopped it off. Because of his incredible patience and fortitude, the House of Tomtom was saved.

Foon decided he was still a little young to be that patient.

He *did* try, though.

He shifted from one paw to the other.

He spun his trident.

He watched the sky.

He practiced a couple of lunges.

He counted to twelve.

"The Phlebbish is deceiving me!" he finally roared. "It is gathering its kinfolk to gang up on me for a surprise attack. No matter; I can take them all!"

He looked upon the site of his imagined bloodbath with expectation.

(The quiet village of sock tents seemed weirdly peaceful for an apocalyptic showdown.)

Just as Foon was about to descend upon them, his Phlebbish came waddling out of a tent on the far side. It looked around blindly for the Stuffy, strange feathery gills tasting the air and writhing revoltingly.

Foon leaped from rock to rock, twirling Focus above him. Not strictly necessary—but it did help with balance a little. And looked awfully impressive.

He landed in a warrior's crouch, right in front of the Monster on one knee.

"There you are," it said, unimpressed. "I didn't learn anything you probably didn't already know. The child is being held on the Mountain of the Lost River in the Bright Lands."

"That is all?!"

"No one much talks to us Phlebbish," the thing said, shrugging its middle set of shoulders. "We only get rumors and gossip if a Gnabird or something comes by. But someone pointed out that there's a Lesser Derker guarding the entrance to our canyon, sent by the Great Pleticon as part of the Revenge Plan. It checks in the Chowgun and Lomers and Vormonths and all the cityfolk who have to pass through our Dark Second to get to your children. No one enters or leaves the valley now without its say-so. It probably knows a *lot* about all this."

"Defense Level probably Five. Maybe Six," Foon said, nodding. "I could take it."

"*Great!*" The Phlebbish looked strangely enthusiastic. "It hasn't let any of us out since the whole stupid revenge thing began. The pusblooms are flowering in the valley now, and we're going to miss them *all* this year."

Foon glared at the Monster.

"And also it could probably give you some info about where we need to go," it added quickly, seeing the look of violence on the Stuffy's face.

"Yes, that is a plan," Foon growled. "Let us go."

☆　☆　☆

The only thing that marked time as they traveled down from the mountains was the weird clock in the unimaginably tall black tower. Its hands moved, but not in any pattern Foon could figure out. Monstrous minutes and seconds. Still, it was something to look at. And it made him think.

"Phlebbish, what *is* a Dark Second?" Foon asked. "Is it like a door, or a portal?"

"Yes," the Phlebbish said.

Then: "No."

"When you open a doorsock on your tent you can go in or out any time you want," the Phlebbish said, frowning as it tried to explain. "A Dark Second is a . . . moment in time. It's a place that's yummy. A time that's useful. It is a . . . feeling? All of these things have to be right for us to get somewhere else. Haunted places keep their Seconds for a long time. Other Dark Seconds come and go much more quickly—on the ebb and flow of Darkness and belief."

Foon thought about this. It hurt.

Time? Place? A *feeling*? All of them had to be right for a door to work?

Although that kind of explained some things, like his Boy's House. Before Foon arrived, Monsters like the Silver Fish and King Derker found their way in and stayed. Once Foon and his comrades had cleared them, they seemed to stop coming. Maybe the Dark Second there was gone forever, now that the House was no longer haunted.

"The Cottonysoft Dark Second is one of only four that I know," the Phlebbish continued. "It's a door that stays. And it was all ours, alone, until the Dark City Monsters needed it for their plan. Selfish jerks. They have *all* the other doors. Hundreds of them! They built the Dark Clock to count the Seconds so they could come and go to your world whenever they wanted."

"So the Monsters in the City know all different ways to get to our world? Er, the Bright Lands? And they somehow use the clock to keep track of them?"

"Of course! The Prime Zargloch knows the most number of doors . . . and will sell their locations for the right price. The biggest Pilshun can read the clock and choose easily. But I've never learned how, nor met any of those Monstren myself. I don't ever go to the City—it isn't delicious. No socks. Lots of Higher Monsters. They'll eat you first, ask questions later. Loud and grumptious. Best to avoid."

"Eat you first? I thought Monsters only fed off children and Grownedups?"

"You see any of those around here?" the Phlebbish asked dryly. "My people may not taste as good as fresh child, but that doesn't stop other Monsters from eating us."

Foon shivered. What a terrible world!

He had to get out of it, and to his Boy, as fast as possible.

FORTY-FIVE

The World of Darkness

Perhaps when he was meditating on great Stuffies of the past, Foon should have also considered the ones who were brilliant strategists. And then come up with a plan that was a little cleverer than *Find the Lesser Derker and hit at it*.

Leaning lazily against the entrance to the canyon on the other side of town was indeed a Lesser Derker. It was narrow and slimy and had a tiny monkey face that came directly out of its chest. Rather than boasting dozens of leg-things along the body like the King Derker, it had only two appendages: scaly tentacles that whittled down to sharp points.

Upon seeing them approach, it didn't bother to snap up straight in readiness or suspicion but addressed them still slouched.

"Stop, stupid Phlebbish," it drawled. "You *know* the Great Pleticon's orders: No one is to come or go from this militarily important area until the Revenge Plan is complete."

"Okay, but—" the Phlebbish began.

"For the Velveteen!" Foon cried. He ran at the Monster, his trident, Focus, aimed at its ugly face.

The Lesser Derker hissed and sprang off its coiled tail.

The Phlebbish fled behind a rock.

There was a *bump* and *clang* as the opponents collided. Limbs, lint, and scales flew. It looked like a mighty battle indeed!

But...

Foon pulled his arm back to strike—and the Monster whipped its tail and body around the Stuffy, squeezing tight.

His trident was caught up against his own body, trapped and unusable.

It was over as quickly as it had begun.

Foon cursed. He should have been stealthier. He should have snuck up on the Monster....He should have done something else, *anything* else. This was exactly the sort of situation that Winkum would have anticipated.

Or even Freya. She was good with setting up ambushes.

The monkey face opened its mouth, revealing a set of fangs much like a King Derker's but smaller. Dark red poison dripped from their points.

Desperately, Foon threw his whole body to the side. Unbalanced, the two enemies fell over onto the ground.

The Stuffy immediately rolled and rolled. When the struggling combatants came to a stop, he pinned the Derker's head so it was beneath him.

The Derker hissed and snapped its jaw, fangs flashing. Foon pulled his head as far back as he could, out of its reach.

"How do I get to the Mountain of the Lost River?" he demanded. "Where is the Dark Second that will lead to my Boy?"

"*You* are the Foon!" the Derker hissed. "*You* are the one the Great Pleticon wants! I will grab you myself and be greatly rewarded!"

"Good luck with that," the Phlebbish called from where it was hiding behind a rock.

Foon twisted and pushed with his whole body, grinding the Derker's head against a rock. Scales and black ichor smeared the ground.

"Tell me how to get to my Boy and I *may* let you live!" Foon growled. He pulled his torso back and slammed his head into the Derker's—horns first.

The Monster shuddered from the blow; its eyes were now heavily lidded and dazed.

It hissed . . . but halfheartedly.

"You will never reach him. Give up now, and maybe *he* will live," it said. "Your life for his."

"Yeah, I wouldn't trust him," the Phlebbish said.

(Unnecessarily, in Foon's opinion. He had no faith in a Monster's promise.)

"Last chance, foul beast! Tell me where the door to his place of capture is, or die."

The thing was so weak now that Foon had no trouble pulling his paws out of its grip and wrapping them around its throat.

The Monster wheezed and laughed. "You want a *door* to your *Boy*? All right.

"In the . . . Desrupt, on the blorth side of the City. There is the *door* that will lead you to your Boy . . . or your Boy back to you. But careful what you wish for, stupid Stuffy."

"You know where all that is?" Foon asked, turning to look at the Phlebbish.

"Yes," it said, a little regretfully. "I do."

"Excellent." Foon threw the weakened Derker to the side and disentangled himself from its scaly tail. "We must go at once. Lead on, Phlebbish! For though the journey may be long, time grows short and my Boy must be rescued—"

"And there goes the Derker," the Phlebbish said with a sigh.

The other Monster was indeed slithering off quickly down the pass.

"I shall be rewarded for my intel!" it hissed gleefully. "I shall tell the Great Pleticon myself and be given so many riches! *MONSTREN OF THE WASTES, HEAR ME!* A STUFFY HAS INVADED THE VILLAGE OF THE PHLEBBISH! TO ME! ALL CLAWS TO ME!"

Without a thought, Foon hurled his trident. It was a beautiful throw: one graceful motion as if his arm was almost part of the weapon. Then Focus broke free and arced, shining, through the air to its target.

The center tine came down perfectly through the Derker's skull, pinning it to the ground.

The Phlebbish swallowed. Loudly.

It looked at Foon in horror and awe.

"Let us go," Foon said lightly. "After I retrieve my weapon."

FORTY-SIX

The Cabin in the Woods

The moment the rain died down again, Clark—and, it looked like, half the cabin—dashed outside to pee.

He was one of the first to make it to the edge of woods, which was incredibly unusual for him. But there was no time to revel in that fact; he just needed to find a secluded tree ASAP.

A quick look around revealed that the trail was a washout. Literally. He almost didn't recognize it at first: a tiny river of mud and sticks that in no way resembled a path. Clark swallowed in despair like his mouth was full of lumpy oatmeal (with no brown sugar or butter).

He looked back at the cabin—it wasn't at all welcoming, with its stone teeth and glass eye-socket windows. The campers' faces that looked could have been the eyes themselves.... What if they somehow were forced to stay there forever? Like ghosts? Trapped, and trapping other campers...

The dead tree seemed way less friendly than it did in the middle of the night, not *safe* or pretty at all. Actually, now that Clark thought about it, that whole thing was pretty weird. He must have been half-asleep when he tried to go outside. Had he really thought that someone was actually asking him to go? *Inviting* him? It was a good thing Evan—or Kai—stopped him.

Despite getting soaked as the rain started up again, Clark trudged slowly and reluctantly back inside. It must have been his imagination that the door snapped shut behind him like a sideways jaw.

The air inside was dark, close, and a little stinky. Fear hung over the heads of the campers and counselors like an actual cloud.

Death by falling branch or exposure was possible outside.

Death *inside* came slower and creepier.

But nobody was packing up.

"What's going on? Any news?" he asked Catherine-Lucille.

"No one's told us what's happening yet. Bunch of idiots."

"Shouldn't we get going?" He tried not to imagine a watery demise or broken neck on the path down. "There must be another way off the mountain...."

"Okay, Shawna just told me," Jaylynn said, coming over. "The counselors never found or took her phone. Anyway, she's got no service at all—no bars. But it was fine on the trip up!"

"I guess the cell tower got knocked down?" Clark suggested hopefully.

"Sure. That explains why the radios don't work either," C. L. said, rolling her eyes.

"ALL RIGHT, CAMPERS, LISTEN UP!"

The one with all the macramé string bracelets was shouting (Robin, likely). She jumped up on the stone hearth so all the campers could see.

Everyone—even the rowdier kids, like Kris—stopped what they were doing and turned to listen.

"We're having some trouble contacting base camp," she said as casually as possible.

Clark did not miss the tightness around her mouth, the paleness of her lip skin.

"We're gonna send Evan back to camp to grab some help and extra supplies and figure out how to get you guys down safely. The rest of us will all just chill out here in the cabin until he comes back. Which is kind of a bummer, but there's a lot of great games we can play to pass the time. We can *expand* our *minds* electronics-free. Plus I have a ton of extra string and can show all y'all how to make these lovely bracelets of mine."

She shook her arms for emphasis and grinned.

It was all very forced.

"Are you kidding me?" Catherine-Lucille muttered.

Clark wasn't brave in front of crowds and was not spurred to action by many things—but panic was definitely one of those things.

"You're not really doing this," he begged/demanded as

he pushed his way through the rest of the campers (who were groaning and sitting back down and generally complaining).

"Hey, there's still two of us to cook and keep an eye on y'all," Robin said, scruffling Clark's hair (but ironically, so it was okay).

"You're splitting up the party," Clark squeaked. "First the communications devices fail, and now you're *splitting up the party.* You're doing everything *exactly wrong,* like in every horror movie ever!"

"C'mon, li'l buddy. How many horror movies have you seen?"

Well, to be fair, most of what he knew about them was secondhand from Anna, who was a bit of a connoisseur. But he felt like an expert. Like an archaeology student who had attended lectures for years but hadn't quite gone out into the field yet. He was prepared.

"Am I wrong?" Clark countered. Which wasn't an answer.

"Oh, you," she said with a smile—which also wasn't an answer.

Then she turned to talk to the other counselors.

"I mean it," Clark yelped, which took the sum total of the rest of his bravery. He *never* talked back to adults except in extreme situations. But things were on the line right now. Things like their lives. "Don't do this!"

Robin (probably) rolled her eyes.

"It'll all be fine," she promised.

Which, of course, was basically a death sentence in horror movies.

FORTY-SEVEN
THE GREAT PLETICON SPEAKS

Despite any rumors to the contrary, there are no, I repeat, *no* Stuffies invading our World of Darkness.

Even if one figured out where and how to use a door, he—or she; I mean, it could be a she, let's not be sexist here—would have no idea where to go, and just be stuck wandering around our glorious, deadly wastelands until he—or she—died under our unsun.

You can rest easy that *on the very unlikely chance* one ever *did* come over here, I would immediately send out assassins to kill him.

Or her.

Once again, everything is going just fine.

The Great Revenge Plan is proceeding splendidly. The Boy is trapped with his equally tasty friends on the mountaintop that has been ours for centuries.

Tonight the Grindel will begin consuming his essence.

So I repeat:

There are no Stuffies in the World of Darkness, but if there were, I would have my Monsters kill him.

Or her.

FORTY-EIGHT

The World of Darkness

Foon frowned at the horizon.

The Dark Clock didn't seem to be any closer—*or* any farther. But now he could see black smudgy things clustered around its base. Buildings or other hideous Dark constructions.

"How much farther, Monster?" he demanded.

"Soon we'll come to the Cystic Swamps," the Phlebbish said. "Just on the other side of it is the Dark City and the Desrupt."

"We must hurry. I am anxious to find the door before any other Monsters find *us*. That stupid Lesser Derker shouted about our presence for your entire world to hear!"

"I haven't been to the Swamps in oodles of tides," the Phlebbish said happily, ignoring him. "It's tasty, though I am not sure you will like it."

"Tasty? You mean you...drink the swamp?"

The Phlebbish laughed. "No, silly. It's *tasty*...for swimming in! Not *actually* tasty. We Phlebbish don't drink much of anything except for spills we sometimes find. Sticky puddles. By the way, we *eat* dust and crinkles and snirkglips, in case you were wondering. Not children.

"Oooh, and sometimes we get rare treats like the pusblooms I was telling you about. And used gum. I love that stuff. I tell you, if there were already-been-chewed gum and socks in our world, I'd *never* go to yours."

Strange. The Monsters that Foon was familiar with were always looking for a way into the World of Light (or *back* in, if you listened to them). Mostly to feed on the things there: children, the rare Adult, good feelings and thoughts. And they had no intention of ever leaving; they wanted to take over the whole World of Light and make it Dark. They wanted to stay and rule. So what was up with these Phlebbish?

Were they . . . *not* evil?

But they were *Monsters!*

Foon scratched his back with the tip of his trident. Sometimes when he thought too hard he got itchy.

"Are you okay? Do you have sores?" the Phlebbish asked. "You keep scratching yourself. I once had an infestation of Grelhooks on my hide that was terrible. My neighbor said the scabs tasted good, but I itched terribly."

Foon, who didn't eat, felt like throwing up.

Also he felt annoyed. He had nothing in common with this Monster! How dare it suggest they were at *all* similar?

He was just about to say something to that effect when the sand in front of them rose up as if it were alive.

Foon jumped back, surprised—which was bad form for a mighty warrior.

He had been lulled into distraction by chatting with the Phlebbish. He could practically hear Freya yelling at him for letting his guard down with an enemy close by. In hostile territory, no less!

(And if DangerMaus had been along, he probably would have heard this thing coming long before it attacked, with his giant mouse ears. Perhaps Foon *should* have waited for the other Stuffies to come....)

Dust and dirt fell in great rivers off the thing that had been hiding under it. Foon didn't recognize the Monster that was revealed.

It was almost completely flat. A flexible sand-colored carapace covered its long body. Despite its similarity to a centipede, it only had three legs: one at the front, one in the middle, and one at the end. But any weakness this might have given the Monster was made up for by a giant pair of silver pincers at its front end—ridiculously large; wider than a human dinner plate.

"A Yechzeken!" the Phlebbish wailed. *"Run!"*

But all this did was attract the big Monster's attention. It dove for the Phlebbish, pincers wide.

Foon immediately threw himself between them. He plunged Focus into the Yechzeken's . . . face?

(It didn't really seem to have one. Just a body that was topped with pincers.)

Clang!

The sound of its mandibles hitting the trident echoed throughout the otherwise silent land.

The Yechzeken screamed in anger.

Foon pulled Focus back and feinted to the left, and then to the right.

Then he *jabbed* to the left, up and (hopefully) into the flesh-meat above the Monster's neck.

But the thing guessed his move—or just got lucky, flailing about wildly. It reared up safely out of the way. The trident glanced off the top of its shell.

Definitely a Midlevel Monster, Foon decided. Despite its not talking. Clever and wily—and extremely deadly with the pincers. A Defense Eight at least.

The Yechzeken pulled back, almost as if it was winding itself up. Then it sprang forward, pincers wide.

Foon fell to the side, hurling himself out of the way. The pincers closed on a rock instead of the Stuffy.

Slicing the rock in half.

Like scissors on tissue paper.

Foon's button eyes widened in shock at the sight.

The Phlebbish began to wail—and then quickly covered its mouth with four of its hands.

The Yechzeken immediately turned to attack the other Monster, rising up onto its hind leg to strike.

Foon took the opportunity to aim his trident very carefully, testing the sight line along his arm. Then he leaned back and threw it with all his strength.

The Yechzeken dove.

The Phlebbish screamed.

Focus the trident landed true to its mark, sinking itself deep into the soft part just under the Monster's pincers. Where its neck should have been.

But this didn't stop the thing's forward motion—the giant crustacean continued to fall toward the Phlebbish.

(The Phlebbish screamed again.)

The Yechzeken's body *just* missed the littler Monster, impaling itself solidly on the trident as it stuck in the ground.

There it squealed and writhed violently, a toeclaw away from the Phlebbish.

Eventually it was still.

Foon breathed a deep sigh of relief, thanking the Velveteen.

His Stuffing sang with victory; he was light-headed with the energy of the fight.

This was what it meant to be a Stuffy warrior!

Wandering around alien worlds with a questionable companion was important, too, of course, as was his quest to save the Boy.... But it wasn't the same as battle. Good against evil, blow for blow. There just wasn't anything else like it.

The Phlebbish was rolling itself into dreadful knots, looping its body around and around.

"You saved me!" it squeaked.

Foon wondered if it would be impolite to point out that he needed the Phlebbish *alive* to find and save his Boy.

Then he realized he hadn't even thought of that when he

jumped in to stop the Yechzeken. He just saw that someone (something) was being attacked by a Monster. And went to stop it.

"You defeated him so handily!" the Phlebbish went on, in awe. "I saw it myself! The legends don't lie! He was a Defense Eight or Nine and you just—wiped the dirt with him!"

Foon modestly didn't say anything and went to retrieve Focus from the corpse. Like most Monsters, the Yechzeken began to fade immediately upon death, leaking black ichor into the sand. The shell dissolved into hundreds of tiny bones. Which was strange, and not how bugs in the World of Light were built.

The giant metallic pincers dropped to the ground when the body was gone—and these did not disappear.

Foon carefully picked one up. The blade was sharper than any weapon he had ever held. It glinted in the un-light like liquid silver. A useful trophy. Maybe someone could fashion it into a scythe. Very carefully he affixed it to his side with some extra hemming thread that hung loose.

"Wow, that looks pretty neat on you," the Phlebbish said.

Was taking a compliment from a Monster unheroic? Foon wasn't sure. He turned and set off for the Cystic Swamps.

The Phlebbish followed, but took one last looked behind them at the bones of the Yechzeken—and shuddered.

FORTY-NINE

The Cabin in the Woods

Catherine-Lucille, Clark, and Jaylynn squatted like thieves over a stash of gathered stuff.

"It looks like most of these batteries are at half charge," C. L. said with a frown. "The LED flashlights should last another six hours, easy. Jaylynn has a hand crank that needs a full wind every ten minutes, and two other kids have those. There is *one* glow stick left and some glow-in-the-dark earrings. Nobody has any Stuffies, and we're down a counselor. Thoughts?"

"Yeah, where *are* the, uh, Stuffies? And the Barbie?" Jaylynn demanded. "Who took them? Okay, Monsters, whatever. Are we going to get them back? Is it the same thing that 'took' D. A.'s action figures?"

"I don't know," Catherine-Lucille said honestly.

"I think it *is* a Monster, and the Monster is all around us," Clark said. "It's the cabin itself, and we're trapped inside."

No one disagreed with him. They had all obviously been thinking the same thing. The three were quiet for a moment, looking at their pitiful pile of things that glowed or lit up.

"If we were adults, we could just leave," Catherine-Lucille growled.

"Oh, it—the Monsters or whatever—would just think of something else to keep us here," Jaylynn said hopelessly. "If that's what it is, that's the way it would work."

"I don't think D. A. is going to be staying with us tonight," Clark said, trying not to give in to despair.

"I'm going to see if we can get some other recruits to take watch in the rest of the cabin," Catherine-Lucille said. "We should probably have two at a time."

"Promise them they can have a flashlight," Jaylynn suggested. "That will help."

"Excellent point. What else can we do?"

"I'm going to light a fire," Clark said without thinking.

The two girls stared at him.

"For real?" Jaylynn asked.

He shrugged. He didn't feel brave, or bold—just determined.

"They *have* to do it. I'm going to make them. We need a fire."

He did *not* say aloud exactly what they needed a fire *for*. To..."clear out the bad mojo," as his mom would say. To cheer everyone up.

But really: to scare away the actual bad things. Unhaunt what could have been a just plain old creepy cabin.

(That was probably a Monster.)

Something.

What he actually said aloud was:

"Tell everyone to grab some dry wood when they go out to, uh, use the bathroom. *Dry* branches and stuff. It's not going to be a big fire, but maybe we can get enough going to have coals to last us through the night."

Jaylynn grinned. Catherine-Lucille looked pleased at his initiative. She even saluted him.

☆ ☆ ☆

Robin and Kai (!) were extremely doubtful at first. But Clark could see the slight pinch of hope in their eyes. Despite their dumb songs and upbeat catchphrases, *they* were beginning to lose it, too.

(Twenty-four hours in a haunted cabin on a lonely mountain will do that to you.)

"What if the flue's all stopped up with squirrel nests or something?" Robin asked. "It could catch fire and we'd all burn."

"There's no flue," Clark replied calmly (but not exactly sure what that was). "There's just a giant hole in the ceiling."

"We don't have any wood."

"There's a stack outside the door, and I'm having people find more when they go outside."

"Neither one of us is an authorized Fire Skills instructor."

"But you're *in loco parentis*," Clark said, remembering the words Anna had used when she pretended to be his guardian so they could do Live Action Role Playing at the state park. "You're completely in charge of our safety and well-being. Which now means making a fire."

The counselors, surprised into submission by this, said nothing.

Clark took it as a yes.

All of the campers were excited to be part of a project, especially one that didn't involve dumb songs, especially one spearheaded by a fellow camper.

Especially one that involved fire.

Tinder was a jumbled mess of illegally hoarded corn chips and illegal cosmetic fluff. Jaylynn herself supplied a daub of Vaseline to smear on them (illegal because it was petroleum-based).

Kindling was easy. Some people claimed they had to use the bathroom more than was strictly necessary so they could gather branches and twigs, all competing to get the biggest bundle.

Fuel was a bit harder.

Even if they kept the fire small, Clark guessed there was only enough wood in the stack for a few hours. The oldest pieces were so light, dried out, and covered in lichen, they would probably flame up and last for twenty minutes at most.

The other wood that his eager fellow campers brought was, in order: wet, green, and wet *and* green (Clark saw some evidence of illegal pocketknives on chipped-off bark and honey-colored inner wood). Kris and another kid brought in a whopping large log that was three feet long, a foot in diameter, and fresh, from that season. It must have weighed, like, fifty pounds. They triumphantly threw it onto the stone hearth, making a noise that practically broke everyone's eardrums.

"Light *that!*" Kris cawed, and made a gesture that Clark decided to ignore.

He simply rolled the log next to the pile of other questionable ones and pretended like he was going to use it. And just like he predicted, Kris and the girl who brought it in forgot about the whole thing thirty seconds later, wandering off to cause trouble somewhere else.

Then Clark began to build his fire.

This would have to be perfect. A masterpiece. Not just because they needed light and heat and warmth and cheer against the night and a way to hurt the cabin Monster.

Also because everyone was watching.

And—this was important—it was the first fire Clark had ever lit all by himself, with no one helping.

He didn't mention that.

Frowning with concentration, he made a little pile of Vaseline-coated cotton balls and fluff.

Then he carefully built a log-cabin stack of dry twigs and Popsicle sticks (and one chopstick, snapped in half) above it.

Finally he balanced two logs above that, supported by two smaller logs and a stone at one end.

The rest of the campers all gathered to watch as he delicately put the final pieces into position. He felt their eyes on him and on the kind of pathetic pile of burnable things he had assembled.

Clark flicked open Kai's lighter (questionably illegal? He

didn't know what the rules for counselors were) and reached into the innermost part of the stack. Using a lighter was sort of cheating. It would have been more impressive with a match.

(But he could also hear Fire Skills Instructor Maya shouting: *When it's fire for survival, there's no such thing as cheating! USE A BLOWTORCH IF YOU HAVE IT.* She appreciated skill but hated the pickiness of snobs.)

After a few moments a piece of pocket lint caught.

It flared up and turned into soot almost immediately.

Clark swallowed and re-flicked the lighter.

"This is stupid. Let me do it," Kris said, grabbing Clark's arm.

"Step away from the other camper, Kris," Robin said. "He's authorized to do this. You're not."

"But I took Fire Skills, too, and I'm sooo much better at it," Kris whined. "Why can't *I* do it?"

"*You* didn't ask," the counselor snapped.

A corn chip chose that moment to hiss and begin to make a pleasing crackly sound.

Everyone held their breath . . .

. . . but then it sputtered and died.

Everyone groaned in disappointment.

"*See?*" Kris said.

Clark took a deep breath and tried again.

The cotton ball just sat there for a moment as the Vaseline melted and shimmered . . .

. . . and then began to flame. A tall, narrow, strong, and beautiful flame that licked the kindling above it.

Clark didn't smile in triumph despite the *ooohs* behind him. He pulled his arm out of the wood and closed the lighter. He *willed* the kindling to light.

A curl of bark began to flicker like an orange firefly.

He very gently blew on it.

He waited.

He blew again and waited.

He would *not* sit back on his heels as if he was done and it would all just suddenly work now.

He would *not* poke at it.

Campers shuffled their feet and muttered impatiently.

"You're doing it all wrong," Kris huffed. "You *built* it wrong. The easily burnable stuff goes on top so it lights first!"

"Not even a little bit true," Clark responded, surprising himself with how calm he sounded. He wasn't angry; he just knew he was right. "You build your fire from the inside out. Maya taught us that on day one."

"No she didn't." Kris sounded angry. So angry it was obvious he realized that he had no idea what he was talking about. "She didn't! You're dumb."

Clark decided to ignore him and just keep on with what he was doing.

Which of course was the one thing Kris couldn't deal with. He stomped away, muttering something about stupid fires.

(But if Clark was also hoping for a response from D. A., for his friend to say something, well—he was disappointed.)

He pursed his lips at the fire and blew again.

And waited.

Several new licks of flame slowly rose from the twigs. These were uneven, lumpy, jumpy. They reached up and slapped the logs above them as if to show off—and then hunkered back down again as if suddenly afraid. Clark mentally encouraged them to move over to the narrow slit between the two logs. This slit would act as kind of a chimney, sucking the hot air up and out the top, pulling more air to sweep in from the bottom.

A tendril of smoke wove its way up, sinuous and feathery. A bright orange glow reflected off the logs from where the wood was catching.

Then Clark sat back.

The logs began to crackle.

"Well done, dude," Robin said, giving him a high five.

The campers all gathered around Clark, praising him, giggling, and putting their wet feet and socks too close to the merry little blaze.

"Lucky mistake," Kris said, coming back and kicking at the burning pile. "I could have done it faster. And better."

Kai pulled him back before he did real damage—or burned his foot.

"Hey, Corporal. You did good," Catherine-Lucille said. "Real good. I made this for you during my watch last night—I was going to surprise you with it at the end of the session. It's not quite done yet, so I'll finish it tonight."

She held out a badge that said FIRE SKILLZ SPRITE, LEVEL I. A tiny red-and-orange flame grinned atop three tiny brown logs.

"Wow, that's *great*! Thanks, Catherine-Lucille!"

A real badge! That he had earned!

But he didn't hug her.

As evening rolled in Clark sat, bathed in the light and heat of his fire, holding his new badge in one hand and using the other to toast one of the Starbursts his sister had given him. They really *were* better than marshmallows...all hot and gooey and fruity and delicious.

His face glowed, matching the flames. He had done it. All by himself. He had made a campfire. And *everyone* was congratulating him.

It was not something he was used to, nor anything he expected to ever happen again. But for this one moment, he felt wonderful.

"Nice job, Clark," D. A. said, high-fiving him.

Better late than never, Clark thought.

"Thanks," Clark said.

"You're kind of amazing. Come play cards with us again later?"

Clark nodded, feeling too good to be annoyed by the request. Everything was pretty great.

All of which would change in just a few hours.

DIY MERIT BADGES

So the Scouts aren't for you. That's okay. You and your friends still deserve badges for everything you've accomplished in life. Maybe it's for finally being able to bust a nollie shove-it on your skateboard; maybe it's for making it through a doctor's visit without acting like a baby when you got your shots. Whatever you've done, you should get a badge and wear it proudly.

"Real" badges are embroidered on heavy cotton canvas (sometimes called duck). They have a brightly colored border of thread sewn around and around the edge to keep the woven cloth from fraying. You may absolutely take the time and effort to embroider your patch and sew around the edges like that... but here's a trick to making it look like a real badge without so much work.

What You Need

STIFF WHITE CLOTH
Canvas, felt, etc. If you don't have it, any light-colored cloth will do since you're using a heavy cloth for the background.

STIFF COLORED CLOTH (felt)

NEEDLE

THREAD
In a color that matches the stiff colored cloth.

DIFFERENT COLORS OF EMBROIDERY THREAD
If you're embroidering the details.

ACRYLIC PAINT
If you're painting the details.

Step 1

- Cut out a circle of the white cloth using the middle circle template ("B").

Step 2

- Lightly draw or write out your badge design in pencil on the white circle. If you want words to go neatly around the outside, you can lightly trace the smallest circle template ("C") on the white cloth as a guide. Remember to keep a little white space between the words and the edge if you plan on sewing it to the background cloth (don't worry if you're just gluing it).

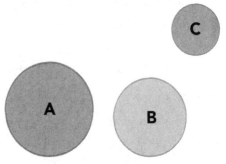

*See full-size template on page 392

- Also, it wouldn't hurt to lightly draw a straight line down the center of the white cloth, and one across it at ninety degrees/a right angle to make a target shape, just to help you keep your design centered.
- If your white cloth isn't felt—if it's woven or knitted—you might want to run a teeny amount of glue around the edge to keep it from fraying.

Step 3

- Embroider or paint your design!
- If you're painting, use a small brush. And, uh, paint it.
- If you're embroidering . . .

Step 3.5

Welcome to the Satin Stitch!

- For outlining your design, words, lines, or small areas, use the backstitch (explained in *Stuffed*). For filling large areas, use a satin stitch. Think of it as coloring in a picture using thick, straight lines. In fact, it might help for you to lightly draw straight, parallel lines in the area to be filled in to give you a guide for sewing.
- As always, the first thing you do is thread your needle and knot the end.
- Note: Embroidery thread usually comes as six separate strands twisted together. It's easier to work with three, so carefully separate out half the strands in the length you need and use that. Unless you don't want to.

1. Bring your needle up out of the front of the cloth, keeping the knot tight in the back.
2. Travel in a straight line to the other side of the area you want to fill in.
3. Push your needle through to the back.
4. Bring your needle back up through to the front again, right next to where it came through the first time (next to the knot for this first time).
5. Bring the thread back down again alongside your first stitch.
6. That's it! Continue until you are done!

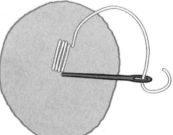

Step 4
The Backing

- Trace the largest circle template ("A") on the brightly colored cloth.
- Center your beautifully designed badge in the middle of it so you get an even ring of color around the outside. (See? *It looks like you embroidered the edge! Like a real badge!*)

- You can either glue your badge down, or ...
- Sew it down to the other cloth with a neat line of running stitches just inside the edge of the badge or ...
- Whipstitch (explained in *Stuffed*) around the outside of the badge onto the background using the matching thread.

Step 5
Attach Your Badge to Something and Wear with Pride!

- Since you have a backing cloth, you can put a safety pin through just the backing and not have the pin come through or show on the top.
- If you have very nimble fingers, you can actually sew a safety pin on with a few stitches through just the backing cloth.
- You could also use a *good* glue (fabric glue, patch glue, etc.), but remember, that's permanent!

Examples of badges:

Expert Needle Skills

Tree Watching

TV Remote Operation: Level 3

Stuffy Troop #28

Read All the Books

Zombie Killing

FIFTY

The World of Darkness

The Cystic Swamps were every bit as disgusting as Foon had imagined.

The black-and-yellow water (?) was thick and oozy and didn't come from the ground or a river, at least not at first. It formed in large sacs that hung off dead trees like, well, like nothing Foon could properly think of. Wetter than spider eggs, far too large to be fruit, too...*sad*like to be mushrooms. They sat there and slowly swelled, getting bigger and bigger, until, shuddering, they exploded. Smeary charcoal or yellowish liquid would fly everywhere, dripping down bark and limbs.

Sometimes the sacs didn't explode—the thick syrupy stuff just seeped out through jagged holes in their sides.

The Phlebbish squirmed off into the murk with a squeal of glee.

Foon couldn't watch, it was so disgusting.

Then he realized the Monster was much faster in the water and could easily escape. He panicked, raising his trident.

But the Phlebbish just turned around and around in the filthy liquid, splashing and playing, before circling back to Foon with a slap of his tail.

"This is the tastiest ever. I feel so full!"

(Foon was relieved to see that the Monster really wasn't drinking the foul stuff—this was just more of his weird and wrong use of words.)

The little Stuffy looked around for a way to cross the fetid swamp. The nubbly islands of half-dead trees were too small to cling to. There were no vines to swing from, even if Foon had any desire to touch the plant life of this horrible world.

Aha!

He spotted a piece of floating junk whose top surface was relatively slime-free and dry. Using his trident to balance, Foon carefully stepped out onto it. The thing—plank? Driftwood? Shoebox?—tipped a little but held him steadily after a couple of terrifying seconds. Whispering an apology to Focus, Foon dipped his trident into the water and poled himself along.

It was almost peaceful—if completely disgusting. He steered himself silently through the bog and the Phlebbish happily floated on its back beside him. Sacs exploded. Once in a while there was the screeching call of some nasty swamp Monster.

"Why *did* you kill the King Derker?" the little Monster asked idly.

Foon almost dropped Focus in surprise.

(Okay, not really. He was a mighty warrior, always prepared for battle. But he did *straighten up* in surprise.)

"He was consuming the Father of my Boy!" he cried. "He was trying to suck the life out of everyone in our House! His intent was to take over the body of the Father and walk in his skin and rule the House for the Dark! All who lived there—my Boy, his Sister, the Mother—were likewise threatened!"

The Phlebbish was silent, thinking about this. It seemed puzzled.

Foon tried again.

"If someone, a Stuffy or another Monster, came and tried to hurt your..." He desperately searched for some similar word. Did Monsters even have families? "...neighbor Phlebbish, what would *you* do?"

"I might run away if it looked like he was going to hurt me next. But maybe I'd try to stop them," the Phlebbish said thoughtfully. "I don't know how. I've never fought anything before. Maybe I'd try to climb onto a cliff above and push a rock down on its head."

Its eye sockets widened in sudden understanding.

"Oh! The Great Pleticon took your child because it wants revenge for the King Derker you killed. But *you* killed the King Derker because he was hurting the Father of your child. And it planned to hurt others in your world. Is this right?"

"*Yes.*"

The Phlebbish asked, in a tiny voice, "Is *this* why Stuffies kill Monsters?"

It sounded scared.

Of course Stuffies were the heroes, good and kind on the side of the Light, noble warriors, shining beacons in the Darkness. Their job was to slay Monsters, the terrible villains who came from the Dark. Thus had it ever been.

But if you were a Monster, a small one...a feeble one... one who never attacked or ate anyone else...Stuffies would seem terrifying. And if you didn't understand why they killed Monsters, they would also seem violent and insane...just like the Monsters they killed.

This Phlebbish had never actually hurt a Boy or Girl.

Once again, Foon wondered about the nature of the Phlebbish.

Because no Monster could be good. Right?

Foon decided to call the Phlebbish *harmless*, and leave it at that. Which was a strange enough thought in itself: a Midlevel Monster that didn't matter.

But if this one showed up—if any of them showed up—in Clark's room at night, what would Foon do? Grab the sock from it and chase it off? Ignore it? Would he still be expected to kill it?

Foon decided it was best to forget it all for now and focus on his quest. He had promised not to kill the Phlebbish if it brought him where he needed to go. That was all.

And time was running out.

FIFTY-ONE
The Cabin in the Woods

At four o'clock the tiny fire was still going, but Evan had not returned.

Outside, the winds and rain lashed the cabin unmercifully. *Inside* it was quiet; a lull or almost-silence as if the campers knew this was the pause before the worst. The faster readers had already started trading books, having finished their own. Clark played a strangely subdued game of Go Fish with Kris and D. A. and a few other kids. He caught Kris cheating but didn't even care. What kind of weirdo asked for cards he didn't have? How did you win with a strategy like that?

At four thirty they had a snack. It was a thin instant soup with little broken pasta bits in it and absolutely delightful. For a few minutes everyone cheered up and the merry clinking of spoons echoed off the stone cabin walls.

By five thirty campers started to whine about dinner because there was nothing else to do.

Clark tended the fire. It definitely tried to go out more easily than it should have. Unnaturally. He had to keep a constant watch on it. Sometimes a healthy flame would just—suddenly—dip and die.

And sometimes the cabin shook.

Sure, it could have been the wind. Or a tree branch.

A couple of the other kids helped with the fire or sat next to Clark and poked it more than was strictly necessary. Jaylynn kept trying to find different food to roast. Starbursts were still the best, but cheese crackers weren't too bad.

Clark wondered what they did in the old days, before TVs and video games and the internet, when they were caught inside for days because of a storm. Especially in a haunted cabin. He thought about the old faceless folk dolls you saw in museums that were utterly terrifying. Maybe they had to be, to combat Monsters in these situations.

At six o'clock they began making dinner. One of the counselors and several campers got soaked washing out the dirty pots from lunch. They came in from the outside looking haggard—as if they had been away for weeks, maybe years, instead of minutes. Dripping, chilled to the bone, and bruised by hail.

"It's going to be tonight," Catherine-Lucille said ominously. "Whatever is happening, it's going to happen tonight."

"I'm not going to sleep a wink," Jaylynn swore.

"So, I'm going to hang out with Kris tonight," D. A. told Clark casually.

"Yeah, sure," Clark said, resigned.

"You can take my guys if you want since you don't have your Stuffies," D. A. offered.

"Uh, no thanks. I'm good. You keep them?" Clark said, just as casually.

"Hey, how's your little boyfriend, D. A.?" Kris asked, whacking them both on the backs of their heads with a stick.

"That is wrong on so many different levels," Clark said as calmly as he could. "It's wrong, and not nice to gay people...."

Kris made a big deal of pretending to yawn.

"Dude, c'mon, be cool," D. A. said, shaking his head—but he still walked off with Kris.

And then the sun went down.

FIFTY-TWO
THE GREAT PLETICON SPEAKS

While there may—*may*—have been a few bumps in our Great Revenge Plan, everything is now back on schedule.

Any assassin who *may* or *may not* have been sent to take down a Stuffy found invading our World of Darkness was certainly not defeated. But even if it was, that stupid Stuffy has—er, would have—no idea what he's going to run up against.

Or she. What *she's* going to run up—

Oh, forget it. The point is, calm yourselves: Of course there is no way he could make it to our beloved Dark City.

And yes, the human children *have* been very clever in their attempts to defend against the Dark. But they are defending themselves against the *wrong* emissary of Darkness—and they do not even realize it.

("Cabin Monster," indeed! Whoever heard of such a thing?)

Our fiendishly brilliant plan has fooled even the canniest of them.

This very night the Grindel will take our victim and eat him—and utterly destroy his stupid Stuffy, Foon.

And we shall *finally* have our revenge.

FIFTY-THREE

The World of Darkness

The disgusting Cystic Swamps finally came to an end. None too soon for Foon, who stepped onto the sort-of dry bank with a heartfelt thanks to the Velveteen.

The Phlebbish, however, crawled out looking satisfied but a little sad, like a child at the end of a long and happy day at the beach.

It shook itself off, beginning at its spade-shaped tail and ending with its nose like a very moist and mutated dog. When it was done, it raised itself up on its hind appendages and stretched out its neck to get a better lay of the land.

The small monster shuddered at what was there.

Foon leaped up onto a rock to look—and *also* shuddered.

The Dark City.

Out of a smeary black smog rose domes and angles and spires of unsettling and haunting shapes. Evil seemed to just *ooze* out of it in the form of shadow, mournful sounds, and terrible fumes. Random fires burned on buildings and street corners, giving off heavy coils of smoke. The Dark Clock loomed above it all like a rocket that would never blast off.

"Some Monsters want nothing more than to go live in the City," the Phlebbish said. "Look at it! I don't know why."

Foon had nothing to say to this and began walking. The Phlebbish sighed and pitter-pattered its six feet quickly to catch up.

"I will have such a story to tell when I get, back if I live," it continued. "About going *almost* all the way to the City, captive of a terrible Stuffy."

"What do you mean, 'if you live'?" Foon asked, deciding to ignore the second part of what it had said. "I have promised your safety."

The Phlebbish cocked its head at him.

"Sure," it said. "And you did kill that one Monster who was going to get me. And that Lesser Derker before that. But the Great Pleticon knows you're here—it totally sent the Yechzeken to get you. Who knows what you—and anyone with you—will face next?

"Also, you could change your mind about letting me live."

Monsters, Foon thought disgustedly. They had no sense of honor. They didn't live by their word and didn't keep promises; they cheated and lied and killed.

And they assumed everyone else did the same.

"Phlebbish, I have given you my word. As a Stuffy. You do

what I ask, lead me to my Boy, and I will not harm you. *No one will harm you—*"

Just as he said that, a primal scream cut through the World of Darkness.

A hooved and horned nightmare launched itself from atop the rocks where it had been hiding, camouflaged. It dove straight for the Phlebbish.

The Monster squeaked and tried to run away—but got tangled in its own six legs.

Foon threw himself in between the two, trident poised to strike.

Then he realized who it was.

Freya.

She was in full battle mode: snorting, eyes wild, teeth bared, ready to tear the Monster apart.

Foon quickly turned Focus so its sharp tips were facing the ground and its pommel pointing to her. A barrier, but not a danger.

"FOON, OUT OF MY WAY!" she bellowed, trying to leap around him.

He moved lightly on his feet, countering her antlers with the butt of his trident. The clangs and ripostes were loud, real, and merry—probably the truest thing the World of Darkness had ever witnessed.

"Freya, at ease," Foon pleaded. "This Monster is my captive and I have pledged him safety while he takes me to my Boy."

Freya immediately stood down.

But her four legs were spread widely, dug into the loathsome dirt of the place. Her head remained lowered, antlers aimed at the Monster who cowered behind Foon.

(The Phlebbish had turned itself into a knot, writhing over itself in fear.)

"You are letting this foul creature of Darkness live?" Freya demanded. "It walks with you like a comrade? Get the information out of it and dispatch it immediately."

"It is not that simple," Foon said. "The Monster is my guide in this forsaken land. I would not be able to find where I need to go, or how to get there, without it."

Freya made a strange noise in the back of her throat. It was like a gargle, but also like the sound right before a human throws up.

It took a moment for Foon to recognize it as *frustration*.

"Fine. It may live," she finally said. "But *you*! Foon! What were you thinking? Traveling into the Darkness by yourself? Without backup or comrades? Without even a warning that you were doing this?"

"My Boy is in grave danger. I had to come immediately to save him. There was no other choice."

"My Girl is in danger, too!" the reindeer spat. "Or did you think there was another reason I am here and not with her?"

Foon stared with his big button eyes; perhaps they would have blinked in surprise if he were really alive.

"But...So you did not go on the camping trip either? You were...left behind, or removed, as well?"

"Yes, Foon. I woke by myself in the middle of the woods, covered in dirt and mud like I had been flung there."

"I didn't know," Foon stuttered. "Doris was there, left on purpose by your Girl. I assumed..."

"Yes, you assumed. You didn't ask. You didn't even wait a moment, gather all the information, understand the situation. The Barbie was also removed from her Girl, and Yellow Dog from his boy, and several others. We all could have gone together, a formidable army of warriors. Instead you rushed off alone."

She sighed wearily.

"Foon, you were foolish. Rarely has a Stuffy ever made it through the Darkness and back out again. And only *one* that we know of has done it without a cohort of warriors with her. If you had died here, what would have become of your Boy?"

Foon lowered his head. Shame washed over him.

"You are right, Freya. My actions were rash. I was not thinking. I was overcome with fear for my Boy."

"You Stuffies talk weird," the Phlebbish said.

The Stuffies ignored him.

"You are a loyal protector," Freya said. "But sometimes being a true warrior means stopping for a moment to consider a situation, and not just running in with your weapon raised."

Exactly like he had done with the Lesser Derker, Foon realized. He had almost lost that battle because he hadn't planned the assault beforehand, or taken a moment to come up with a better strategy.

"True. But you were about to kill our only guide," he couldn't help pointing out. "And ... *you're* here by yourself.'"

"You are impulsive. I have a temper. We both have room in which to grow. As for the other Stuffies separated from their children, the Great Bear decided that they should remain behind as a second wave in case our rescue attempt fails."

"Is she going to kill me?" the Phlebbish whispered.

"She will not kill you," Foon said tiredly. "You will lead us both through the Desrupt to the Dark Second that will take me to my Boy—and her Girl."

Freya's eyes widened. "So many words I don't know. Perhaps your guide is useful after all."

"I am *so* useful," the Phlebbish promised eagerly.

FIFTY-FOUR

The Cabin in the Woods

At nine—everyone was going to bed later than Camp I Can policy—Clark went outside to brush his teeth feeling almost okay.

He had banked the fire so it was a happy smolder, just like Calcifer in *Howl's Moving Castle*. The whole cabin was filled with its cheery glow. And it no longer smelled fetid and weird; it was smoky and homey. Catherine-Lucille was taking first Fire Watch to tend it (and finish up his badge).

Robin and Kai promised that no matter what the weather was—or whether or not Evan returned—they were all going home tomorrow.

Everything was going to be all right.

Clark sighed, did a final spit of his super-minty toothpaste, and went back inside the cabin.

He stopped in the doorway, gaping at the scene that was unfolding dramatically among the campers. For a moment he was confused; it was strangely similar to what had happened before, back at camp, when his friends were fighting.

But this time Catherine-Lucille was facing off with *Kris*, and D. A. was watching. And the two counselors were nearby, their arms frozen in ready positions, looking angry.

And the fire was out.

Kris was standing on top of what would have been the coals, his heels grinding out what was left of the orange glow.

"What the heck?" Clark yelled.

"It was late and no one was watching it," Kris said sullenly. "I thought it was going to catch the cabin on fire."

"You *idiot!*" Catherine-Lucille yelled. "*I* was watching it! I was right here! You waited until I went back to my bag to grab another needle! I saw you! It was like you were *planning* it!"

"Okay, everyone, calm down," Robin (most likely) said, going over to put her hands on the visibly shaking girl. One black look from Catherine-Lucille squelched that impulse immediately.

"I had banked it properly!" Clark shouted. He felt lost in a tsunami of different strong emotions. Anguish at the fire being out. Rage that Kris had put it out. Fear that it was now out.

He tried to sort his thoughts, to get to the most productive one.

"Let me go restart it," he said, moving forward.

"I think we're done with fires for now," the other counselor (Kai) said.

"We can't have campers setting themselves on fire," Robin agreed, but angrily, looking at Kris.

"No," Clark said. "Please."

"As soon as we get back to camp, Kris, your parents are getting a full report," she continued as if he hadn't spoken.

Clark should have felt better when she said this, but it didn't really matter. The point was that the fire was out. It was the only real protection they had left against the Monster.

And D. A. had just watched the whole thing. Without saying a word.

For some reason that was the final straw for Clark. Not Kris killing his fire, not Catherine-Lucille's wet and angry eyes, not even the counselors giving in and giving up.

"You . . . idiot!" Clark swore, unable to even think of a more original insult. He stomped over to his sleeping bag.

"You stink," another camper said to Kris, turning her back to him and walking away.

"That was the worst," a second one spat—also a girl.

"Not cool," a boy chimed in, hands on hips.

"All right, break it up, everyone," Kai said, sensing a dangerous mood in the room. He took Kris by the arm protectively, but the boy shook it off, glowering and sulking.

"Hey, Corp, I'm sorry," Catherine-Lucille said, hurrying over to Clark. "That was on my watch. He's bigger than I am; that's no excuse, I know. . . ."

"No, no, it's okay," Clark said, sighing. "He's like a force of nature. There's nothing you could have done."

"Oh, there's something *I* can do," Jaylynn said, looking evil. "A bowl of warm water and his fingers. He'll pee himself in his sleep. Works every time."

☆ ☆ ☆

But at midnight it was *Clark* who had to pee.

It was so stupid.

He woke up with an actual cramp.

Got to go

He looked around the cabin, wondering who was awake. If anyone had actually spoken aloud, or if he imagined it.

Catherine-Lucille was silent and working on the badge over by where the fire used to be. Jaylynn was snoring. A lot of kids were uncomfortably, lightly asleep. There were whisperings and movings, the swish and swirkle of sleeping bags.

In the absolute silence that fell between these noises Clark almost thought he could hear the cabin breathing.

He groaned, realizing that while there was little chance of returning to sleep because of Monsters, there was absolutely *no* chance because of his bladder.

He crawled partway out of his sleeping bag.

Come on, don't be a baby

Go out, do your business, and then you can go back to sleep

Well, it seemed like a good idea. He might as well, now that he was fully awake.

Catherine-Lucille looked up at him from where she was sewing, squint-eyed and bent over in the dark.

He pointed at the door. She nodded.

He made his way tippy-toe over the other campers and paused to look out the window. The rain had stopped but the wind was still strong. Clouds skidded across the sky as if driven by terror or someone with whips. The moon flickered in between them, which should have been a comfort. It wasn't. It seemed to cast no actual light and the woods were still blacker than black. There was no way Clark was going to enter them, even for privacy.

But he really didn't want to pee out in the open, where anyone could see from a window.

I'll protect you

Oh—there was always the dead tree.

He *could* stand in the shadow of its branches, and be hidden or camouflaged.

No one will see you

No one would see him.

As Clark stood there, debating—and the need to pee increased—a sleepy, fluffle-headed D. A. stumbled over to the door and joined him. Clark distractedly noticed the slide-on sandals that his friend's mom made everyone wear when they were in the Lee house. Funny that his friend would pack them.

"Hey, um, whatcha doing?" D. A. asked, rubbing his eyes.

Clark was irritated that his "friend" was talking to him so casually. As if nothing had happened. As if the fire was still burning.

"I have to go . . . outside, but I don't want to go outside," he admitted reluctantly.

Oh, you want to come outside

"Oh," D. A. said. "I want to come outside. Too. And nothing's keeping *me* from going. Not rain or wind or other post office stuff."

He pushed the door open with swagger and stomped through. Clark noticed the new similarity between his friend and Kris. It made him angrier.

But he followed.

The moon shone for a brief second and the branches of the dead tree looked like friendly, welcoming arms.

C'mere

Clark stepped forward.

"Hey," D. A. suddenly said, startling Clark. "Whyncha stay here, out where it's open. I know you hate shadows and scary stuff. I mean, who doesn't. But *I'll* go there, under that creepy tree."

Creepy tree? But it was so pretty with its shadows....

D. A. was still talking. "I'll do my thing facing the cabin, so I can keep an eye out for other campers coming outside. And any peeping toms at the window."

"Really? No, it's okay, I'll just…"

"Don't worry about it!" D. A. said, clapping Clark on the shoulder. "I…I feel bad about the fire and all."

Clark wasn't really listening.

"Okay…"

Feeling a little disappointed somehow, he nevertheless did what his bladder demanded. True to his word, D. A. went over to the tree but kept his attention on the cabin door.

When he was done, Clark turned to go back inside, feeling weird and spacey.

"Hey, Clark?" D. A. called. "I really am sorry about your fire. That was a jerk move."

He sounded like he meant it.

"Thanks," Clark said, unsure what else to say. Unsure what else to believe. He headed back to the cabin.

As he opened the door, he looked back to where D. A. still stood in the shadow of the dead tree.

D. A. waved.

Clark waved back.

The door shut between them.

And Clark went to bed, a strange feeling of terror and dread blossoming like a sick rose in his stomach.

FIFTY-FIVE

The World of Darkness

No doubt they made a strange sight, Foon thought: two Stuffies and a pale Monster traveling together across an ugly, dead land under the black unsun.

At first Freya insisted on walking behind the Phlebbish, keeping her antlers lowered and aimed at his backside. Ready to strike. But soon it was obvious even to the suspicious reindeer that the Monster was in mortal fear of Foon—and now her. It would not try to escape. It was resigned. This was its life now until it was freed.

Such a strange creature.

The land slowly rose until the travelers were on a mesa above the polluted plain where the Dark City squatted. Soon they could see—and hear—strange and Monstrous details emerging from the oily haze. There were roads, buildings, and large objects of no clear purpose. Also sounds: screams, guttural roars, and murmurs and hisses that rose and fell on the wind.

"What is happening?" Foon asked, curious.

"It sounds like the entire City is outside somewhere, crowded together—Shadow Square, maybe. That's the main place for public gathering," the Phlebbish said. "Probably something about the Revenge Plan. Not a filling or scrumptious place for you to be—or for a tiny Monster, like myself. Let's keep moving so you can get your children and I can go home."

"This could provide fascinating intel," Freya said. "I don't know if the Lorekeepers have firsthand accounts of the Dark City and what goes on there."

"That is true," Foon said, nodding. "We need to hurry, but who knows when such a chance will come again?"

"I don't like the sound of this," the Phlebbish muttered.

"Go scout it out quickly, Foon," the reindeer said, ignoring the Monster. "And report back. I will keep an eye—and my antlers—on the prisoner."

"At once," the other Stuffy agreed, and began to lower himself down the escarpment.

He could hear the Phlebbish and Freya arguing all the way until he reached the bottom.

"So you're his Ruler?" the Monster asked.

"What foolishness are you talking about, foul thing?"

"You ordered him and he went. You're his Ruler."

"It was a good idea, and logical, and he agreed. That is all.

We are equals. Neither one of us is a captain or a leader of a cohort. And we are all companions in the war against the Dark."

"What if he disagreed with you?"

"Then we would discuss it until we came to an agreement."

"Oh! You kill each other to see who's right?"

"No! You stupid thing…"

As he scuttled down the stony cliff Foon wondered which of the two would give up in frustration first. Somehow, although each spoke words the other understood, the meaning behind those words was completely alien to the one listening.

A Foon-length from the ground he dropped and landed softly on all fours. Keeping low, he scuttled through the debris and garbage that ringed the City, hiding in shadows when he could. There wasn't so much a *road* leading to the main entrance; it was more of a path through the waste.

Massive, ugly gates rose into the haze-choked sky. Cautiously, silently, Foon approached.

Stuffies don't dream the way their human charges do. They are also not subject to nightmares. But the Dark City was exactly what Foon imagined a nightmare would be like.

For starters, everything was icky and run-down. And looked like it had been for eons.

The giant arch at the entrance of the City was the only thing that was finished and expertly made. It was a big, unwieldy curve on top of two squat columns made out of some heavy black stone. Like a rainbow had given up and gone evil, fattened on its own misdeeds. A primitive statue of a Monster stood on the apex of the arch, screaming at the sky with its claws out.

There were no walls around the City; the gate was only a symbol. Or maybe an afterthought. Foon crept around it anyway, refusing to go through; who knew what evil magic the portal might have silently contained.

The streets were paved unevenly with painfully sharp cobblestones. Between them oozed a foul-smelling dreck.

The buildings were all different shapes (round, square, squat, thin, rugose) and all incomplete. Everything looked like the builder lost interest halfway through. When they were painted it was only in shades of awful black, grungy green, sick grey, vomity red.

The thick smog found its way into every alley and doorway. Piles of refuse grew to Monstrous size on corners.

Trying not to breathe or smell, Foon crept his way toward the sound of the crowd. Eventually he came to a large plaza— probably the Shadow Square that the Phlebbish had mentioned.

It was completely filled with Monsters.

Foon's sock jaw dropped at the sheer number and types of them.

They were all…

moving squirming swaying pawing clawing braying screaming hissing heaving

And had…

tentacles claws teeth and hoofs wings oily spray beaks flaking horns

Foon wished he had a Lorekeeper with him. While he tried to memorize the showiest Monsters he didn't know, there were dozens and dozens more.

Standing before them was the most hideous one of all.

It was huge; bigger than Stuffies, bigger than the Boy's car, maybe as big as the House. Its body was massive and flabby and slick and green. Something that wasn't blood flowed just under its skin, causing its flesh to wobble and pool in unnatural ways.

This giant Monster moved through the crowd on four thick stubs like the legs of a grub. Its noodle-thin, very long neck ended in a tiny face with giant evil yellow eyes. Its mouth was pulled out of shape by two giant fangs that weren't symmetrical; one hung from the middle of its upper set of teeth, the other from the left side of its cheek.

This was the Great Pleticon.

"Brethren and sistren and isthren of the Darkness, our time of revenge is at hand!" it hissed, waving its head back and forth far above the crowd. *"Our mighty, foul deeds now come to fruition! Foon shall rue the day he was ever made!"*

Most of the crowd cheered.

"All this revenge on just one Stuffy?"

This was called out by a Trakel, a toadlike Monster with six tentacles on its face and a Defense of eight. Foon had dispatched one with help from some Fang and Dark Horse. They were *nasty*.

"I mean, who cares?" the Trakel asked, shrugging.

Actually, Foon was sort of wondering the same thing. Some of the oft-repeated tales of his adventures *might* have gone to his head a little, but he knew that in the grand scheme of things, in history and legends, he was only one small Stuffy in an ancient line of truly epic heroes.

Plus he had only been made a year ago.

The Pleticon paused thoughtfully, considering an answer.

Then, almost faster than could be seen, it whipped the head at the end of its long neck down at the Trakel. Its mouth opened wider than should have been possible.

With a sickening *crunch* it bit the other Monster in half.

The Pleticon flung the two halves far away, over the buildings of the City.

Foon watched in stunned silence.

The Great Pleticon paused for a moment and let the ichor drip off its fangs.

Then it answered the now-dead Trakel.

"One of my favorites in the Horde, my biggest, oldest, most darling King Derker, was killed by that Stuffy. Which was bad enough. But it was about to lay eggs! A whole new generation of the most fiendish of fighters! And now that generation is lost forever.

"Too long have we crawled around the edges of the Light, grabbing our prey here and there, fighting quick pitched battles against Stuffies.

"No. More.

"This time we will shake them. We will make a statement—we will have mighty revenge on them for killing one of ours. We will enter the World of Light and make them pay. With this strike we shall start paving the way to a final, glorious battle in which we will defeat the Light forever!"

The Monsters all cheered, snorted, growled, and huffed at

that. Perhaps out of real enthusiasm. Perhaps out of desire not to be bit in half.

"So let us celebrate our first victory! The trap has been sprung, our prey is caught and at our mercy. At this very moment, the human child that Foon once protected now begins to be devoured!"

At this very moment?

Foon backed away, sick and panicky.

His left hind paw accidentally kicked a piece of garbage. It skittered so quietly compared to the noises and howls in the square....

And yet.

A Vorleck (Defense Four) standing at the front of the crowd in a pack of its own kind suddenly stopped cheering. It turned its almost doglike head and snuffed the air, frowning.

Foon shrank back against the wall where he hid.

The Vorleck swung its ugly face back and forth, trying to catch his scent.

Foon quickly slunk back along the wall, down the road, and tiptoed around the gate. As fast as he could he ran to the cliff and clambered up it again. Only at the top did he finally look behind him and breathe a sigh of relief: He didn't appear to have been followed.

"Well, what did you see?" Freya asked by way of greeting.

"More Monsters than I ever hope to see again, gathered in one place," Foon answered. "It would take an army unlike the world has ever seen to defeat them."

"Why would you come to the Dark City to defeat them?"

the Phlebbish asked. He said "them," which was strange, because it wasn't *us*. Weren't they all Monsters? "They are *here* in the World of Darkness. Our world. Not in your Bright Lands."

"But they come to our world and hurt people there," Freya snapped.

"Not all of them. Who would run the shops?"

Freya opened her mouth to snarl something unhelpful—but probably correct—so Foon quickly interrupted.

"We must go *now* to rescue my Boy—the Great Pleticon said he was about to be devoured!"

"Lead on," Freya said, prodding the Phlebbish with her antlers. "Let us quit this evil place."

The Monster trotted quickly ahead, as eager as the two Stuffies to get away from the awful City.

FIFTY-SIX

The Cabin in the Woods

Clark woke up with a jolt.

It was deep in the middle of the night and the wind had entirely stopped.

Everything was silent.

Silent!

The storm was over.

For some reason, that didn't make Clark feel better. Everything seemed empty, devoid, *wrong*.

Why hadn't Catherine-Lucille woken him for his watch?

He sat up on one elbow and looked around, heart racing. Close by, Jaylynn shuddered in her sleep and kicked her foot like an unhappy puppy having nightmares. The one flashlight still on was dim, its feeble light casting long, spooky shadows.

Catherine-Lucille was sitting up on the hearth, fighting sleep and losing. Her head kept nodding down to her chest and she would yank it up again—eyes closed.

He looked over at the counselors. Robin and Kai were asleep spread-eagled, arms flung out to either side of their bags. Their mouths were slackly open. They looked like the campers they were supposed to be protecting: innocent and unguarded. Relaxed.

"Useless," Clark muttered.

But otherwise everything *looked* okay, nothing was weird or wrong. . . .

And then he noticed D. A. was missing.

FIFTY-SEVEN

The World of Darkness

The three tiny creatures slowly made their way through the terrible Desrupt.

It wasn't baking hot or deadly dry or plagued with sandstorms.

It was just kind of grungy.

Its fine sand flowed more like liquid than actual sand (and Foon was pretty sure he caught tiny streams of it flowing *up*hill). Sharp things hid just beneath this top layer; more than once Foon wished he had Freya's hooves. Even the Phlebbish was having trouble winding itself around the jagged garbage that was buried in the landscape.

Also, it *was* pretty warm.

Foon wished he had a bandanna like Clark sometimes tied around his Stuffies' necks. While they were too bright and not really his style, it would have been very useful to wrap over his muzzle. He didn't breathe, exactly, but he could smell things, and the little bits of not-sand were getting into all his seams.

"This place is the worst," Freya grumbled.

"What?" the Phlebbish asked as a small debris tornado whipped up around them.

"THIS PLACE IS THE WORST!" she shouted.

"THIS IS THE WORLD OF DARKNESS," Foon shouted back. "NOT THE WORLD OF HAPPY GOOD FUN TIMES."

The Phlebbish looked insulted.

"The Desrupt *is* difficult. But the whole world is not like this. I have yummy times at home. Often right after I molt I—"

"DON'T WANT TO HEAR IT!" Freya snapped.

There was silence for a while after that.

☆　☆　☆

"We are getting soon," the Phlebbish said eventually.

"You mean close?" Foon asked.

"No," the Phlebbish said.

"Yes," it then decided.

"Kind of?" The Monster looked pained. "It's almost time. But it would be closer if you could believe in the Dark more."

"Foon, do you understand anything it is saying?" Freya snorted in disgust.

"I don't understand all of it," he admitted. "But I almost understand the . . . drift of it."

"Can you two even believe in the Dark?" the Phlebbish asked hesitantly. "It's stronger with belief, or hopelessness...."

"*NO!*" they both shouted.

"Then it will be a bit longer," the Monster said with a sigh and a shrug of four of its appendages.

FIFTY-EIGHT

The Cabin in the Woods

"Where's D. A.?"

Clark gave Kris a (small) kick in the side, and pointed to his friend's empty sleeping bag.

"Mmmh mmph nnfph," Kris mumbled, rolling over.

"*Where's D. A.?*" Clark asked again, giving him a (bigger) kick.

"Go away." The other boy didn't even bother to open his eyes. "Went to pee..."

"*I know!* That was *hours* ago! Did he ever come back?"

"I dunno, geez...."

And with that Kris turned over and went back to sleep.

Clark ground his teeth, torn between frustration and panic.

He picked his way over to Catherine-Lucille. Her eyes were half-closed and glazed. Her sewing was on the floor.

"Hey! Wake up!" Clark said, no longer bothering to keep

his voice low. "D. A.'s missing. I don't know if he ever came back to the cabin after we went outside...."

Catherine-Lucille's eyes finally snapped all the way open.

"Clark! I'm sorry! I fell asleep. What time is it? I don't know how I...I'm the worst!"

At any other time he would have been rapt with attention.

Catherine-Lucille was apologizing for something! *Desperately!*

"Okay, yes, but listen: *D. A. is gone.* We gotta go look for him!"

She nodded and rose without another word. Together they snuck through the cabin, taking wide steps over the sprawled, sleeping bodies. They paused at the door and looked at each other; it was obvious they were both thinking the same thing: *What is out there?*

Finally they went outside, cringing at what they might find.

It wasn't what they expected.

It was a spectacularly beautiful night on a mountaintop.

But...it was like a beautiful night looked at through a filter of something else. Something *evil.* A scene inside a snow globe, ninety degrees off from reality.

Everything was too still; even the leaves didn't rustle. It was the height of summer and not a single insect chirped. The moon shone, cold and brighter than Clark had ever seen it, but the color was somehow wrong. Its rays made everything sickly, the same way old fluorescent lights could flicker in a headache-causing hue. The sky was black and filled with stars—but blacker than it should have been, considering the bright moon. There wasn't a trace of blue in it anywhere.

Clark didn't look too closely at the stars. He was afraid he wouldn't recognize any of the constellations.

And everything was bone-dry, which was strange considering all the rain and how wet it was just a little earlier.

"D. A.!" Clark shouted. He tried to ignore the way his voice died in the air.

"Derleth!" Catherine-Lucille yelled, probably hoping the use of his real name—which he hated—would get a response. "Derleth August!"

"D. A.!" Clark shouted again.

There was no response. No movement. Nothing except the terrible blue light and the night.

"Where else could he be? Where would he *go*?"

Clark felt a rush of panic: What if D. A. had tried to go back down the path to get back to camp? By himself? In the middle of the night? On the washed-out trail?

But Catherine-Lucille grabbed his shoulder, spinning him around to look where she was pointing.

D. A. was . . . right where he had left him.

Under the giant dead tree.

It seemed even taller than before. Its clawed branches looked like a skeletal fist being shaken at the sky.

The boy was sitting on the ground, legs pulled up to his chest, arms wrapped around his knees. His eyes were open and staring (but not blinking. Ever).

There was nothing...*wrong*. Exactly. There were no Monsters, no puke, no blood, no Bad Adults, nothing obviously amiss. But Clark felt a jolt of hot fear rocket from his stomach to his head and back down to his stomach again.

"D. A.!" he cried.

D. A. turned his head toward them—without seeming to see anything.

Then he turned back. To continue looking at nothing.

"Get up, *idiota*," Catherine-Lucille growled, anger taking over her fear. She grabbed his arm. "You had us worried."

"no im fine here" he said.

"D. A.?" Clark begged, tugging his other shoulder. "C'mon. Come on back into the cabin."

He didn't say *Are you sick?* or *Were you sleepwalking?* because none of it was probably true, and speaking lies out loud in this night, even comforting ones, would be pointless.

"im okay here" D. A. repeated, halfheartedly shrugging them off.

"Right." Catherine-Lucille looped her arm under his armpit and motioned Clark to do the same. Together they stood up, pulling their friend along with them.

Only, he didn't budge.

It wasn't like he was glued to the ground or anything they could immediately explain. It was more like he was too heavy, or it was all too hard, or not worth doing, or...

There was just no way he was moving from that spot.

Clark put his hands through his hair in frustration and

looked for something he could do—maybe find a fallen branch to pry D. A. off the ground, or at least poke him with it....

And then he saw it.

Everything suddenly came into focus.

"C. L.," he whispered. *"Look."*

He pulled her back so she could see the situation properly. At first she just scowled, not understanding.

Then her eyes widened in fear and wonder when she saw what he had.

The too-bright moon cast stark black shadows of the tree's curling limbs.

Shadows that made *the shape of a cage.*

D. A. was plunk in the middle of the shadow cage, black bars and stripes of branches keeping him tightly in.

"The *cabin* isn't haunted," Clark whispered.

"The tree is!" Catherine-Lucille finished.

FIFTY-NINE

The World of Darkness

It was more than a "bit longer." Many minutes or hours passed (in that timeless place it was hard to tell) before the Phlebbish cried out: "Look! There it is! The Dark Second!"

The little Monster rose up and up into the air until it was standing just on its hind pair of legs, balancing with the tip of its tail touching the ground, peering into the distance.

It immediately pulled itself back down, looking way less excited.

"Uh-oh," it said, gulping.

Foon and Freya quickly stepped forward even as their Monster shrank back, writhing and whimpering behind them.

Foon wasn't sure what he was expecting. In the World of Light, the Dark Second he had come through looked like a broom-closet door. In the World of Darkness, it was a crack in the rocky wall of the Phlebbish canyon. So he was expecting some sort of stony formation, maybe a "natural"-looking arch or cave, filled with the darkles he had seen in the other doorway.

Instead there was nothing. No rocks, no arch, no doorway. Just empty wasteland ... and something that was *not* a tree.

This not-a-tree was pointed and fleshy like a snowflake made animal in the worst possible way—or a starfish that was being pulled apart by its legs.

Two ... *appendages* stretched up from the sand, rooted in the ground. These pulsed malignantly. Three more appendages reached for the sky but sort of faded out at the tips. It looked like they were attached to something invisible, stuck there. The whole thing hung and swayed, caught between the dirt and air.

In the middle of it, stretched between the "arms," was a hole. Mostly a hole; there was a little bit of flesh surrounding it. Planted in that moist and gummy flesh were rings of sharp triangle teeth that gnashed and snapped together metallically in what Foon now realized was a *mouth*.

Inside that hole was ... blackness. And moonlight. And stars. And shadows.

"What. Is. That," Freya sort of asked.

"A Grindel!" the Phlebbish moaned. "We should leave now while we can!"

"Is it real?" Foon asked, curious. "I can see through parts of it. And its mouth is strange."

"Oh, they're real, all right," the Phlebbish said. It was keeping its face toward the Stuffies while turning its body around the other way, preparing to run. "They look like that because they live between the worlds, ours and yours."

"How do they move?"

"They don't! They eat whatever comes near them, in either world. Monster, human, animal, torlock…"

"What's a torlock?" Freya asked.

"Later," Foon suggested. "All right, it's a big, terrible Monster. But what of the Dark Second you said would take me to my Boy? And the doorway that was supposed to be here? You lied to me—or the Lesser Derker did! There is no door here!"

"I didn't! This is what the Lesser Derker meant when it said 'Careful what you wish for.' Don't you get it? Can't you see its black mouth that leads to both worlds? *The Grindel* is *the door!*"

Freya and Foon looked at each other, understanding and horror slowly dawning on them.

"The only way through is when it *eats* you! It's probably grinding through your Boy's essence as we speak—if it hasn't devoured him already!"

SIXTY

By the Tree

"The Monster is in the tree," Clark said, sick with dismay.

"Or the Monster *is* the tree," Catherine-Lucille said. "I've never heard of such a thing, but just look at it! It totally caught D. A. in its shadow."

There was no doubt about it. The crosshatch of black bars on the ground around D. A. was, unmistakably, a cage.

Clark glanced back at the cabin. It looked even more like an evil skull now, rounded out with a strange smile as its door, in its stones.

And yet it was harmless.

He looked back at the tree and D. A.

"*This* was the whole point of everything," he said slowly. "Everything weird at camp this year. To get us trapped up here without our Stuffies. To catch one of us."

"The weather's involved, too, somehow," Catherine-Lucille

said thoughtfully. "It got worse so we *had* to stay here a second night when it didn't get what it wanted."

"And no senior counselors like Fire Skills Instructor Maya along on this trip . . . and then we lost one of the lesser counselors. . . ."

"No senior counselors anywhere really this year. And no experienced camp director keeping an eye on everything . . . and you said Miz Shirley was acting all weird, like maybe she was taken over by something. . . ."

"And the Monster stuff we were worried about?" Clark asked, voice cracking. "The slime, the Crellans . . . We thought they were invading *camp*."

"I guess the Monsters were all just setting up everything for this, putting everything in place. Scoping us campers out. Maybe even choosing the victim!"

Clark swallowed. *He* should have been the one trapped there, in the shadow cage. The strange voice he'd thought he heard, calling him outside . . . It should have been him. D. A. had— almost knowingly—saved him.

"What do we do?" he whispered.

"I don't know," Catherine-Lucille said.

Which was terrifying. She knew more about Stuffies and Monsters and things that went bump in the dark than anyone else. She knew how to protect against them and how to defeat them.

And now she was as helpless as Clark.

"Should we try to, I don't know, wake him up . . . ?"

"He's not asleep," she pointed out. "Not really. *Hey*. Hey, D. A.! Wake up!" She cupped her hands around her mouth and shouted into his ear.

He didn't respond.

All three friends were silent—for different reasons.

"Go get the counselors," Catherine-Lucille finally suggested. "Go wake them up and bring them out here. Maybe…maybe they're grown up enough that this is all nothing to them. Like once they see the tree and the shadow they'll just see a tree and a shadow and then that's all it will be. And they can drag him back into the cabin."

"You think?"

"I don't have any other ideas. Do you?"

"Nope."

Clark rose and marched across the short space between the tree and the cabin with his fists clenched, arms close by his sides, refusing to admit to the fear that was consuming him. Refusing to see the weird moon above. It was like pretending not to be cold for the first few minutes swimming in the lake. All lies, but it got you through.

Inside the cabin, everything looked normal. There were a few snores, but otherwise campers and things were silent and still.

Clark ran over to the counselors, not caring if he stepped on anyone this time.

"Hey, Robin, Kai, wake up, hey, we have a problem," he whispered, unsure why he was keeping his voice low. The more awake the merrier. Clark would have given all his allowance money right then to be yelled at, to be made fun of, to be ridiculed. If only someone got up, went out, screamed a lot, and led a confused D. A. stumbling inside and everyone went back to sleep.

"Wake *up*," he hissed, shaking Robin's shoulder.

The counselor smacked her lips wetly twice without opening her eyes, and rolled over.

"Kai! Get *up!*" Clark kicked the other counselor on his side, none too softly.

"Mmmblemph," Kai said, sleepily brushing at Clark as if he were a mosquito.

"Come on! *Get up!*" Clark cried, using his outside voice. He knelt down and took the counselor's—slightly greasy—head in his hands and shook it.

"Ehh," Kai said and promptly began snoring again.

Clark stood up and grabbed at his own hair, drowning in shock and panic. How was this all really happening?

What could he do?

What else *was* there to do?

Who else was there?

No one. If he and Catherine-Lucille couldn't get through to D. A., there just wasn't anyone else.

Oh.

Wait.

There *was* one other person.

Ugh. But…

Clark ran over and began to shake him.

"Kris, wake up. Kris, c'mon!"

Kris had a sleeping bag with little army symbols all over it, Clark noticed distractedly.

"Kris! *WAKE. UP.* Get up!"

"Whhh-wha?" Kris said, yawning in the most disgusting, spittle-filled, large-mouthed way possible.

But he sat up on one elbow and blinked his eyes blearily open.

That was success.

"It's D. A. He's in trouble. You gotta help!"

"Izza middle of the night...."

"KRIS!"

"All right, all right..."

It took the other boy what seemed like *hours* to push himself out of his sleeping bag. Clark nearly screamed. At one point Kris wavered and looked like he was about to fall back down. Clark grabbed him by the arm. Digging his fingers in.

"All right, geez, get off, Little Miss Grabby-Pants!" Kris grumbled, swatting at him.

With a few more ridiculous yawns and some very inappropriate butt scratching, the other boy finally lumbered along after Clark and out of the cabin. He didn't bother picking his big feet up over other sleeping campers. One girl yelled "OW!" in her sleep—but that was all.

Then they were outside and the moonlight hit Kris in the face.

"Whoa," he said, for just a moment drawn out of himself by the eerie, evil beauty of the night.

"Over here, c'mon." Clark pulled his arm again.

Kris shrugged him off but followed.

He stopped when he saw Catherine-Lucille crouched down next to D. A., holding his hand carefully through the shadow bars.

"What the frig is going on here?" he asked in confusion.

"D. A.'s sick or something, he won't come in. Can you help us?" Clark begged.

"Why'd you bring *this* loser?" Catherine-Lucille demanded with a snarl.

"The counselors wouldn't wake up...."

"Hey, hey, what are you doing?" Kris asked D. A., kicking at him with his toes. "You're being weird. Your little friends are being weird."

D. A. turned to look up at Kris with a vacant smile and wide, wide eyes.

"hey kris"

The other boy looked shocked at the strangeness of this response, eyes going wide and eyebrows practically jumping off his forehead.

"Dude, cut it out," he said, almost begging. "Just cut it out. Come back inside before you, like, get peed on by a fox or something. Stop being so weird. What's wrong with you?"

"no its okay i like it here"

D. A. returned to looking at nothing, resting his head on his knees.

"Is he really sick?" Kris demanded. "Like the flu or something?"

"We don't know," Catherine-Lucille said carefully. "Help us bring him in?"

"I'm not touching him if he's sick," Kris said, pulling away from D. A. (and showing a whole new side of himself Clark never would have imagined).

"'A fox could pee on him or something,'" Catherine-Lucille mimicked.

Kris grumbled and put an arm under D. A.'s shoulder. The two friends went around the other side and grabbed his other arm together. All three braced themselves and tried to stand.

Nothing.

They strained and pulled and heaved.

Still nothing.

The moment they relaxed, D. A. slipped like a fish back down to the ground.

"Ugh, limp noodle! Cut it *out*, man!" Kris swore, yanking hard on D. A.'s arm in anger.

D. A. let his arm be pulled until it was almost all the way around the wrong way, about to be popped out of its socket.

"Why you being such a weirdo?" Kris yelled. He dropped the arm and shoved D. A., hard.

Clark went to stop him, but Catherine-Lucille held up her hand: *Let him.*

D. A. tipped partially over toward the ground...

...and stayed there.

Eyes still wide open at nothing, unmoving. He just stayed hanging there at an impossible angle.

"This is stupid. I'm out of here," Kris declared, stomping back to the cabin.

"Wait, what? No!" Clark ran after him. "You have to help us!"

"You want to freeze out here with your dumb friend, go ahead, I'm out." He threw the cabin door open, hard. "It's the middle of the frigging night. I'm going back to sleep."

And the door slammed behind him.

Catherine-Lucille and Clark were alone.

SIXTY-ONE

The World of Darkness

Foon was sick with rage.

"This Grindel is in both worlds?" he demanded. "So it is both here now, with us, and on the mountain in the World of Light, consuming my Boy?"

"Sadly, yes," the Phlebbish said, backing away from the murderous-looking Stuffy (but keeping an eye on the bigger Monster).

"Well," Foon said with a deadly smile. "We shall just have to kill the Monster *here*, then!"

Burning with violence, he rushed forward, trident raised. From deep within his Stuffing came a mighty, meaningless war cry.

(Not even *For the Light*, which was his usual. Or *For the Velveteen*.)

"No!" the Phlebbish cried. *"You can't..."*

"Foon, wait! We need a *plan!*" Freya yelled.

But Foon didn't hear them.

The Grindel screamed back.

This wasn't an ordinary scream; it was more like a wall of sound that plowed through the air, rippling and distorting everything in its path. A howl beyond hearing, a shriek that shook the earth.

Foon's horns crumpled under the weight of the noise. But still he leaped, holding his trident high.

Freya galloped behind him, a stalwart and loyal comrade, whatever her misgivings were. Her hooves sparkled in the un-light.

It shouldn't have been too difficult a fight—the Grindel couldn't move. Even if it managed to somehow attack, the Stuffies could always retreat to just out of its reach.

Foon brought Focus forward as he came down from his leap, aiming it at the center of the mouth hole. Freya followed suit with her antlers.

The shiny tip of his trident had just touched the blackness of the maw when the thing howled again—but silently this time.

Foon felt shock waves of *nothing* bowl him backward into the dirt.

Freya was tossed aside like a wadded-up piece of paper.

Both Stuffies went tumbling end over end, falling hard onto the stinking dust of the Desrupt.

The Grindel drew back, stretching its five appendages as if it were taking a deep breath. Then let loose another howl.

Foon bent over and covered his horns, trying not to—listen to? Feel? Accept?—the alien scream.

Oh, how stupid and rash he had been.

The Grindel was extremely powerful.

The Phlebbish had *said* so. It had tried to tell them.

It wasn't a normal Higher Monster. It felt *ancient*. It didn't speak and yet somehow seemed even more evil than the King Derker. The Grindel was primal Darkness, a corrupt thing that had been around since before forever had begun.

What was such a Monster? A Defense Twenty? *Thirty?*

"GETupgetUP!"

Someone was yelling at Foon.

He shook his woozy head. It was strange; his Stuffing felt fine. There were no wounds or cuts in his cloth. He just felt ... out of focus....

Wait, was that the *Phlebbish* yelling at him? That was strange.

"Get up, Stuffy!"

Foon rubbed his eyes; he saw the six-footed Monster anxiously pattering back and forth a little ways off. Why was it so far away? It was like there was an invisible wall the Phlebbish couldn't—or wouldn't—go beyond.

But it was still yelling at him.

"Get up now! Now! *Now* it attacks!"

If that *wasn't its attack*, Foon thought blearily, *what is?*

The Grindel howled again.

Foon braced himself ... but nothing hit. No wall of noise. No shock waves.

The scream wasn't loud and destructive. It was ...

Subdued. Timid.

Questioning.

Why

it seemed to say.

Just ask

I

don't kill

Foon forced himself to stand up. It took all his effort, and he swayed a little. Freya was also slowly rising onto all fours, shaking her antlers to get the sand off—or to wake herself up.

All your answers are within me

I contain worlds

Travel through me

Just

  Ask

Just ask? What did it mean?

The Phlebbish was shouting again.

It was like everything was reversed. The little Monster's wet mouth opened and closed and nothing came out . . . but Foon could hear the Grindel speaking as plainly as the Great Bear. All else was silent.

Your Boy can be found through me

Just look and see—I speak the truth

It opened its maw widely and stretched.

Foon stepped forward numbly, toward the hole ringed with teeth.

SIXTY-TWO

By the Tree

A thin silvery thread of spittle slowly dribbled from D. A.'s lower lip like webbing from a sick spider.

Otherwise he hadn't moved at all in over ten minutes.

"At daybreak whatever is happening to him has to stop, right?" Catherine-Lucille said in a strangled voice. Her fear, her not knowing what to do, scared Clark more than almost anything else. "Monsters and ghosts and whatever—they can't stand the sun. The counselors will *have* to wake up and someone will have to do something if he doesn't snap out of it. Right?"

"I want to do something. *Now,*" Clark said, frustrated. "He needs us to."

"Keep thinking, Corporal. We'll come up with something— we *have* to. In the meantime I'm going to go get D. A.'s sleeping bag to keep him warm."

Catherine-Lucille saluted crisply and then marched into the cabin.

Clark settled down on the strangely cold and rigid ground. His breath made little puffs of smoke like a dragon—which would have been cute if only it wasn't the middle of August. Much, much tinier puffs were coming out of D. A.'s mouth, and much less often. But at least he was breathing.

"Don't worry, buddy," Clark whispered. "We're here with you."

But that's when it happened.

D. A. suddenly looked—different.

Not a lot. It was very subtle. Easy to dismiss as shadows and the overactive imagination of an overtired Clark.

His friend's skin had . . . *silvered* somehow.

It might have been a trick of the moonlight. Or he had just grown pale with cold or sickness.

Maybe.

But—and Clark was pretty sure he wasn't imagining this—his friend seemed to *shrink in* a little. Around the cheekbones and jaw and eyes. There the skin wasn't silver; it was bruisy black. Like a bad piece of fruit.

Like he was being drained from the inside out.

Clark looked to the door of the cabin, willing Catherine-Lucille to hurry.

He stifled a sob.

It was still many hours until morning.

SIXTY-THREE

The World of Darkness

Foon stood on his tiptoes and leaned forward, looking deep into the Grindel's mouth.

His head was almost over the first row of pointy teeth.

He saw . . .

A Boy! It was! Just like the Phlebbish said! And it was—

Not his Boy.

His Boy's . . . *friend.*

Foon looked at Freya in confusion. She looked back, equally confused.

This was the Boy with the baseball cap, whose legions of action figures warmly welcomed the Stuffies at sleepovers. The Boy whose pink unicorn, Uni, had a magical suit of armor and was very strong both in Attack *and* Defense.

But why was it him, and not Foon's Boy?

This whole thing was the Monsters' plan for revenge on *Foon.* The Grindel was supposed to torment and destroy *his* Boy in return for killing the King Derker. What happened? Did a Monster mix up the two Boys?

Freya flicked her ears and gave him a look: *What does it matter?*

Nothing, of course. This was still a Boy in trouble.

Foon shook his head to clear it. Actually, this glimpse of the other Boy was a good thing. It had surprised him, shaken him up. Stopped him.

If it had actually been his Boy, Foon might very well have stepped into the Grindel's maw to get to him.

This Monster was extremely clever. It couldn't move from where it was "planted"; it didn't leap or fly or throw barbs or spit or attack outright at all. So it *lured* its opponents in with hypnotic lies. It numbed their brains with its scream and then spoke without speaking. And it sounded so real and comforting. . . .

And the Phlebbish!

It had tried to help! It had yelled at Foon. . . .

He didn't have a chance to finish thinking about this.

Freya, also apparently thinking clearly again, was done with inaction. The reindeer slammed her antlers into the Grindel with the full force of her stocky body. She aimed just below its mouth, into the stinking flesh from which its "legs" sprang.

The Monster howled.

No!

Come and see. . . .

Don't hurt....

Foon hurled his trident at it, trying to ignore the words that slipped evilly into his Stuffing.

His weapon struck the Grindel above its maw, sinking into where a nose would have been on something else. A wound symmetrical to the one Freya made.

The Monster shrieked again—but not the mesmerizing sound to lure the Stuffies in. This was a cry of pain, louder than anything yet: high-pitched and deadly. Foon grabbed his horns, folding them down to block the noise.

Freya was having trouble disentangling her antlers from the sticky sinew of the Monster. She swung her head back and forth in a panic, trying to break free. Slimy beige strings stretched and pulled until they finally snapped back into the body of the beast.

None of which stopped her from slamming her head into it again.

"Hold a moment!" Foon cried.

Freya froze, antlers buried in the flesh of the thing.

Foon ran and leaped, flipping up onto the reindeer's back. From there he jumped up again to grab his trident, which was still stuck in the Monster's flesh.

It didn't come out. It sort of *twanged* in place while the tines stayed buried deep.

Foon thought quickly.

He grabbed Focus's now-springy handle and used it to launch himself into the air, head over horns. He landed on top of the Monster, between two of its "arms" that disappeared off into the sky.

The Grindel writhed and twisted, trying to avoid the attacks that now came from both above and below.

Foon leaped up, flipped, and dove down, paws-first, digging his claws and horns into the Monster. Its flesh split open and foul ichor seeped out of the wounds.

A moment later Freya finally pulled her head free—ripping the thing's leg entirely off.

The Grindel shrieked and the noise seemed to shatter the world. Grains of dust and debris on the desert floor vibrated and danced above the surface in strange patterns.

Foon stumbled and fell off the Monster. He tumbled down, down to the ground...

...and landed on sharp spikes of broken glass.

SIXTY-FOUR

By the Tree

Catherine-Lucille came out of the cabin carrying supplies. She had *two* sleeping bags, her flashlight, and a giant bag of peanut M&M'S. None of which made Clark feel better.

"I tried waking the counselors again—*nothing*," she said, unceremoniously dropping the pile of loot on the ground. "I wish we could record this all somehow. As a warning—"

"There's something happening to D. A.!" Clark interrupted.

"Holy crow," Catherine-Lucille swore when she saw him. "He looks like...like...he's being drained by a vampire or something!"

D. A.'s jaw was very slowly falling open, as if its small weight was too much to hold. His eyes were like dull marbles in sunken black hollows.

Above them, the ugly, dead tree twisted and groaned in the

wind. Except that there wasn't any wind. Out of the corner of his eye Clark thought he saw the black hole in the trunk stretch.

He looked away and then back—nothing was moving. The hole was the same shape and size as before, the tree was still.

D. A. let out a groan.

It wasn't very loud, like something in a car that wasn't working quite right, or when you sit on a deflating basketball. But it was low and creepy, and beads of ice-cold sweat popped out on his forehead.

"Go *away!*" Catherine-Lucille shrieked, losing her usual cool. She leaped up and began punching the tree, smashing her knuckles bloody. Of course it did nothing.

Clark's mind raced desperately, looking for ideas. What could they do? Against Monsters they couldn't even really see? This thing was either inside the tree—or actually a dead tree. Hard and invincible.

A *dead tree.*

Wait…

Clark began to have an idea of *exactly* what they could do.

SIXTY-FIVE

The World of Darkness

The Grindel was still howling.

Freya fell back on her rump, knocked down by the noise, her eyes wide with pain. She writhed and scraped the ground with her hooves, unable to cover her large and sensitive ears.

Foon woozily lifted his head up. By luck—or the Velveteen—his body hadn't been impaled by the glass. His side was sliced open; some stitches in his feet were cut through. One glittering shard pierced his right horn and stuck there.

With the ground still spinning and Stuffing spilling from the wound on his torso, Foon still managed to stagger to his feet.

Despite his blurred vision he noticed something strange. When he was in *front* of the Monster he had been able to see through its mouth to the World of Light, where the captive Boy was. But the *back* of the Monster was just that—back. Thin, dog-poop-colored flesh stretched tautly over whatever strange muscles held up the remaining leg and arms.

The Grindel twisted and howled and squirmed. The nubby root where its leg had been flailed uselessly, spraying a mist of acid over the landscape.

Eventually the screaming quieted.

The howling became a humming.

All right

Come attack me face-to-face

Come and face me like a real hero

If I am to die, let it be by a hero's weapons

A real hero

Not a coward who would strike me from behind

Foon

Well, that *was* true, wasn't it? Only a coward attacked from behind. It was the ploy of bullies and assassins. How would that sound in songs? That he, Foon, *snuck up* behind a Monster to slay it?

"I am no coward!" Freya cried, slamming her head into the Grindel's mouth. Ignoring its remaining leg, which should have been her target. She was in an almost berserker-like frenzy and not thinking.

Her antlers clanged against its teeth and the shock pitched her backward onto the ground.

Foon watched it all in a daze. Hadn't the Monster said *his* name? Not hers? Who was it calling a coward?

Feeling disoriented and sick, he limped around to the front of the Monster. Where its deadly maw was.

Because he would face it like a Hero.

But the Grindel wasn't paying attention to him. It pulled itself back on its remaining leg and arms, stretching like a rubber band.

The Monster opened its mouth wider and wider...and bore down on the reindeer.

SIXTY-SIX

The Cabin in the Woods

Clark ran into the cabin and mostly tried to step over the sleeping campers—but didn't waste a lot of time trying *too* hard.

(A few moaned as he passed or stepped on them, but that was all.)

He made his way to the hearth. The fire was out, really out. Clark grabbed one of the blackened "pokey sticks" and scattered the coals back and forth with it, looking for any sign of life.

Aha!

One of the logs had burned unevenly. Its smaller end was black...but dusted with orange at the tip. Still smoldering a little!

Clark picked up the log by its cooler end and, holding it like a torch, carefully made his way back out of the cabin. Painfully slowly this time: He didn't want what little fire there was left on the log to go out.

When he finally made it to the door, Clark opened it with his foot, shielding the log from the wind.

Catherine-Lucille was right where he had left her, standing angrily above the moaning D. A. Her eyes widened in surprise when she saw what he carried.

"Clark, what are you going to do?"

It was one of the few times she had ever used his name.

He didn't answer, running past her—

And thrust the burning tip of the log straight into the dead tree.

SIXTY-SEVEN

The World of Darkness

Many things happened at once.

The Grindel's teeth glittered in the unsun as it dove at Freya, mouth open wide to gobble her up.

The Phlebbish screamed: "Big-horned thing, *move!*"

(Was it actually waddling up to Freya? As if to push her out of the way?)

Suddenly the Grindel pulled back, away from the reindeer. It gibbered and wailed in pain.

Foon didn't understand. He hadn't seen anything happen to the Monster, to make it retreat. It wasn't something Freya did; she was still dazed and not really moving.

But wait—what was that?

Was Foon seeing things?

No! There was a strange black burned spot on the Monster's remaining leg! It was already beginning to weep bright yellow pus.

But *how?*

Neither Stuffy had wounded it (and neither had the Phlebbish)....

While Foon was wondering this the Grindel quickly changed its tactics.

Come

it suggested.

Come...

Peace

Don't fight

Join your Boy

Be together

Forever

Isn't that what you want?

Yes, more than anything!

Unable to control his legs—which seemed to be controlled by his heart—Foon was once again moving closer to the Monster's terrible maw.

He struggled and tried to stop himself, but it did no good. His feet were obeying the Grindel. He was inches away from the terrible Monster.

But his arms were still free.

Foon suddenly remembered the shiny-sharp pincers he had taken from the dead Yechzeken. He ripped them from where they were hanging on his side, ignoring the pain as his thread ripped.

Then, with his last bit of willpower, he forced himself to slice them deep into the Grindel's flesh.

The Monster prepared to scream. It opened its mouth wide, wider, wider still, until its body was so stretched and drawn out that the thin light of the unsun could be seen through it.

Grimacing with the effort, Foon placed both his paws around the curving blades. Bits of Stuffing leaked out around his claws. He pulled down. Hard.

The pincers tore down through the Monster's body like a dull knife through a banana peel. Fetid ichor dripped out in hissing rivulets.

Freya forced herself up onto her four legs, leaning against the Phlebbish for balance. With the last of her own strength, she struck *up* with her antlers against the Grindel's remaining leg.

It was ripped up out of the soil, thin and spindly and wriggling like a roundworm.

Everything froze: For a moment it looked like the Monster would snap up on its arms, still hooked somehow onto the sky. Like a window shade, up and away from the Stuffies.

Foon cried out in despair. It would escape!

He desperately seized hold of the Monster with one claw and grabbed the pincers with the other. Then he swung hard, flipping up and backward onto the top of the creature.

With a quick *whick-whick* he sliced through one of the stretched-out arms.

The Monster seethed and shrieked and howled. It bounced and cavorted like a horrible circus act: something hanging from a trapeze by two rubbery ropes. Its vicious mouth gnashed and snapped with ugly metallic sounds.

Foon was thrown to the ground—and so was his trident, now finally freed from the foul flesh of the thing.

Freya lunged, catching the body of the Monster on the deadly prongs of her antlers. She whipped her head around, throwing herself onto her front knees.

With a terrible wet sound, the Monster's body snapped off its last two arms and came crashing to the ground.

Foon grabbed his trident.

"FOR THE VELEVTEEN!" he cried with a ragged breath, and ran at the soft, toothy mass now squirming on the Desrupt floor.

He plunged Focus hard into the Monster, twisting it in deeply.

The thing writhed and ebbed, its now limp "body" quivering on the sand. Steaming fluid pooled around its entrails.

Instead of a howl, all that came was a thin whistly noise.

Finally, eventually, the thing was still.

Freya, Foon, and the Phlebbish all looked at one another uncertainly.

It *seemed* to be dead.

The two Stuffies crept forward to look into the deadly—but now silent and still—mouth that led to other worlds.

SIXTY-EIGHT

By the Tree

Clark jabbed the burning log over and over again into the side of the tree, leaving char marks on the bark. He only stopped when Catherine-Lucille put a hand on his shoulder.

"Corporal, look!"

D. A. had slumped to the ground—and was blinking.

"What the," he began.

"Where the," he continued.

"Whoa," Catherine-Lucille said with awe. "It totally worked! D. A.! You all right?"

Clark almost collapsed in relief.

Above them, clouds were skidding across a moon that now descended naturally into the west. The dead tree . . . looked just like a dead tree. Silver and ancient and unmoving. The giant black hole in its trunk had a nest in it. For a racoon, or squirrel, or something equally cute and furry.

Clark grinned. "You okay, buddy?"

"Yeah. No. What?"

D. A. scratched the back of his head and looked around, eyes still a little unfocused. "I feel terrible. Like, weak and gross, like I just threw up a lot. And cold. And that tree...I had the worst nightmare...."

He looked up at it wonderingly. But unlike Clark, he didn't smile. He shuddered. It turned into uncontrollable shivering.

"Can we go inside?" he begged.

"Absolutely," Catherine-Lucille said cheerfully, grabbing one shoulder. Clark took the other, and together they helped him back to the (*un*haunted, Monster-free) cabin.

SIXTY-NINE

The World of Darkness

Foon saw his Boy and his heart leaped.

He was fine, and *helping* the other Boy, no less! The three children were as close and tight as the very best comrades.

And...what was that in his hand? A brand? A...burned-out torch?

Foon thought about the black wound that had appeared on the Grindel's leg.

His Boy had wounded the Grindel somehow! He was the reason the Grindel had stopped attacking Freya!

His Boy had aided Foon in the battle! Without even knowing it...

Overcome with joy, Foon started to step into the mouth of the dead Monster, now a harmless portal to the World of Light.

Then he stopped.

"Why do you delay?" Freya asked. "Let us go and be with our Boy and Girl!"

"No," Foon said, feeling his little Stuffy heart clench. "We are...not supposed to be there. We would step through, and then fall into our Stuffy sleep. We would appear out of thin air with no reason for our appearance. It would not be the reunion that I long for with all my Stuffing.

"It would...not be right."

Freya dipped her antlers in disappointment. "Yes, you are wise. They are not meant to know."

"So that's your Boy?" the Phlebbish said curiously. "I like his hat."

"That is not my Boy, that is my Boy's friend," Foon explained wearily. "My Boy is the one there—with no hat."

"And that is my Girl," Freya said proudly.

"But—wait," the Phlebbish said, its lower two-thirds squirming and working around itself in confusion, four hind legs pattering in the dust. "Did the Grindel grab the wrong kid?"

"It would appear to be that way." But Foon was too exhausted to care anymore. Everyone was safe—that was what mattered.

"There must have been some mix-up," Freya said thought-fully. "Perhaps our enemy is even dumber than we thought."

"But...but...but..." the Phlebbish said. "If it wasn't your Boy... When the Grindel tried to lure you into its mouth, you *saw* it wasn't him. That it wasn't your Boy. It was someone else's. So why did you fight?"

"It is still a Boy," Foon said. "And I will fight for any Boy or Girl who needs my protection."

"And he is my Girl's friend. He is like family," Freya said. "Hurting him is like hurting my Girl—or me."

The Phlebbish regarded the Stuffies silently for a moment.

"Huh," it finally said. "So…this is like that thing when you asked if I would help should someone attack my neighbor?"

"It's called love," Foon said with a tired smile.

"Or loyalty, or kinship, or kindness, or sisterhood," Freya added quickly.

Foon noted this with amusement. Freya was brave and true-hearted and fierce—and embarrassed easily at any mention of *love*.

He would tease her mercilessly about it at the next Circle of Fire.

"And now you must lead us back to the…Cottonysoft Dark Second so we may return," the reindeer added, trying to change the subject. "The sooner we leave this horrid world the better."

"If the Pleticon and the others are at all smart, they would be keeping an eye on this situation," Foon agreed. "And will soon send an army after us. We should flee this place at once."

"And then I am free!" the Phlebbish said in delight, making figure eights with its body.

☆　☆　☆

The journey back was much quicker.

Possibly it was because Foon and Freya had an idea of where

they were going this time and could march alongside—or in front of—the Phlebbish.

Or possibly it was because the tale of a terrible pair of Stuffies defeating a Monster of unknowable strength on its home turf had traveled fast in the World of Darkness—and everyone kept out of their way.

If the Pleticon sent anyone after them, those Monsters never appeared.

Foon was quiet the entire way back, drained and spent—and turning something over in his mind. When they reached the Cottonysoft Dark Second door (the darkles were still there), he finally asked his question aloud.

"Phlebbish, why did you help us? Why did you try to wake us from the Monster's magic grip? Why did you push Freya out of its way? You could have just let us be taken—and then escaped."

"Oh," the Monster said, as if also surprised by the thought. "I guess I wanted to see your quest turn out all right. Now that I'm part of it. But I also didn't—I didn't want to see you hurt!" Its fronds spread in wonder. "It would leave me not-full."

"Not full? Hungry?" Freya asked in disgust.

"Yes. Finishing this with you makes me feel full! This is an ending that's super tasty."

It made a funny face, mouth skin pulling back over where it should have had teeth. Maybe it was a kind of smile. Maybe it was like smacking its lips. It rubbed its belly with four of its slimy, fat fingers.

The reindeer shook her head, obviously revolted.

Foon took one last look at the terrifying world they were leaving: the Dark Clock, the dark sky, the unsun, the tenebrous clouds, the garbage and filth. It was truly the opposite of the World of Light. And so strange that any creature—even a Monster—would wish to stay there, and call it home.

"Good-bye, Phlebbish," he said formally. He did not bow or put his paw out—this was still a Monster, regardless of how harmless it was.

"Good-bye, Stuffies," the Phlebbish said back. "This is the most interesting thing that has ever happened to me. I hope nothing like it ever happens to me *again*."

Freya snorted a good-bye, which was perhaps a little rude, but then again, she hadn't spent as much time with the Monster as Foon had.

As the two Stuffies stepped through the doorway—and the darkles floated around them—something else occurred to Foon.

"*Sated*...full...tasty..." he said slowly. "Freya! I think I understand now! Monsters do not have a word for 'good.' Or 'happy.' Or 'love'!"

"Well, of course not. They are evil creatures of the Darkness," Freya said with a shrug.

"Yes, but—when the Phlebbish said something made him full or was tasty, it's as close to 'happy' or 'good' as it could get. Almost the same thing, I suppose."

"So?"

"I just...It is sad," Foon said helplessly. "The thing does

not even have the idea of good. Only of being "hungry" or "not hungry." I wonder if, given enough time, it could learn. The truth of the world. The truth of the Light."

"Monsters learn the truth very quickly," Freya said, "when they are impaled on my antlers."

Foon sighed and put the thought away for another time.

SEVENTY

THE GREAT PLETICON SPEAKS

No Stuffy came into our Dark World.

Certainly not *two* of them.

They have not, I repeat, *not*, defeated a Lesser Derker, a Yechzeken, and definitely not a Grindel.

They did not upset the Great Revenge Plan.

If they did, which they didn't, I certainly wouldn't bother sending more troops after their pitiful little selves. Or maybe I would, but my assassins would totally chase the Stuffies down and kill them. So it doesn't matter, does it?

The Great Revenge Plan is still on.

In fact... it's... even revenge-ier than before! We will not have revenge on just one stupid Stuffy. We shall finally wage war on *all* the Stuffies! The entire World of Light shall be ours! Our time has come! Yes! We shall rule it all!

What was that?

You want to know *why* we didn't "wage the final war" before? Why we bothered at all with this one stupid Stuffy?

[*CHOMP RIP CHOMP CHOMP CHOMP CHOMP*]

[*Burp*]

SEVENTY-ONE
From Cabin to Camp

The next morning campers woke up cranky but excited to leave. The sky was blue, a warm wind whispered across the mountaintop . . . and everyone seemed to have forgotten about Evan returning and the whole rescue plan.

Robin and Kai stomped around yelling for people to pack up and not forget anything and certainly not leave behind any garbage. There was oatmeal again and it was nasty.

"Somebody should get a ranger to cut down that snag there, that dead tree," Robin said as they lined up outside. "It could fall at any time."

Clark couldn't agree more.

He, Catherine-Lucille, and D. A. were mostly quiet, exhausted, and a tiny bit awkward after the strange night. Jaylynn and D. A. talked about baseball a little.

Then Kris came galumphing up, slapping D. A. on the back. "Ready to go, amigo?" he said, all grins and goodwill.

Catherine-Lucille winced at his pronunciation of the Spanish word.

"Yeah, think I'm going to hang with Clark and C. L. And Jaylynn," D. A. said.

Not *today*, implying it was their turn. Or that it was just for now. Also not apologizing. There was no anger, only a statement of facts. Clark wished he could be honest and even-tempered like that.

"*These* guys?" Kris demanded. "*We* have so much more fun together."

"We have fun, totally. But they stuck by me while I was— sick. Adios, *amigo*."

Kris looked at him for a long moment. Then his face slowly blackened into some dark emotion. Realization, regret, anger—it was impossible to tell.

"Whatever, loser," he grumbled, and stomped off.

"While you were *sick*?" Catherine-Lucille demanded.

"I mean, yeah. So hot and sweaty and then freezing and I was sleepwalking.... It was really weird. And scary."

"But..."

Clark put a hand on C. L.'s shoulder and shook his head. *Give it up.* Their friend was safe, they were heading home... *that* was what was important.

Catherine-Lucille bit her lip in frustration and annoyance. Then she let it all out in a ragged sigh, shaking her head.

The four friends walked down the path behind everyone else, laughing and joking when energy allowed.

On their first water break, the tiniest, cutest little girl on the trip—she couldn't have been more than eight—came up to D. A. and tugged on his shirt to get his attention. She held out her hands. Lying there cradled as carefully as an egg was his clone trooper and Hondo.

"I'm sorry," she said, on the verge of tears. "I found them when I went to go to the bathroom they were just lying on the cabin floor and I took them and I *knew* they were someone's but no one said anything and I took them and I'm sorry and they're beautiful and I'm sorry."

D. A. took the little action figures back with wonder.

"It's okay, little buddy," he said, scruffling the girl's hair. "I know how awesome these guys are. Don't do it again, though, huh?"

The little girl sniffed and skipped off, her relief so great that she seemed weightless, about to fly.

Clark thought about how he assumed none of the girls near them would have taken the action figures. Well, he would certainly not make any assumptions like *that* again!

(And he wouldn't tell his sister about the mistake, either.)

"The action figures weren't hurt...'cause the *cabin* wasn't haunted," Catherine-Lucille said meaningfully.

"The *tree* was," Clark finished, nodding.

"You're going to need to fill me in," Jaylynn said, crossing her arms.

"Oh, we will, Private. We will," Catherine-Lucille said with a (small) smile.

☆　☆　☆

When they finally got back down and canoed to camp, the first thing the friends did was look for their missing Stuffies and doll. They found them almost immediately, in the CONFISCATED box in the office at the Hobbit House.

"These were scattered all over the camp," Miz Shirley said in surprise when Clark, Catherine-Lucille, Jaylynn—and quite a few others—demanded them back. "We thought they had been abandoned. And anyway, it's against camp policy to return contraband until the end of the session. When we do, it's directly to the parents."

Catherine-Lucille's face went red. Jaylynn opened her mouth and closed it, gaping like a fish while the rage built up.

Clark was annoyed but a little curious. This wasn't the woman he had talked to before *at all.* This woman's eyes were bright, she spoke sympathetically, and she smiled. More Monster mischief that was now all fixed, he decided. He wondered just how far this plan to get rid of the Stuffies and trap the kids—and eat one—went.

Well, that was a good topic for the next secret club-without-a-name meeting. Right now they had other problems.

Clark took a deep breath, summoning all of the sneaky adult power of his big sister.

"But the unexpected extra night in the extremely *allergen-*filled cabin really broke down the self-empowerment skills I had been working on."

"Especially with the asthma," Jaylynn quickly put in, wheezing.

"I need...my...*physical token of love* to restrengthen the ideation of resilience and emotional fortitude that my parents were so *proud* I had fostered here. At Camp I Can. It would be a shame to see all that go to waste."

Miz Shirley frowned.

It was obvious she knew something underhanded was going on.

But she was almost there; she just needed one more little push....

"Also," C. L. added, "having *so* many extra kids without enough counselors—or any senior counselors at all—on a mountaintop during a storm that you guys should have known about? Not sure parents would like that, either..."

Miz Shirley went white. Ghost white.

"Here," she said, shoving the box at them. "Don't tell the others."

Clark grabbed Foon and hugged him tight, not caring who saw him or what other people were doing. The sight of his crumpled horns and mismatched, sock-y skin, filled him with warmth until he almost burst.

"I don't know how that happened," he whispered. "I'm so sorry, Foon. Believe me when I say it wasn't me who left you behind."

He brushed the dust off of his Stuffy's body—and saw something strange. A silver crescent, sharp and metal, in his paw as if on purpose.

Did someone else play with him after he was left behind?

Was this a counselor's joke?

Clark wondered...

D. A. was waiting for them outside. Everything and everyone at camp seemed back to normal. Catherine-Lucille was looking at Jaylynn's Barbie, admiring the subtle military bent of her outfit. Jaylynn was hugging Freya.

Fire Skills Instructor Maya was screaming—really letting loose, not her usual yells—at Kai and Robin and Evan (the last who had mysteriously reappeared, alive and well and utterly unhelpful). James stood by, arms crossed and nodding seriously. He gave his friends a wink and a thumbs-up.

"*ABSOLUTELY DISGRACEFUL.* If I had been along, *none* of this would have happened. All those campers in your charge—and your decision-making process was *abysmal.* No disaster planning, or following standard procedure of what to do in the event of communication failure. No following protocol at all. Have you idiots ever even gone camping before?! Oh, hey, Clark."

Her rage instantly disappeared. She turned and gave him a cheery wave and a smile full of teeth.

The shamed counselors sagged in relief.

"Don't relax," James suggested. "You're in deep doo-doo."

They immediately looked frightened again.

"Great job with the fire, I'm told," Maya said, slapping Clark on the shoulder. "Technically unauthorized because there were no Fire Skills–approved senior counselors there, but from everything I've heard, you did it all correctly and safely. Definitely skipping you ahead to Advanced Primitive Cooking Skills. Youngest camper ever to do that! Wish I had something to give you. You kept good spirits up and the bad spirits away—just like a real Keeper of the Flame."

Her eyes burned a little too brightly as she said that last bit, but Clark thanked her anyway.

"I made him a patch," Catherine-Lucille said. "Like a scout patch but cooler."

Clark picked up his pack to show her.

"WOW. I like you," Maya said immediately to Catherine-Lucille. "Take Fire Skills this week with me."

"Okay," C. L. said with a rare, surprised smile.

"*AND THE THREE OF YOU CAN KISS YOUR END-OF-SUMMER BONUSES GOOD-BYE IF I HAVE ANYTHING TO DO WITH IT!*"

With no hesitation or transition, Maya had turned on the counselors again and resumed screaming.

The four friends tiptoed quietly away.

"I'm so glad you got Foon back," D. A. said. "And Freya."

"Yeah. I wonder who took them," Clark said.

"Or *what*," Catherine-Lucille added.

"Yeah, dude, can we talk about that later, too?" Jaylynn asked. "I've always had suspicions, but..."

"Absolutely," Catherine-Lucille said. "At the secret club-house. The new one. Also we need to discuss getting back the big swing that James said the camp used to have...and maybe talk about inducting some new members...?"

"Hey," D. A. said to Clark, grabbing his arm and pulling him aside. His light brown eyes were wide with worry. "I was, um, kind of rude last night. This weekend. A total butt. I'm sorry. I really am."

He wrung his hands, one of the least D. A. gestures Clark had ever seen him do.

"We cool?" he asked hopefully.

"Yeah, sure," Clark said. The little hurts and betrayals from two days ago seemed like nothing after last night. He couldn't forget them. But they were forgiven.

"Dude. Thanks, man." D. A. grabbed him in a bear hug, squeezing tightly for a moment before letting go.

They didn't talk about Stuffies or Monsters. Clark wasn't sure D. A. would ever talk about them—really—again. But they would talk about other things. And he had a strange feeling that even with that gone, they would be closer friends than they were before. Something had changed in D. A.

He had finally realized who his true friends were, and what true friendship was—even if he didn't entirely understand it.

SEVENTY-TWO

The Circle of Fire

"...and what were the buildings in the Dark City made of, do you think?"

An exhausted Foon tried to think of how to reply. Apparently "hideous rock" wasn't good enough for the Annals of Stuffy History.

Great Bear put his big, gentle paw on Lorekeeper Brush-Tailed Phascogale's tiny shoulder.

"Our heroes have answered enough of your questions for now. There will be time for more later. Let them rest and celebrate their victorious quest."

"But this is the first time in our present era that anyone has gone into—and returned from—the Dark!" the Lorekeeper cried. *"WE HAVE A FIRSTHAND ACCOUNT!"*

"Do I look like an architect?" Freya asked, tossing her head.

"The buildings were dark and ugly. Next time come with us, that you may see it for yourself."

The Lorekeeper's eyes grew wide in fear. The bear carefully eased him away from the two heroes.

Freya and Foon were offered the seats of honor at the fire next to the Great Bear but declined. Freya said she wanted to sit comfortably where there was enough room for her to fold all four of her legs under her. Foon said he wanted to be closer to the clean, hot fire for its warmth and purity.

Neither was strictly the truth.

Freya preferred the glory that came with performing a duty well and honorably, not the prizes and adulation after.

But Foon seemed more *uneasy* than humble that night.

Their closest friends were gathered around them: the saber-toothed tiger, Baby Monster, the miniature fantasy adventurers (and the equally miniature space adventurers), Doris, Ren Faire Beast, DangerMaus (and DangerMaus Number Two, and Number Three, and...).

But there was one who was missing. Foon made his excuses and left the circle, seeking the tightly knit clique of dolls at the other end of the fire.

Curious, Freya followed.

The dolls, also curious, stopped their talking immediately and looked up at him. One doll in particular.

"Barbie," Foon said, mustering a different sort of courage than he needed in the Desrupt. "I owe you an apology."

"Me? What for?" she asked in surprise. The other dolls looked surprised, too, but it was more because a Stuffy had come over and was speaking to them. "*All* of our children were in some sort of danger—my Girl, too, who was separated from me. We owe you thanks, not forgiveness."

"You should have been there with me," Foon said. "You *all* should have been. Freya knew this and she found her way to me. But I should have asked you. I was rash, and perhaps my Stuffed head was a little too full of the praise from our comrades. I did many foolish, thoughtless things that good comrades could have stopped.

"But it is not just that I needed you, that I could have used your strength and skills. Coming on the quest was your *right*. Your child was in danger. It is a shared task protecting our children. Not the panicked, vain quest of one bigheaded Stuffy."

The Barbie smiled—a strange, plastic smile, with a funny look in her makeupped eyes, but a smile nonetheless.

"I didn't hold it against you, Stuffy, but I do appreciate the apology. Perhaps you should take this apology and turn it into a learning experience, that we all may benefit from your mistake."

Foon sighed. "Every time I think I have become the hero I wish to be—by defeating a Lomer, by killing a King Derker, by earning my silver trident, Focus, by venturing into the Dark—I find it is *not* the end. Just another step in my journey. How many more steps are there until I stop making mistakes?"

"I suspect that if you're lucky and live long enough—you

never stop making mistakes," the Barbie said, laughing. "Life is growth, Stuffy. Change is life. There is no such thing as perfection."

Foon smiled. "Strange to hear that from a doll. Some humans think dolls are perfect versions of themselves. In perfect, unchanging plastic."

"Oh, we age, too, Stuffy, if we are loved," the Barbie said. "It usually shows in our hair first."

"Three cheers for the heroes who made it out of the Dark!" Baby Monster cried from across the fire. He held a little pennant in one of his feethands and waved it wildly while balancing nimbly on the other.

"Hip hip hooray!" the saber-toothed tiger cried, clapping her paws together.

All the Stuffies cheered. Freya and Foon traded a tired, amused look. They would both be the Stuff of legends after this night.

But for now, they were surrounded by friends and warmth— and looked gratefully forward to a good Day's sleep.

EPILOGUE

Miskatonic University was impressive—in a creepy sort of way. It sat on the top of a hill in an old New England town, all marble and alabaster and brick buildings covered in ivy. Above it were roiling grey clouds that seemed constantly on the verge of breaking forth with a terrible storm. Below it, the steep, cobbled streets were lined with bookstores and third-wave coffee shops and dark, intriguing alleys with boutiques that sold art supplies and comic books.

"I. Love. It," Anna said, her face pressed up against the car window.

It wasn't bad for the setting of a superhero's origin story, Clark thought. He was too old to actually hold up Foon to look out the window with him, but he hugged the little warrior tightly in his lap.

Anna was leaving him—and her dolls and Stuffies.

And not even the pool at the hotel they were staying at could make up for that.

Grandma Machen must have sensed something with her own grandma superpowers, because she put her soft, dry hand on Clark's and squeezed. He felt childish—but also comforted.

They had to park far away from the dorm because of all the other families parking at dorms. And all four Smiths (and Machen) had to carry all of Anna's things up to her room—third floor, no elevator.

"That'll get you in shape!" Mrs. Smith said cheerily, hauling an oversize purple beanbag chair.

"Ungh," Mr. Smith said, three boxes piled up on his arms, blocking his view.

The room was tiny. The walls and ceiling were covered in so many layers of glossy white paint that the moldings melted into each other like warm icing. The floor was wood, ancient and worn. The beds had ugly metal frames and the desks were somehow both too modern and too old. The windows would have been large and pretty but had bars across them.

The other girl's things were already stacked on one side of the room: piles of boxes and laundry baskets, books and blankets. Her bed was already made (in shades of dusty rose and soft pink). Nestled in the thick duvet were carefully placed fluffy pillows—and *Stuffies*. But cute, "perfect" ones, like an expensive velvet brown teddy bear, the kind a boy would give to a girl on Valentine's Day on TV.

"*Eww,*" Anna growled.

Once again Clark worried about the fate of the roommate.

His sister set her jaw and chose a box, opened it purposefully and methodically, and put the things from it onto her own bed. The black velvet duvet with the runes, the sheets that looked like they were spattered with blood (she did it herself, like the pee prank), the pentagram-shaped purple pillows she had ordered off Etsy...

...and her Stuffies.

Not all of them. Just Siouxsie the Man-Eating Rabbit and her scariest vampire doll.

Still...

Clark's eyes widened with joy.

Anna gave him a little smile.

"Guess I'm not quite grown-up *yet*," she said.

Then she stuck her tongue out at the pink bed, making a rude noise.

"Let's get you guys some curtains," Grandma Machen said, running a finger along the top of a window and inspecting it for dust.

"I think I saw a linens and supply store on the way here—it was next to that burger place, the Crave Loft," Mrs. Smith said eagerly.

"Hey, I think the other family's coming," Mr. Smith said, returning from his investigation of the shared bathroom. He tried to sound optimistic. "They seem...uh...normal."

"Well, no kidding," Grandma Machen said. "Look at that ridiculous, poofy pink bed."

Anna started moving around the room strangely. Nervous, excited, formal…like she was being watched or trying out for a play. She clasped her hands and patted things.

Mrs. Smith put on a giant smile so bright her teeth actually glowed, even against the ugly bare lightbulbs hanging from the ceiling. She grabbed the earpiece out of her ear.

Grandma Machen smoothed her hair.

Clark stepped out of the way, into the corner by the poofy pink bed.

And then noticed something else sparkling in the room besides his mother's teeth.

The perfect velvet teddy bear, lying on the big pink heart pillow…

…had fangs.

~~BONUS MAKE!~~

~~ENCOURAGEMENT~~ BANNERS!

~~YAY ON YOUR TRUE SELF WITH A BRIGHT-COLORED REMINDER HANDMADE BY YOU!~~

~~S~~ession canceled due to technical difficulties. Sewing machines broken because of ~~Glimers haunting them.~~

TOTALY NORMAL BREAKING AND MALFUNKTSHUN.

THERE ARE NO SUCH THINGS AS MONSTERS!!!!

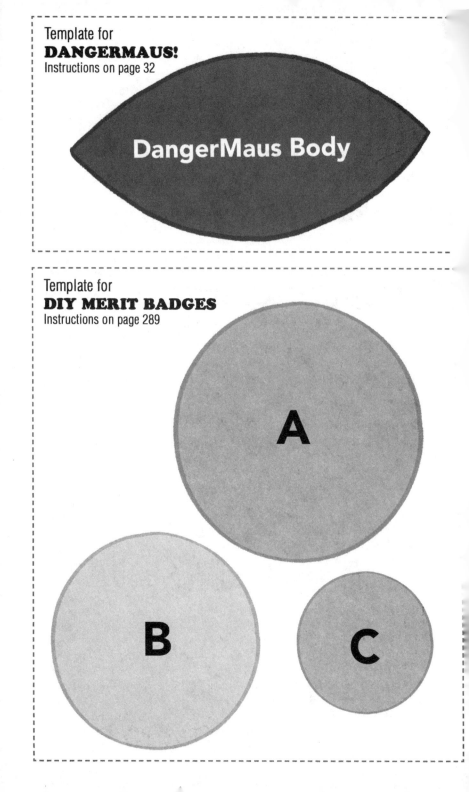

Template for
DANGERMAUS!
Instructions on page 32

DangerMaus Body

Template for
DIY MERIT BADGES
Instructions on page 289

A

B

C